Divinity Games

LOU GILMOND

Armillary Books

First published by Armillary Books 2025

Armillary Books
Summertown Pavilion, 18–24 Middle Way, Oxford, OX2 7LG

A CIP catalogue record for this book is available from the
British Library.

1 2 3 4 5 6 7 8 9 10

ISBN 978-1-914148-71-2

www.fairlightbooks.com

Printed and bound in Great Britain

Cover Design © Nick Castle

MIX
Paper | Supporting
responsible forestry
FSC
www.fsc.org
FSC® C013056

...And old friends

Prologue

It was the first time they had gathered together. Clarissa Colbey looked across the crowd and shivered.

To ensure the night's success, the Chairman had arranged everything. Divas had been flown in from around the world and, at great expense, the canopy of the open-air theatre had been removed. At even greater expense it would need to be replaced in the morning. The programme had been scrutinised and changed. Nothing could be too heavy or too long, the Chairman had said, because privilege has no patience. Nor can it be corralled, yet somehow he had managed it.

There they all were, in their rows, in jewels and furs. As the orchestra slipped into the pit, the gossip was of the cost of horses, the shortage of pilots and the difficulty of finding staff one could trust.

They were perhaps fifty or so in number, and did not fill the opera house, yet they huddled in the centre rows. And right in the midst of them, in the best of the best seats, was Clarissa's daughter, Chloe Colbey. She had shrugged off her wrap and the folds of cashmere had fallen to the seat behind. Clarissa saw that those nearby couldn't stop staring – at her daughter's natural beauty, her slim face, her pale cheeks and the blush she had applied with a careless hand. She knew they were stung with envy.

'To be so young again,' one of them whispered and was met with a collective sigh.

But Clarissa knew it wasn't just her daughter's youth they coveted. They didn't drink in her face so as to better describe it to their plastic surgeons. It was the aroma of freedom that ensnared them. A freedom that she wore as other women wore perfume. They saw her belief that good things could be achieved without resorting to liposuction and Botox, to tucks and discreet procedures, to pre-nups and nannies and drivers and florists, to cash stolen from husbands and offshore trusts hidden from wives, to multiple houses, cars, flights, boats, parties, races.

She didn't even have a tan. It was the first time the Owners had gathered together in one place, and Chloe Colbey, soon to be wed to the Chairman's son, had not even taken his private jet to the Caribbean to get herself a tan.

Clarissa, who was not as stupid or wicked as many supposed, looked up at the night sky and mused on all this. Not that she found a star. The lights of the city had drowned them all out. Perhaps the Chairman had arranged that too.

Somewhere a peacock cried out, and, as the conductor stood and tapped his baton, Clarissa realised she had heard it before. She'd been thinking through the consequences of a decision she'd just made. Now, where had that decision got her?

'Mummy!'

Clarissa looked down to find that the auditorium's lights had been dimmed and her phone was buzzing with a call. There came a tut from behind.

'Yes, alright,' she muttered, standing quickly and making her way along the row of knees. She was forced to suffer several more tuts before she reached the stairs at the end.

It *was* bad form, she knew. But then, she considered, as a medley of overtures began, it was really bad form to muddle up operas. So they were all philistines anyway.

Down in the corridor next to the exit, the families' security staff stood like awkward gatecrashers in the shadows.

'Everything alright?' one of them asked, but seeing who it was, he coughed and looked away. 'Sorry,' he said. 'I thought you were...'

Clarissa did not listen to the rest. She hurried on, out into the foyer. No one was there. Not a ticket collector. Not a cashier. Not even someone to man the sweets counter. The Owners' privacy was always of top consideration. Clarissa crossed the empty room, hurried through the double doors to the steps outside and peered out into the moonlit night. In the distance, she could see the lights of the Owners' limousines, come to wait in case any should wish to go home early.

They had arrived at the venue in a series of helicopters, each one taking turns to touch down on the sports ground at the bottom of the park, from where the Chairman had led the way to the opera house.

'There's no one in the park but us,' he'd reassured them. 'In fact, there's no one on the streets for miles around.'

Of course, he didn't count those who were laying out the picnic of lobster and Krug on trestle tables in front of the theatre, or the bodyguards who stood, arms crossed over their bodies, biceps bulging, at a discreet distance.

Now, the tables, the rugs, the food, the champagne bottles and glasses were all gone, as were those who had served the picnic. Those who accompanied the families from country to country and from house to house had tidied it all away as if it had never been, and then tidied themselves away.

As Clarissa stood in the darkness, she felt rather than heard the silence of the suburbs that surrounded the park. Was anyone leaning out of the window and catching a dream of opera floating on the breeze? There was a stay-at-home order in force for the whole of London that night. Genuinely also the Chairman's doing, or at least the company's. Might those people in their houses even now be turning to their housemates to ask who the hell the performance of opera from the famous Holland Park could possibly be for?

Clarissa looked at her phone. The caller had hung up before she'd even reached the foyer. Where is he? she thought, as the peacock cried out again. It was making its way across the moonlit lawn, dragging its long tail stoically behind, its little crowned head bobbing back and forth.

The bird heard him coming before she did. Off it went, skittering away from the trees that ringed the lawn just as the shape of a man came crashing through them. On seeing her standing there on the steps, he paused, altered his direction and stumbled on. Clarissa hurried down and was about to run onto the grass towards him when a shout came from her right.

'I see him!'

Two men had appeared round the far corner of the opera house. At the same time, another came crashing through the trees in the far distance, obviously in pursuit, while a fourth came running round the corner of the building from the opposite direction.

As one, they made for the lumbering shape. But while the fugitive ploughed on, the young men took erratic paths to reach him. They leapt in the air, like dancers of a corps de ballet. While he was silent, they whooped and cheered and called to one other. Yet, for all their dance, surely and steadily they closed in. For a moment, Clarissa wondered if it was part of the night's performance – the players escaping the confines of their stage and putting on an impromptu show just for her. But when they finally reached the man, he fell among them and at once they began kicking him.

They were close enough now that Clarissa could see them clearly, and she marvelled at how young they were. The one who kicked the most savagely was... what... fifteen? But he clearly had a desire to thrash like an angry five-year-old with a toy bat. In his frenzied stamping, his arms flailing about, he knocked his own glasses from his face. They went flying off into the darkness. Clarissa heard a bone break.

'Enough!' she said, stepping forward, her stiletto sinking into the grass.

The sound of her voice, the authority within it, surprised her as much as them. Like hounds at the whistle, they lifted their heads and all of a sudden the beating was over. Two of them hauled the man up by his arms and held him so that he dangled between them. His head was lolling to one side. His face was bloody, his nose broken and his clothes torn. An acrid smell seeped out from him.

With a sudden roar, he wrenched out of their grip and fell forward onto Clarissa, grabbing at her hand. With a snarl of annoyance, two of the attackers stepped forward and pulled him back among them.

They were Mobsters. She had seen it straight away – the cropped trousers, the billowing shirts. Each wore his hair in a topknot, not dissimilar to that of the peacock that had fled. And each wore dark glasses. All, that is, except for the one who had lost his. The young one. There was blood on his fists and in a wide stripe across his cheek. He came up to her, and he was so close she could smell his sweat and exhilaration.

'And why aren't *you* safely in your home?' he asked. His cheeks were ruddy, and she tried to place his accent but couldn't.

She thought of the empty foyer that stood between her and the Owners and their guards. With the opera going on, they wouldn't hear her, even if she screamed as loudly as she could.

'Well?' he persisted. 'Or do you need a reminder of the rules too?'

The boy raised his arm in a mean and teasing fashion, but another, the leader perhaps, took hold of it and placed the lost glasses in his hand.

'Put them on,' he said.

The brat did as he was told and after looking up and peering at Clarissa, he bowed his head and took a step back.

'I'm sorry,' he mumbled. 'I didn't know you were...'

Clarissa wasn't certain she could speak. She was as breathless as all of them.

Elite. She was elite.

'No,' she said. 'You didn't, did you?'

Thank God, she thought. Thank God I'm elite. And despite everything, even as she shook, a dirty pride filled her. Yes, she felt sorry for all those people in the city who had to do as they were told. Who had to stay inside their little boxes, their poky new-build houses with plyboard walls, their crumbling two-up-two-downs and gardenless flats when they were told to. But she had made it so that she wasn't one of them. And that was down to her. Which was why she was here, listening to opera, while he...

'Be more careful next time,' she said.

On hearing her voice, the captured man fought to lift his head and looked at her with the one good eye he had left.

Seeing it, the leader said, 'Sorry you had to witness that. We've got to make sure people stick to the rules.'

'And what do you intend to do now?'

'Make sure he goes home, where he should have been in the first place.'

She looked at each in turn, trying to find a chink of doubt or empathy in any of them.

'Leave him with me. I can take him indoors.'

The boy sneered. 'I don't think so.'

'You shouldn't have beaten him,' Clarissa said. 'You had no right to.' She waved her phone at him. 'I'm going to call the police!'

'And do you think they'll come?' the leader replied, and laughed at her.

Clarissa looked around at the dark and empty park.

For a moment, she thought about hurrying inside and begging *them* for help. Just one or two of those professionally trained men would do the job against these self-appointed lunatics. But even as she thought it, she dismissed the idea. They would not agree to come. Didn't their happiness depend upon this exact sort of thing being kept at a careful distance?

Despite the boy's apology, and the leader's civil tone, there was still menace in them. She saw it in their postures, the way they held their bodies, like dogs waiting for a second go at the prize. They would happily have a go at another prize given half a chance, if one should fall in their path. The leader knew it too.

'Go inside,' he said roughly. 'It's not safe for citizens to be out. Even if they are Owners.'

She wanted to tell him it was a sham. She opened her mouth to say the words. She wanted to ask why they were allowed to break the curfew. Why, if it so was dangerous to be out on the streets, he and his fellow Mobsters were allowed to roam about and set upon people.

'You're not allowed to lay a finger on me,' she said.

The Mobster looked up at the building behind her, his eyes searching its cornices for a listening eye. There was bound to be one up there. They were everywhere these days. But of course he had forgotten that the glasses he wore fed into the same system. She heard a tinny echo of an instruction fed into his ear and at once the leader waved his hand. Without another word, he set off across the lawn, back towards the trees from where he had first appeared. The two with their captive followed, dragging him between them. Only the brat lingered.

'Where are you taking him?' she called out to the leader, but he ignored her.

The brat stood and peered at Clarissa.

'I've never met an Owner before,' he said. Then he lifted up his hand, a finger extended, and moved it silently in front of her face. 'You have no tags. It's like... It's like you don't exist.'

They stood and looked at one another. She had an urge to grab his glasses and grind them into the ground beneath her foot.

'Where are you taking him?' she said, this time to the boy.

'That is not for you to know,' he replied. 'You may be an Owner – but we are the chosen ones.' And at a shout from the leader he turned and ran off after them, whirling in circles, his arms outstretched, and disappeared into the undergrowth after the others.

Clarissa turned back to the opera house. She trudged up the steps and stood in the still empty foyer. She wasn't sure she could go back in, go back past the disinterested bodyguards, back to the auditorium. She opened the door a crack.

The rows of diamond chokers glinted as the lights were turned onto the crowd and a change of scene was announced. Philistines, she thought, as they rose to cheer the arrival of a new diva to the stage. As the soprano began to sing, she recognised the form of her daughter making her way through the bouncers in the dark.

'*Thy hand, Belinda, darkness shades me.*'

Chloe stood at the open door and looked in a puzzled fashion at her mother standing there in the foyer for no reason. 'Who was it?'

Clarissa did not respond, but Chloe persisted.

'Was it Daddy?'

'Yes,' Clarissa muttered, as the Diva's aria came through the open door.

'*More I would, but Death invades me.*'

'Is he OK?'

'Of course he is.' When Chloe looked behind her, uncertain, she added, 'Go back to the stalls. I'll be there in a minute.'

Her daughter did as she was told.

What else could Clarissa say? That the bundle of torn clothes, bloody flesh and broken bones who had been dragged off to goodness knows where, for goodness knows what, had been Chloe's father. That it had been her husband of thirty years.

Ex-husband, she corrected herself.

Clarissa found a velvet chair beside the cashier's office and sank down onto it. She realised she was still clutching the programme of the evening, and looked down to see who the soprano was. A tear fell onto it.

Yes, it had been Harry Colbey who had been beaten and dragged off.

But there was something gripped in her other hand. Slowly, Clarissa opened it; she looked down at what was in her palm and smiled. Harry had paid quite a price to get it to her, but for Chloe's sake, she was glad he had.

PART ONE

Thirty-six hours earlier

Wednesday 19 June

I . I

The longest day of the year was not far off, and although the window of the room in which Harry Colbey slept was west-facing, it was already washed with a bright, early-morning light that was threatening to wake him. The MP turned with a grumble to the wall and pulled the blanket over his head.

Where had he been? Lost in an English wood, that's right. There had been rickety bridges and babbling brooks. There had been a lake swept by dwarf willow trees, and the birds had been full of summer song. Hadn't there been a clearing? And a picnic? One with pork pie, strong, hard cheddar and lashings of ginger beer? No, that's not right – ginger wine...

'Damn this whole thing,' he said with irritation, throwing off the blanket. In the office next door, someone was vacuuming with an unnecessary aggression.

Rolling over and levering himself up, Colbey faced the four wood-panelled walls of his parliamentary office, and groaned. The chimes of Big Ben sounded out. Colbey counted them. 6am. When might he be allowed a little peace?

Just as the thought occurred to him, the door at his feet banged open, hitting the bottom of his bed, and even though he had known it was about to happen, Colbey jumped. A cleaner was trying to force her way in.

Fortunately, Colbey knew the door wouldn't open far enough to allow her and her damned instrument of torture into the room. The unseen malevolence tried a few more times before giving up. She had obviously come to the conclusion there was something in the way, though presumably she didn't realise it was a grumpy MP, still clad in his pyjamas.

Colbey did not feel bad about it. There were plenty of dusty rooms in the House of Commons, after all.

He heard her unplug the Hoover, the echo of it running along the skirting boards between the two offices, and listened as the door of his outer office opened and closed. Thank God, he thought. He was about to lie down again when he heard the office door open and close once more and Tilly, his office manager, come breezing through. It was definitely her – she was humming a cheery tune, slightly off-key. Colbey groaned one last time as the door of his office banged up against the bottom of the bed again.

Tilly's head appeared through the gap.

'Are you awake?' she said.

'I am,' he replied, archly.

He wasn't sure how old Tilly was. She was one of those country folk who start on the twinsets and tweed at boarding school and stick stubbornly to it as fashions, seasons and even decades pass by. She appeared to him the same today as she'd been the day she had first started working for him. Her hair was neither grey nor blonde, but some indeterminate shade of yellow, and although she had to be at least sixty, she had the energy levels of a much younger woman.

'I thought I'd get in early and get a head start on the day,' she said.

'Right,' Colbey replied. 'Good idea.'

Above him, the porcelain base of a corner sink loomed and for once he remembered not to bang his head on it as he levered himself up to a seating position. His camp bed creaked ominously.

Tilly disappeared for a moment and when she returned, squeezing her ample bosom through the gap, she had a cup of coffee in her hands and a duster over her arm.

'You are, without doubt, an angel sent from heaven,' he said, as she handed him the coffee.

'The cleaner couldn't get into your room.'

'I know.'

'I thought about suggesting she lose a bit of weight.'

'And did you?'

'No, though I should have done. She said she hadn't been able to dust. Do you mind if I...?'

Colbey took in the room with a flourish of his hand. 'Be my guest.'

He watched as she set about the surfaces of his office – the mahogany desk with its green felt top, the old-fashioned cupboards, the framed prints of parliaments of yesteryear. It was hardly in her job description, but that sort of thing didn't bother Tilly. If there was something that needed to be done, she would find someone for the job or else do it herself. Without doubt, he had the best office manager of any MP in the land. She looked after his constituency diary, booked venues for his surgeries and acted as his agent during elections. Since his wife and he had divorced, Tilly had also taken over Clarissa's old duties as his secretary. And a far better job of it she did too, he thought, and then was struck with guilt. Clarissa hadn't been so bad. Not way back when... when she was full of enthusiasm for the role and determined to help him in his chosen career.

Colbey reached under the bed, pulled out an old-fashioned desk calendar and crossed off the day's date. I expect they get better treatment in Wormwood Scrubs, he thought miserably, and started counting back the days.

'So how long's it been, then?' Tilly asked. She had her back to him and was giving the window behind the desk a good wipe. That woman had eyes in the back of her head.

'Two hundred and eighteen days.'

Tilly gasped without pausing her dusting.

'Two hundred and eighteen days! You'd get less for a hit and run.'

'I don't see what that has to do with anything.'

'Well, you haven't done anything wrong. Yet here you are, all cooped up. And a young man still.'

'I'm hardly young, Tilly. I'm over fifty for a start.'

'Nonsense,' she replied. 'I've had two husbands since I was fifty.' Colbey did some mental arithmetic. So that would mean she was… 'You need to get yourself out there,' she went on.

Colbey took a sip of his coffee and frowned.

'I can't go out, Tilly. You know that.'

'But—'

'Someone, or more correctly something, has meddled with my life. They've cancelled my credit cards, taken away my bank account, stopped my train pass, my gym membership… even my library subscription has disappeared.'

'I know, but—'

'They have created deepfake lies and slander showing me with prostitutes and underage girls. Every police officer in the country is told to arrest me for any minor infraction they can drag up from my past – every light I might have hopped as it was turning red, every second I might have failed to put my seatbelt on, every lost library book…'

'But—'

'And the minute I set foot outside the Houses of Parliament, they send swarms of drones to chase me down and attack me—'

Tilly roared, 'Not "out"! *"Out"*!'

Colbey took a gulp of his coffee and tried to calm himself.

'I mean out on the dating scene. Plenty of lovely ladies work here on the parliamentary estate, you know.'

To which Colbey rolled his eyes. Tilly might be a super-efficient powerhouse of an office manager, secretary and parliamentary agent, but he didn't need her starting to act as his matchmaker too.

'As it happens,' he said, trying his hardest to be haughty, though it didn't come naturally to him as he was a good-natured soul on the whole, 'I'm already seeing someone.'

Tilly whipped round. 'You dark horse,' she said.

Taking the duster with her, she stalked out of the room. He heard her turning on her computer in the outer office and, admitting defeat, thought he might as well get out of bed. He was in relatively good shape for his age, but even so it was a struggle to lever himself out of the low camp bed. As soon as he was up, he went over and shut the door, then hunted among the sheets for the remote control for the television, which hung above the bed.

Although he worked steadily through the channels, Colbey could find nothing but a grim procession of warnings about terror attacks. Apparently, they could come anytime, anywhere. It sounded like a Martini advert from the eighties. Dirty bombs in suitcases, foreign interference in national infrastructure, poisoning of the water supply with lethal pathogens. Finally he found a kids' channel and, letting the cartoons run, folded up the camp bed, stowed it against the far wall between the sink and his desk and started on his morning routine: thirty press-ups, thirty sit-ups, thirty jumping jacks, then a slow roll down to touch his toes and a slow roll back up again. He cleaned his teeth in the sink, gave yesterday's stubble a quick shave, found a clean shirt and underwear in one of the cupboards and changed into his grey suit.

He was just tucking his pyjamas into a drawer when Tilly came in again with the post in her hands. This time the door swung gently open onto its backstop.

Tilly looked disapprovingly at the cartoons, picked up the remote and switched through the channels. There it all went again. Dirty bombs in suitcases, foreign interference in national infrastructure, poisoning of the water supply with lethal pathogens. Finally she found the House of Commons station that the television screen was intended to show. It allowed the MPs to watch proceedings in the chamber while still in their offices and provided warning bells when it was time for them to hurry along and vote. As it was still early, the screen showed an empty chamber: the two facing rows of green leather seats, the microphones hanging like vines from the ceiling, and at the far end the empty throne of the Speaker, who chaired the debates.

'We're all in mortal peril, are we?' Tilly said. 'What a lot of nonsense. They just don't want us to go out in case we ruin their green targets.'

'Yes, perhaps that's it.'

Tilly threw her hands in the air.

'And who are they? That's what I want to know! First they say it's the Russians. Then they say it's the Chinese. It's not like we haven't had this threat all our lives. I was a child of the war, after all.'

Colbey did some more mental arithmetic and decided it couldn't be true.

'You won't find any disagreement from me,' he said.

'And if there really is someone out there meddling with the gas pressures and derailing trains, they ought to get to the bottom of it. That Neville Jameson. Calls himself a Prime Minister. Couldn't organise a gymkhana in a pony yard.'

'Indeed.'

'All these stay-at-home orders dropped on us any time, any day.'

Colbey eyed the post she had in her hands. Tilly went and put it on his desk, before picking up a stiff card she had discovered there. It was an invitation for dinner that night with his daughter's prospective in-laws.

'You didn't tell me Chloe was getting married!'

'They're just engaged at the moment,' he said. 'A long engagement, I'm hoping.'

She raised her eyebrows. 'No man ever fell in love with his son-in-law, they say.'

Colbey could only admit it was true.

'And what does Mama think? She's doing awfully well for herself from what I hear.'

Colbey didn't reply, but went round to sit at his desk and leafed through the post. There was nothing interesting in it.

'Didn't she move to that new development in west Chelsea, with the massive walls and security guards?'

'I believe she did.'

'Is it true they have a helipad next to the river? And that they fly from there direct to the south of France or wherever it is they're off to next?'

'As ever, you have your ear to the ground, Tilly.'

'Bit tacky, isn't it?'

'Why Clarissa does anything is not really my business anymore.'

'Right you are. Well, I'll let you get on.' She pulled her phone out of her pocket and looked through it. 'I've heard Number Ten are holding a conference for the press lobby in the Star Chamber. Invites went out last night. It's to be first thing.'

'First thing?' said Colbey. 'That won't go down well.'

'Daily updates, first thing each morning, during our time of uncertainty, apparently.'

Colbey tapped his chin with his finger in thought.

'I wonder if Jameson has invited the hacks from that blasted Mouth of the Mob website. Our Prime Minister seems determined to work with them.'

'Well, you can go along and see, can't you?' Tilly said.

The Mouth of the Mob was a website that had posted deepfake images of Colbey with underage girls the previous year. An unprofessional lot they were, with no interest in the truth. Each of their so-called 'journalists' had their own account on the site and was allowed to post whatever nonsense they chose to make up. The more ridiculous, the better for them, because the more outlandish the gossip was, even if only a tiny fraction of it turned out to be true, the more their personal ratings rose. It had taken months of legal work, not to mention thousands of pounds in court fees, for Colbey and his lawyer to get the images taken down and an apology issued.

'You need to be in the House for the first session anyway,' Tilly went on. 'The Speaker has picked you for this morning's urgent question.'

At least that was good news. The Speaker was a fair man. He made sure that even those who were independent like Colbey still had the chance to ask questions in the House. After all, the Speaker had said, when challenged by a government toady, the independent MPs' constituents needed representing as much as anyone else's.

Tilly scrolled through her phone. 'Then you have this new Cross-Party Committee on Democracy and Privacy or whatever they're going to call it, in Meeting Room Three of Portcullis House at eleven. And then... good news...'

Colbey looked up at her hovering there with a grin on her face.

'I've saved the best for last.'

'Tell me?'

'The Speaker has asked you to come to his rooms for one o'clock. Inspector Albury says he's ready to report back.'

Colbey sat back in his chair and stared at Tilly.

'Really?'

'Yes. Two hundred and eighteen days later, the Inspector is finally there.'

'Do we know...?'

'I'm afraid not. The Speaker's secretary said they hadn't been given any advance information.'

Colbey looked up at the window. They had asked the police to investigate his harassment months ago. The Speaker of the House and the Serjeant at Arms had chased many times, only to be told that the handle of the machine was being turned and that they must be patient. He had almost given up. Was about to make a formal complaint to the judiciary. Had, in fact, already made a series of complaints to the Attorney General.

Tilly looked at him with a mix of pity and joy. He really couldn't take it. He was afraid he might start to cry. A grown man blubbing in front of Tilly Harringer. It mustn't be done. How to get rid of her for a moment?

'Is there any chance of a bacon butty?' Colbey said.

'Ketchup and mustard?'

'Yes.'

'Anything for you, my dear Harry.' She carefully put the card down on the desk and went to leave, but paused at the door. 'You can't hide in here forever, you know. Not if your little girl's getting married.'

After she was gone into the outer office, Colbey got up and looked out of the window. He could see down into New Palace Yard, and across to the gates of the Parliament Square exit. Beyond it the world was going about its business as usual. It had no interest in him, trapped here on the parliamentary estate.

Cars and buses ran endlessly around the little green square, eternally circling the statue of Winston Churchill hunched over his cane.

A few feet above the traffic, an endless stream of drones plied their trade, delivering takeaway coffees and sandwiches, stationery and post, and all the other useless tat that the city seemed unable to do without. Since their trial the previous year, their numbers had grown exponentially. First it was emergency deliveries – blood and organs between hospitals. Then it was post and sundries. Then came the police drones.

Turning his back on the Square and facing the room, Colbey picked up the stiff card and toyed with the sharp corner of it.

The hideous meet-the-parents affair had been concocted by Chloe and her fiancé. A table had been booked for the six of them at some fancy club in Mayfair. Did his parents even know that Clarissa and he were divorced, he wondered? But it was all moot. He couldn't be there and felt terribly guilty that he hadn't told her yet. Knew it was going to cause upset. But better to drop out at the last minute and say a work problem had cropped up than confess he was unable to leave the Houses of Parliament because he was the target of unwanted harassment and was trapped there until they got to the bottom of it. Chloe mustn't know that. He had told her he had been busy with work these last few months. A lump came to his throat. He must pull himself together. Tilly was still bustling about out there.

It wasn't that he didn't like her intended. Emir was his name. Colbey had only met him a couple of times in passing, before the two became serious about one other, so it wouldn't be fair to judge yet. It wasn't even the fact that Emir's family were shareholders of the very company he was campaigning against and which owned the IT system waging the campaign of harassment against him. It was more the fact that the family was obscenely wealthy.

Not that he had anything against wealthy people. He represented all his constituents as well as he could, rich and poor. It was just that it wasn't the life he had wanted for her. To be the wife of some spoilt rich kid who grew up travelling between European houses before being jettisoned into Harvard and a top job in the city.

She was such an accomplished girl, determined, clever, yet sensible with it. A little ditzy sometimes, he would admit, but... she could be so many things. Achieve so much in life.

This marriage, this connection. She didn't see it, but it wouldn't open doors for her. At least not the right ones. Instead, it would lock her in a gilded cage. It would make her… a questionable applicant for any serious job application, any serious career. Always Emir's family would appear, lurking like a set of unpleasant gremlins behind her, putting people's backs up and making them not trust her. But what did he know?

He looked down at the picture of Chloe on his desk as the outer office door opened and closed. Finally, Tilly had gone to get his bacon butty.

Colbey folded the invitation in two and put it in his breast pocket, then hurried over to the door of his own office and quickly closed and locked it. Then he knelt down on the ground.

With his shoulder, he shoved aside the little cupboard in which he had stored his pyjamas, revealing a faded patch of flooring. He tapped at the end of a floorboard and prised the corner of it up. Then he slipped his hand into the cavity, pulled out a phone, and hurriedly turned it on.

A message came through.

I am here and so is Easterly.

Colbey sank back onto his heels, turned the phone off again and slipped it into his pocket.

'Thank God,' he said. At last, there was hope.

I.2

Esme Kanha stood in the basement of St Thomas's hospital and waited for the body of her colleague, Reginald Easterly, to arrive. He had been a well-respected MP and a cheery soul, although perhaps not with the best attendance record.

At the end of the corridor, clear plastic flaps blew about in the wind and each time they lifted she saw the corpse's progress as it was unloaded from the back of a truck, placed onto a wheeled gurney and raised up to the level of the mortuary corridor. The man who had arranged all this was Karolinski. At least she hoped it was Karolinski. Like her, he was dressed head to toe in scrubs, his mouth masked and his eyes covered with gauze. As he came up beside her, she looked down on the gold foil of the CadSeal mortuary bag and tenderly placed a hand on it.

'How did you—?'

The man waved a warning finger and pointed into the air around him.

'Not here,' he said.

He was as plummy as Harry had said he would be. Eton, perhaps. Or St Paul's. Yes, it was Karolinski alright.

He manoeuvred the gurney to pull it through the mortuary doors, pushing his backside up against them.

'Are you sure you want to come in?' he said. 'You don't have to, you know.'

Kanha clutched the gauze sack that held her handbag, in which was a video recorder. It fell to her to witness. In reply to Karolinski, she took the other end of the gurney and helped him wheel it into the room. It was bright in there compared to the dingy corridor, the same strip lighting now reflecting off all the silver surfaces – the cadaver lockers, the mortuary racks, six sets of hanging scales and the long row of autopsy tables.

A man in scrubs stood in the room, and Kanha was pleased to see that the medical examiner was already prepared. He had picked a table to be his workspace and his equipment sat on a rolling tray by his side. His rather large belly was swathed by a blue apron and from his mask the dark curls of a beard were trying to escape. He raised a gloved hand. 'Greetings,' he said to them both. Then he moved quickly and efficiently to help Karolinski remove the corpse from the foil bag and place it on the table.

The smell was not as bad as Kanha had expected. She had steeled herself, remembering the stench of a badger's corpse that had once lain on the lane outside her constituency home and which had caused an immediate gag reaction. But this was not like that. As the bag opened, the room filled with an aroma of garlic washed through with something chemical, but death still lurked underneath. Kanha put a hand over her mouth and, seeing that the camera in the room had been covered, took the gauze from her eyes.

'Is it safe to speak?'

'Yes. I've made sure of it.' The mortician also glanced to the corner of the room. 'The security camera is disabled and I've covered it with lead-lined cloth to be sure. The instructions were very clear.'

Kanha approached the autopsy table and steeled herself again. If these two men could look at the corpse, so could she. She looked up at the examiner in surprise. Easterly had been dead for eight months, yet his skin was still intact.

'Why has he not…?'

The examiner grunted and after cutting open the suit in which the MP had been buried, pressed down on the skin of Easterly's chest. 'Airtight coffin,' he said. 'It's the blowflies that do the work. And they don't reach the deceased until the casket becomes compromised over time.'

He rearranged the dead man's arms, using brute force. 'Though now that he's been exhumed, that will change,' he added. Then he picked up a dictaphone and began taking notes.

'It was my fault, you know,' Kanha said.

The medical examiner paused, his finger hovering over the button. 'I very much doubt that.'

She touched the cold metal of the table.

'It was my choice to involve him. And that led to his death.'

She wanted to ask the examiner if he could already tell what had caused her colleague's death, but she didn't want to prompt him.

'We only have a short time,' she said.

'I know. I'll be quick,' he replied.

Kanha took the video camera from her bag and recorded his work. Fifteen minutes later, twenty at the most, he turned to the sink on the wall, stripped off his gloves and washed his hands and forearms.

'Give it here,' he said.

Behind him, Karolinski stapled up the suit, before manoeuvring Easterly back into the gold foil, then went to a dispenser on the wall to change his gloves as the examiner took the camera.

'Here,' the examiner said to Kanha, winding back through his work. 'You can see the cuts on the subject's face. Not deep enough to reach to the dermis, but deep enough to have stung. They're too blunt to be the work of a metal blade. I would hazard a whip or a fine strip of plastic. There are so many, so close together, it has to be a spinning implement. Like the plastic string of a strimmer.'

'Or the propeller of a drone?'

'Yes, that's it. That's exactly what it is. And more than one drone, is my opinion.'

Kanha leaned forward as the coroner spun on.

'See here. The cuts on his face are also on his hands.' He lifted his arms, the camera held aloft. 'The victim—'

Kanha tried to stay calm. 'You think he's a victim?'

'Yes. The victim held his hands up to protect his face. See here,' he said. He spun on again. 'I've lined up this series of cuts across his hand with another set across his ear.'

She didn't want to lead him, but she had to know.

'If he was set upon by a swarm of drones, would that be consistent with what you're seeing here?'

'It would. You can even see cuts repeated over and over, shifting position each time as the machine hovers.'

'Would the cuts have killed him?'

'No. They would have hurt. It would have been disorienting. But it was the fall that killed him.'

Easterly had been found at the bottom of the cliffs near his home. They had said it was suicide. She had known it was not. She had known.

'The fall to the rocks broke the bones of his torso and arms, and staved his head in. That last was the cause of his death.'

Kanha felt an anger sweep over her. But they hadn't time. She looked at her watch.

'Let me check you agree,' she said. 'He stood with his arms raised to protect his face from the drones as they swarmed him. He stumbled. He got too close to the cliff edge. He fell.'

'I agree. It's the most likely scenario.'

'The scratches couldn't be from the fall? From branches perhaps?'

'No.'

'And you'd be willing to testify to that?'

'Of course. Why wouldn't I be?'

'Because…'

The examiner put a hand on her shoulder.

'I understand from Lord Silverman that skulduggery is afoot here. But murder is murder.'

'Thank you,' she said.

The medical examiner stood back and removed his mask, so that she could see his face. 'If things are that bad, tell Lord Silverman he owes me a game of dominoes,' he said and grinned.

Kanha smiled at last. 'I will,' she said, taking back the camera from him.

'Thank you for arranging this.' She waved at the empty autopsy room and the covered-up security camera in the corner. 'Would you be happy to record something now, a statement covering what you just said, in case…'

'In case they bump me off too?'

Kanha was silent and he shrugged his shoulders in agreement.

As quickly as he could, the examiner presented his views while Kanha filmed. When he was done, Kanha said, 'Now tell the camera who you are – your name, where you were born, what school you went to. Who your parents, siblings and best friends are.'

The examiner did as he was asked, and Kanha finished filming and threw the camera in her bag.

'Thank you,' she said. 'There are so many fake people online now, generated by AI, that any videoed witness has to be verified with at least ten reference points. It's important to set a context of humanity if this evidence is to mean anything.'

The examiner did not offer to shake her hand, but instead held open the doors to allow Karolinski to wheel out the gurney with Easterly on it. He gave her a wave goodbye, and Kanha paused and thanked him again. When she turned, Karolinski was already gone, so she hurried after him, catching up as he arrived at the open end of the corridor.

'We don't have long until they send someone to find out why there's no power to the block's street furniture,' he said, lifting the plastic straps. 'Traffic lights and CCTV, that is.'

'And why isn't there any?' Kanha asked.

'I broke into the substation and turned it off.'

He gave a satisfied grunt when he saw that the traffic lights at the end of the service lane were still out. That meant the security cameras dotted about the buildings would be out too. Instinctively they both looked up at them.

Kanha touched the gold foil that contained Easterly one last time. 'I'm sorry, Reginald.' she said. Then to Karolinski, 'How will you get him back in the ground?'

He wheeled the gurney onto the service lift and pressed the button to lower it down to the street where the lorry was parked, its back doors still open. Kanha jumped down beside him. She found her clothes folded up in the back and changed as quickly as she could.

'It will have to be tomorrow night,' he replied, loading the gurney.

She threw her scrubs into the lorry. 'Does his widow know it will take that long?'

'She does. She's at peace with the fact.'

After Karolinski had closed the doors at the back of the lorry, he turned to her.

'Why him?' he said. 'Of all the MPs they could have murdered, why him?'

Kanha considered his question. There were many MPs who were either unsettled by the government nudging the country towards a surveillance state or openly against it. In fact, Easterly had been neither of those. But at Kanha's request, the old MP had raised a question in the House asking how privacy could be maintained while the government was watching and listening to its citizens at every step they took. The question had gone viral, a popular song woven into the footage, and the next thing they knew Easterly had fallen from the cliffs near his home while out walking his dog. He was not the only opposing MP to suffer harassment, but the first, as far as she knew, who had been murdered.

The system the government used to watch the nation was intelligent enough to act in an autonomous manner and had taught itself to become the best hacker in the world. She already had proof it had murdered a journalist by hacking into his car and forcing it into a river.

For eight months Kanha had been begging Easterly's widow to allow her to disinter her husband so they could arrange an autopsy. The police had said it was suicide, but she had known it was foul play.

'Why him?' she said, and then answered her own question. 'He was just in their way.'

Karolinski nodded.

'Now. You and I had better get on,' he said in his plummy voice, and he climbed into the cab of his lorry with a wave of farewell, telling her to take care of herself.

When the vehicle had trundled off, Kanha hurried down the service lane after it, but at the far junction where it turned right, she ducked into an alley that led to the embankment on the south side of the Thames. She quickly went over to a bench that faced the grey waters and sat down, making sure to match the position she had been sitting in when she had risen from the bench an hour earlier.

Like the river, the sky above her was grey, from a low covering of clouds that might or might not bring rain. She looked up at the listening eye ten yards away. Its power should still be out. The system watched at all times, so when it switched back on its intelligence would hopefully assume she had been sitting on the same bench for the last hour.

Why? Why would she be sitting there, all on her own, so early in the morning, halfway to work?

She had once been an MP at the top of her game, a government Chief Whip with pretentions to the leadership role. But fortune had changed. Now she was just an out-of-favour backbencher. She had no social life. No friends to speak of. No obvious partner. Only a cat at home for company. The logical conclusion would be that she had been contemplating running over to the parapet and throwing herself into those swirling grey waters.

At least, that was what she wanted it to think. The reality couldn't be further from the truth.

Always she worked to hide her real feelings and her true intentions from anything that could watch, anything that could listen, anything that could read – because it all fed back to the same system. It was harder to hide her heartbeat, particularly now they were putting smart lightbulbs into public spaces with sensors that could monitor the vitals of anyone nearby. But she could only do what she could do.

She had opposed the use of the system by her own party's government, and for that reason, not only had her star fallen but she had been placed on a watch list. The system kept a close eye on her at all times. And faced with a blank patch it wouldn't be happy. It would probably send...

Yes. Sure enough, Kanha heard the familiar hum. She resisted the urge to look up. There was a drone approaching. The system had come to check on her. It hovered above her, not bothering to hide the fact.

Kanha got up and walked over to the river and put her hands on the low stone wall. The system couldn't care less if she threw herself in. Wouldn't call for the emergency services to come rushing to her aid. Wouldn't call a Samaritan to come and talk her down. As far as its logical cells computed, her death would be one less inconvenience to the government, to the system it used, and to those who owned it and profited from it. A result in fact. A tick passing from synapse to synapse.

But Kanha had no intention of throwing herself in.

It was murder. It was murder, she chanted in her head. They were ready to act. With the medical examiner's evidence added to what they had already gathered, they had all the proof they needed. For the journalist who was killed, for Harry Colbey, who had been harassed to within an inch of his life, for Easterly and for all those citizens of Britain whom they represented, she would get justice.

I.3

Licking the last of the ketchup from his fingers, and checking he hadn't spilled any on his fresh shirt, Harry Colbey hurried down to the ground floor of the Palace of Westminster and out into the corridor that ran through it like a thoracic spine. To his left lay the House of Commons, of which he was a member, and to his right the House of Lords. Between these two debating chambers was an octagonal stone room with a domed ceiling. It was here that Colbey paused beneath the gilt chandelier and collected himself.

He had not been invited to the press conference, but judging from the number of MPs who were hurrying past him towards the Star Chamber, he was not the only one who had caught wind of it and decided to gatecrash. That was a good thing. He could hide among them.

'Who's doing the presentation?' Colbey asked a passing MP.

'The Prime Minister,' was the reply.

Colbey mused. It was unusual for Neville Jameson to take a press conference himself. He was not a confident speaker. Certainly not sharp enough to field questions from the lobby press. He hurried to catch up with his old colleague – for he had once belonged to his party too – and joined in step with him.

'Why Neville?'

The MP shrugged. 'I don't know. I got an email saying I was invited. Did you, then?'

Colbey had not walked out into the Star Chamber Court before. Despite its name, it was just an interior courtyard of bare grass enclosed within the House of Commons. Far above them, the outside faces of stained-glass windows could be seen, and below that it was all stone. A claustrophobic sort of place. At one end of the courtyard was a platform with a lectern and a screen behind, and rows of seating filled the rest of the space.

Colbey slipped away from his old colleague. Looking around, he saw that the invited MPs were all keen supporters of the Prime Minister. But most surprising was the sight of the audience – row upon row of hacks from the Mouth of the Mob website, known as Mobsters. They were easily identified, with their floaty shirts, Tintin trousers and long hair pulled up into topknots. Colbey searched in the crowd for familiar faces. He knew most of the lobby press journalists well. They were there, but they were scattered about, and mostly at the back.

Colbey made his way over to Quentin Tidy of the *Times*, who sat looking cross in a crumpled suit.

'What are you doing back here?' Colbey said to him.

'Tell me about it,' Tidy grumbled and waved his hand over the ranks ahead. 'Those arseholes have been given the front seats.'

Colbey shook his head to show his disbelief and Quentin shifted about in his seat.

'There's going to be hell to pay when my editor finds out about this, I tell you. Bloody Number Ten. They've gone too far this time.'

The Prime Minister's Chief of Staff fussed about on the stage, moving the lectern and then moving it back. On the screen behind him, the coalition government's slogan ran on a constant loop: *safety through modernity*. He raised his hands in applause and the Prime Minister, Neville Jameson, came running up the far side of the chairs. The Mobsters leapt to their feet with a cheer and Jameson had to wave his arms like he was slowing down traffic to get them all to take their seats again. As their applause died away, the tail end of a squabble could be heard: the *Daily Mail* representative was complaining to a junior member of the Number Ten team.

'That's just how it goes,' the SPAD was saying. 'Stars rise and fall, you know.'

But realising the Prime Minister was there, he quickly fell silent and backed away as the lobby journalist grumbled, 'We'll see about that.'

The Prime Minister was a tall, thin man, not quite a beanpole, but certainly standing a head above most. He wore his hair greased to the side, and Colbey thought how much better dressed he was than he used to be.

'Thank you all for coming,' Jameson started, but at a prompt from his Press Officer he said a little louder, 'Sorry, can you hear me alright?' He tapped on the microphone and the audience winced as the speakers buzzed.

'I won't keep you from your breakfasts for long. But due to the recent step up in terror attacks...' he trailed off, and looked behind him. 'Yes. We will have *safety through modernity*. And our party, together with the Whigges, are already showing how well-fitted we are for the job.'

'Here in Britain, under my coalition government, we have become the safest country in the world. Crime rates have fallen to record lows, arrest levels are at a record high, and if and when terrorists choose to strike again, we will be ready.

'But you know all that. So let's get on to today's exciting announcement. And it's this...'

A forest of Mobsters raised their phones.

'The state-of-the-art Alcheminna system, which is already linked up to many of our government services – health, immigration, administration, policing, the management of our energy networks – is going to be made available to all of you too. To all of our British citizens. What I'm thrilled to announce is that…' – and here he rocked on his toes and the phone cameras tilted up and down – 'this morning we began to roll out a delivery of free smart speakers, with Alcheminna's systems pre-installed, to every household in the country.'

The MPs at the back applauded and hooted, and Tidy rolled his eyes. 'Is this a press announcement or a political rally?' he muttered, but was shushed by those Mobsters around him.

'These free smart speakers will not only be connected up to the government's version of the Alcheminna system but will also carry the company's other AI products as standard. Products I know many of you already use, such as their personal assistant product, which comes with free email, free text, free search, free therapeutic care. Thanks to this government, every person in our nation will be able to gain access to the benefits of the modern world. Free medical advice, free legal advice, free security advice. By the end of this week, Britain will be the most technologically advanced nation in the world.'

Jameson turned round to draw everyone's attention to the screen, which filled with an image of a family gathered around a grey block on the dining table.

'Small, isn't it?' he said. 'Wireless – wireless charging. One for every room in the house. I like to think of the system, particularly here in its smart speaker form, as being like a new family member. A wise old grandparent, perhaps, who is always there in the corner, ready to give help and advice. Ready to warn of danger, any time, night or day.'

On the screen behind him, a picture of a man sitting in an armchair appeared. He had wiry, curly hair and was dressed in slacks with a cardigan over an off-grey shirt.

'No,' laughed Jameson. 'That is not any old grandparent. That is Henri Lauvaux, the CEO of the company that made the system that is keeping us all safe.'

Henri Lauvaux's smiling face disappeared and was replaced by an image of children playing in a garden.

'That's the fun stuff. But the other important thing to know is that these government smart speakers will also help keep us safe, by allowing the government to immediately let people know when there is danger about.'

The cartoon image of children playing in a garden turned to one of a mother looking on in alarm as the smart speaker blared out a siren, little lines coming off it to represent the sound. The mother ran to the garden and called her children inside. Jameson watched the crowd as the clip played.

'Following last year's terror attacks, both the train derailment and the gas explosions, we are on an amber terror warning across the country...'

Now he continued more loudly and Colbey thought that, despite the new suit, there was some hesitation in his manner, as if he had practised giving Prime Ministerial speeches in his bathroom mirror, and hadn't quite convinced himself he was the part. As if he was nervously waiting for someone at any moment to leap up from the crowd and call out that he was a fraud. He raised his voice and pointed a finger out at the crowd.

'Be vigilant! If you think someone isn't who they claim to be, then act. You can use the smart speaker to call for help. Just say... "Help!"'

Jameson smiled and the audience dutifully laughed. To more applause, he finished off with, 'Now. Do I have any questions?'

The PM's Chief of Staff made a show of pointing at his watch. He seemed to be offering the PM some glasses, which Jameson was refusing.

'I think we have time for two.'

Tidy of the *Times* immediately rose and called out, 'Prime Minister!' But he was ignored. Jameson picked out a Mobster from the ranks of those who stood, and her question came gushing out of her.

'Prime Minister, will the smart speaker let us know if there is a stay-at-home order in place?'

'Good question,' the PM replied, and even the MPs around Colbey glanced at one another to laugh at such an obviously planted question. 'I should have said. If the smart speaker sounds a warning, it means your area has moved up to a red alert, and you must *stay at home* for your safety.'

The forest of Mobsters' arms was raised into the air again, and as Jameson looked them over, his index finger hovering over his choice, Quentin Tidy stood and bellowed, 'Prime Minister! The associated lobby press must be allowed a question!'

Jameson glanced at his Chief of Staff and was given a nod.

The crowd fell silent, and many swivelled round. As amateur journalists, some of whom had been invited into the House of Commons for the first time, the Mobsters were as keen to film the *Times* asking a question of the Prime Minister as they were to film his speech.

Tidy stood, taking his time to do so.

'Prime Minister. This is the first time you have been clear that both the train derailment and the gas explosions were attacks of terror. Do you have any further intelligence you can share with us?'

Jameson glanced not at his Chief of Staff this time but at his Press Secretary, who shook his head.

'No comment on that,' Jameson said. 'And please keep to the news we're announcing today. So, one more question then on the topic we are trying to cover today.'

With a frown and a mutter of 'Disgraceful,' Tidy took his seat again.

This time Jameson picked a Mobster on the second row, and as she stood, Colbey thought he recognised her. She had definitely once been a Mobster, but he had a feeling she was freelance now. He'd seen her reports here and there in the mainstream press. It was hard not to recognise her what with that shock of pink hair she favoured.

Seeing her stand, Jameson's Press Officer frowned and started to inch his way around to her. He was obviously wondering how his seating plan had gone awry.

'Prime Minister. Can you comment on rumours that Henri Lauvaux, the CEO of Alcheminna, and his fellow shareholders have become obscenely rich due to the large number of government contracts they have secured? And can you comment on the fact that they are now using that wealth to buy influence all over Britain?'

Jameson muttered loudly enough that Colbey heard it even from his place at the back. 'Who the hell is that?'

By now the PM's Press Officer stood next to where she sat, at the end of her row.

'Who do you represent?' he hissed. 'I thought you were with the Mouth of the Mob.'

'Can you comment, Prime Minister?' she said. To the Press Officer, she hissed back, 'I'm a lobby journalist. I have a press pass, you know.'

Good for you, Colbey thought.

'But you said you were with the Mob.'

'No I didn't. You just assumed because I used to be one of them.' And to the Prime Minister she said again, 'Prime Minister, could I please have a comment.'

Jameson looked beautifully blank and was clearly about to say 'No comment,' when the Press Officer shook a finger almost imperceptibly in the air, so Jameson stepped back to the microphone.

'Alcheminna is a legitimate company that follows the same laws as every other company in Britain. It won the government contracts through a regulated and transparent process.'

'Prime Minister, I didn't ask about the company,' the journalist persisted. 'I'm talking about the shareholders and their hangers-on.

I have eyewitness statements asserting that their family members are free to move about during stay-at-home orders.'

'Alcheminna's systems are crucial to the security of the nation,' Jameson said. 'And as such its workforce may well be afforded different status.'

He saw his Press Officer wince over the word 'different', and at once the lobby press journalists picked up on it.

'Prime Minister!' Tidy called out. 'What other kinds of different treatment are they afforded?'

'Prime Minister!' called another. 'Why the families too?'

At this, even the mobsters couldn't help themselves, with one shouting out, 'Prime Minister! Is it true that three members of your cabinet are shareholders too?'

'That's all we've time for for now,' Neville Jameson said, moving quickly to leave the stage as his Chief of Staff leapt up and called the press conference to an end. Like the Prime Minister he was deaf to the questions, and quickly enough they petered away to nothing.

Colbey laughed, seeing that the Prime Minister's loyal Mobsters had happily recorded all that too. When you remove all the rules, there are no rules, he thought. Already they were hurrying off to dictate copy or be the first to get articles or analysis up on the web. However loyal they might be to the government, they were more loyal to their Mobster rankings.

Colbey made his way through the departing crowds towards the journalist with the pink hair. It seemed she had won her argument with the PM's Press Officer, who had tried to take away her pass and was now walking away with a grumble, saying, 'We shall see about that.'

'Hello,' Colbey said to her. 'Good question.'

She cocked her head to one side. 'Harry Colbey, right?'

'That's right.'

'You used to be with them, didn't you? But had the whip removed after that sex scandal.'

'It was a deepfake – I have the proof. The Standards Committee agreed.'

'But Jameson withdrew the whip from you all the same.'

'Yes. He did. Didn't think I represented their party's modern views. I'm an independent now. Seems you are too?'

'Got fed up at the Mouth. It used to be great, when Johnny ran it. Citizen journalism, searching for scoops. Out and about in the world, search for the truth. But that all changed after his widow sold it.'

Colbey looked at her in surprise.

'She sold the Mouth of the Mob? Who bought it?' he said.

'Take a guess.'

'Oh,' Colbey groaned. 'Not…?'

'Yes, you guessed it: Alcheminna Systems.'

Colbey looked up at the square of sky above them. There was now a mackerel of white among the grey clouds.

'We missed that,' he said.

'They hid the trail through an offshore company in the Caribbean.'

'I'd love to know which one. Will you tell me?'

'Sorry. I sold the scoop to Quentin Tidy. He's going to run a piece on it in the next day.'

'So you're freelance now?'

'Yes, trying to be official. I went back to college and everything. The trouble with the Mouth of the Mob since Henri Lauvaux took it over is that they push what they want to the top, not what real people vote for. The whole thing is fixed.'

'Well, at least there is still a free press,' Colbey said automatically, but then thought of how they had been pushed to the side in this meeting. 'Democracy doesn't function without it.'

Jade pushed her pink fringe from her forehead. 'I know. I went back to journalism school, like I said. A free press and an opposition. That's what makes a democracy strong.'

'And a few other things…'

'Yes, yes. We have the Lords who scrutinise the laws, the judiciary who carry them out—'

'You'd be surprised how many people are invested in democracy,' Colbey said. 'It's a strong machine.'

Jade stopped and watched the cartoon that was still running on a loop on the screen. 'But it's being picked at around the edges, isn't it?' she said.

Colbey nodded. 'Yes, but we're working to fix that.'

Jade looked at him. 'Do you have anything I could use for an article? It's hard, trying to get established.'

'You can have my deepfake evidence if you want? I tried to get the papers interested, but apparently I was just another sleazy MP. Yesterday's news.'

'Figures,' she said. Then she added, 'I'm sorry. I don't think I'd be able to find a home for it.'

They watched as the cartoon flicked back onto the smiling face of Lauvaux.

'Have you ever met him?'

'A few times.'

'So what drives him? Is it greed?'

'Greed?' Colbey shook his head. 'Not at all.'

He thought about his last conversation with Alcheminna's CEO.

'Henri Lauvaux believes it is only a matter of time before the world turns to a new order. Where there will be those in front of the cameras, and those behind them. I don't mean in the sense of your cameras here, the phone and television cameras. I mean in the sense of the eyes and ears of the government. There will be those who are watched and those who will be doing the watching. He decided the best way to make sure he was one of the watchers was to build a system for the government and own it. He calls the system "Divinity".'

'And the other shareholders?'

Colbey looked around; there was no one left in the courtyard but them.

'I'll set you on the path,' he said. She looked at him eagerly as he went on, 'They call themselves the Owners. The system looks out for them. And you're right. They don't follow the rules. In fact, they receive... preferential treatment. While those who are in opposition to the system receive unfavourable treatment.'

'Such as?'

Colbey thought about how to explain the campaign of harassment he had endured since he had stood up against them. He thought of the warnings that came up on police systems whenever he passed an officer, suggesting he needed to be stopped and searched. The way that nothing worked for him. Even traffic lights would not turn green for him.

'Little things,' he said, 'that make life impossible. Make you want to give up and let them have their way.'

'Can you prove it?'

'We will soon, hopefully.'

'We?'

'I've said too much.'

She seemed to think things through as she stared at the cartoon.

'Jameson's three new party members are shareholders of Alcheminna, or Owners as you call them. They're bold enough to declare it openly on the list of interests. Ewan MacLellan – that piece of work who used to govern our country and should never have been allowed back as an MP, let alone into the cabinet – is one. Then there are two others who were given British citizenship, jettisoned into safe seats at the last two by-elections, and immediately given ministerial positions.' She turned to Colbey. 'Will you show me the proof of your harassment when you have it?'

'Maybe,' he said. 'Do you think you would be able to find a home for that?'

She broke into a grin and ran her fingers through her hair. What was she? Thirty, perhaps. This was what he wanted for his daughter. Independence, a job where she depended on her own skills, her own wits.

'For sure,' she said. She dug a card out of her pocket and pressed it into his hand.

'Jade. Jade Harrelson. When you are ready to share, I will be waiting.'

'OK,' he said.

He watched her walk away. Then he looked up the sky again. There were a few patches of blue starting to show through. Colbey had a sudden urge to feel the sun on his face. Where was it? Not in that window of sky above him. He sighed. Oh, to be young and still full of fight, he thought. He got wearily up. It was ten o'clock and there was work to be done.

I.4

Jameson and his Chief of Staff sat in the back of his Prime Ministerial car – a bomb-proof Range Rover with the most comfortable black leather seats.

'Bloody associated press,' he said, as they were driven the short distance from the Houses of Parliament to Ten Downing Street. 'They've got a shock coming for them.'

Jameson didn't listen to the man's reply. His stomach was rumbling and he was thinking about requesting a second breakfast. Would the day chef know that the night chef had already cooked him one?

They took the back entrance into Downing Street and his Chief of Staff bored on. I won't let him in the car with me next time, Jameson thought. Can't run the country with someone wittering on at me the whole time. As they pulled up at the building, Jameson felt his usual swell of excitement at the fact that he was Prime Minister. It had happened so quickly. Sometimes he needed to pinch himself because it couldn't possibly be real. One minute, he had been a no-hope candidate for the party leadership elections, the next enough of his fellow members had voted for him that he was a shoe-in. Hah! That showed that smarmy Esme Kanha, didn't it? She'd thought she had them all behind her.

Then out of nowhere came the opportunity of a coalition with the Whigges. Alright, perhaps not out of nowhere. Perhaps the Frenchman and his clever little system had engineered it piece by piece. Yet by grasping the opportunity, it was he who had seized power for them all. Kanha wouldn't have done that, would she? Wouldn't have grasped the nettle and agreed to work with that arrogant fool of a Whigge leader, Sanjay Arun?

Jameson strolled through the back corridor into the hallway behind the famous black door and onto those famous black and white flagstones, and found that his Chief of Staff was still going on. Something about the Foreign Office.

'Right,' he said, stopping and looking down at the chap. 'What is it *you* think we should do?'

The man told him.

'Well, go and do that, then,' Jameson said.

The man seemed uncertain.

'Don't you trust your own judgement?' Jameson tried to hold back his sneer. He had been working on his facial features in the mirror of late, and had realised that sometimes he had a sneer when he talked. He didn't want that now that he was Prime Minister. A sneer wasn't very Prime Ministerial.

Finally, the man agreed, and went off to arrange whatever it was he had wanted to do in the first place. He's far better qualified than me to make the call, Jameson thought, and then congratulated himself.

Delegation, that was the key. That was always the key to a successful leader. Gather those around you who are clever and capable and get them to work for you, not the other way round.

He trotted up the stairs to his office. He would ask for a second breakfast, he decided, but the other question was what should he have for lunch? He liked to challenge the chefs at Number Ten by making random requests. Sushi today, he would sometimes tell his secretary. Or roast beef. Or tapas. Or whatever came to mind, day and night. After all, he was the most important man in the country. It was his right to eat as he chose. Well, he thought, maybe not the *most* important. There was the King, after all, although his role was ceremonial. And then there was the Frenchman himself...

Jameson's office was upstairs, looking out onto the garden at the back. He had debated long and hard which room to take, as he knew he would be judged by the Number Ten staff on his decision. He had been unable to make up his mind. He had made them gather together the best of the furniture that he had chosen from all of the rooms and take them first to one room and then to another – desks, chairs, pictures. After three changes of room, they had ended up where they had started and he'd chosen that one for his office.

Later he was embarrassed to discover it was the same room that Rolt, the opposition leader, had used, and he had been about to move again when his Chief of Staff pointed out it was also the room that Ewan MacLellan had chosen. And if it was good enough for MacLellan, Jameson thought, a hero of his...

So he had decided to stay put.

His secretary sat at a desk outside his office. A pretty thing by the name of Anastacia. I have plans for you, he thought, as she greeted him and took his dark raincoat from his arm.

'Can I get you anything, Prime Minister?'

'Breakfast. I'd like bacon, scrambled eggs, black pudding and fried bread.'

'Right away. There's fresh coffee in your office.'

She gave him a slightly fake smile. But he wasn't bothered. He was Prime Minister now and that was catnip to these young girls. She has only taken a job like this because she's drawn to powerful men, he thought. Probably looking for a husband. Well, let her try and catch me. Jameson smiled at the prospect.

'Something funny?' she said.

'No, no.'

She gave another fake smile. Mm... maybe he should bombard her with flowers. He stormed into his office and closed the door behind him. That sort of girl likes that sort of—

But he was pulled up short.

The bloody Frenchman, Henri Lauvaux, was sat at his desk, in Jameson's own chair even.

He felt a spasm of annoyance at seeing the weathered face, the wiry hair that surrounded it.

Worse than that, Sanjay Arun, his Home Secretary and fellow coalition leader, sat at the side of the desk with his feet up on Jameson's green felt. A short man. Jameson was surprised his feet could reach.

They didn't even acknowledge his entrance. They were using the big screen that hung on the far wall to hold a meeting with Divinity.

He wasn't sure what upset him the most. That they ignored him. That the Frenchman sat in his chair. That Arun had feet on his desk. Or that the two were holding a meeting without him.

He glanced at the screen. The Divinity AI was the jewel in the Alcheminna fleet, a multi-personality system. It had taken Jameson a while to get to grips with it, but he understood it now. In its development, the company – or the AI itself in fact – had scraped or been fed data about every citizen in the country: texts, emails, telephone calls, work presentations, social media posts, heart rates, medical files, police records, school reports. It knew everyone better than their own mother did. All their little tells that only an expert or an AI trained in facial recognition would spot had been fed in. Lies on a conference call, a hurt look when sitting under a security camera – the system saw it and noted it. Every vocal inflection. Every kiss or lack of kiss in a text. Every time someone's heart beat faster because they had bumped into someone they wanted, the AI was party to it. Who they loved, who they liked, who they didn't, who they hated. It stored not just friendship links – that was old hat – but the nuances of relationships between everyone. The system knew it all. And then... it was designed to put on these personalities and 'think' like the person. 'Look' like the person. 'Sound' like the person. 'Act' like the person. And there was no putting the genie back in the bottle now. Divinity knew them all inside out. Could be them if it wanted to. Could speak like them. Look like them. Spill their secrets. The possibilities were endless...

Today, Lauvaux and Arun were quizzing Jackie Rolt. Not the real Jackie Rolt, of course. But the version of the opposition leader that existed in the Divinity system.

'Good morning,' Jameson said. 'I hope I'm not interrupting.'

They ignored him and carried on their 'meeting' with Rolt. And in her bluff Northern tones, Rolt was telling them exactly what her next step was to be. She had not given up on challenging the validity of the coalition.

Somewhere she or one of her team must have let that slip in front of a phone, a listening eye, perhaps a passing delivery drone. It was hard now that there were listening cameras everywhere, to keep things private. Knowledge is power, Lauvaux was always telling him. To know someone is to control them.

Letting their discussion wash over him, Jameson went to make himself a coffee. Although it was not yet midday, he put some brandy in it. I won't offer them one, he thought. I shouldn't have to wait on them. By rights, they should leap up and wait on me.

Arun glanced over his shoulder at Jameson. 'Black for me, old man.'

Jameson ignored him. He hovered next to the screen with his coffee and looked pointedly at the Frenchman.

Henri Lauvaux was a tall man, dressed as usual in his cords and off-white shirt, and it took him a moment to extricate his long legs from under the desk and ease himself out of Jameson's chair. The Prime Minister stood for a moment wondering if he should pretend he wasn't too fussed, but when he saw Arun glance at the empty seat he hurried over and sat down.

'Help yourself,' he said to Arun, waving a hand at the coffee station.

He hated Arun with a passion. The leader of the Whigge party was more arrogant than he had any right to be. He had just been lucky, that was all. He had been in the right place at the right time. That was the only reason he was in any position of power at all. If Jameson had not been short of a majority – if he had not been forced to enter into a coalition with the Whigges – then the man would have remained what he was. A cocky, jumped-up minor player of a minor party.

He hadn't wanted to give the Whigge leader the Home Office, had plenty of staff loyal to him whom he would have preferred to dole it out to, but the Frenchman had insisted. And he had to keep Lauvaux happy. Him and that many-faced, ever-watching devil in a box that came with him.

Jameson watched them interrogate the opposition leader, taking turns to ask her questions. Eventually, Arun got bored and said, 'That's all we need, isn't it? One last thing, Rolt. You got any little quirks in the bedroom? Whips? Dress-up?'

Lauvaux smiled and waved his hand, and the screen switched back to the waiting icon.

Sometimes, Jameson wondered whether he might be able to get the little devil in the box for himself and do away with Lauvaux, but the thought of it frightened him. How would one control the devil once one owed it, without Lauvaux to give it instructions? And he wasn't sure the Owners, those shareholders of Alcheminna who officially owned Divinity, would leap to his command as quickly as to Lauvaux's. But I'm the one who allows them to live as they choose, he thought. I'm the one with the majority in the House. I can change any law I want.

Although it was on standby, the devil, or Divinity as Lauvaux called it, was still there, listening to them. Lauvaux had put a little dot of a smart speaker down on the desk because the security camera in Jameson's office was old fashioned and did not have listening capabilities. He glanced at the TV screen in the corner of the room, its conference eye built in to the top. It would be watching them too. He thought of the watch that Lauvaux insisted he wear at all times. Divinity would be monitoring his heartbeat, and it would know that when he had walked into the room it had started to beat a little faster with annoyance when he found them there in his office. Why had his secretary not told him they were there?

But it would soon be his devil too. He was not an Owner yet, as he did not have shares in Alcheminna. But he had been promised them, so it would all be worth it later.

They were done. Lauvaux clicked off the screen with a signal of his fingers and sauntered over to the side table. He poured a cup of coffee for himself and another for Arun, which he handed to him.

'I want you to call a cabinet meeting tomorrow,' he said to Jameson. 'And I will be there. I think it is about time I started to take the meetings myself.'

'But...' Jameson felt his bottom lip tremble. 'Is that necessary? Surely I can manage the cabinet.'

'No.'

Jameson felt his grip on things sliding. 'But in what capacity will you be there?'

'What does that matter? They all understand the situation, don't they? They have all agreed to the plan?'

'Yes, of course.'

'Which is why Divinity chose them.'

'But...'

'Yes?'

'What will the staff of Number Ten think if you're in the meeting?'

'Whatever you tell them to.'

'And what will that be?'

'Whatever you want it to be.'

Jameson took a gulp of his brandy-infused coffee. It scorched his lips, but he needed the alcohol to cool the buzzing in his head, to slow the beating of his heart, the thumping that the devil was monitoring.

Arun grunted. 'Just tell them he's a special advisor.'

'But special advisors aren't allowed to speak in cabinet meetings,' Jameson protested.

'Who is going to tell anyone that I speak?' Lauvaux said, and Jameson looked down at the desk, feeling the beady eye of Divinity on the top of his head.

'You're right. But—'

Lauvaux said irritably, 'Just hold the meeting at Chequers if this is going to cause you an issue. We'll have it this evening.'

'Yes,' said Jameson, with relief. 'That would be easier. Thank you.'

Why am I thanking him? he thought. And how had Lauvaux even gained entry to Number Ten? Perhaps Arun had signed him in, but Arun did not have the right to do that. Perhaps he shouldn't enquire. Perhaps he wouldn't like the answer.

Lauvaux pulled up a chair and the three of them worked on the plan for a while. Divinity was in everything now. It sounded like a prayer, but it was far from that.

'When will we move to the new order?' Jameson asked.

'The new order is already in place,' Lauvaux said.

'Yes, but when will we push the button to make it official?'

Lauvaux considered. 'We are not ready. There are a few things that must be handled delicately. A few problems that need sorting.'

Jameson knew exactly what he was talking about. 'Harry Colbey,' he said.

Lauvaux shook his head. 'There will always be opposition. But soon you will find they will not be able to pierce your skin when they try to bite.'

Arun picked up a pen and tapped it on the desk. 'We're not ready,' he said. 'In some of the inner-city estates people are covering up the listening posts. Spraying them with cement.'

Lauvaux frowned. 'Cement? We can't have that.' And turning to Jameson, he said, 'Put through some legislation. Make it a life sentence for compromising the safety of fellow citizens by damaging a listening eye.'

'Well...' Jameson started. 'I suppose I could raise it as an emergency bill.'

'Good.'

'I've ordered in more police drones,' Arun went on. 'To patrol the estates. But the kids keep shooting them down with air rifles and despite the system urging them on, the officers are reluctant to move against children.'

'What about the other idea, then?' Jameson said. 'Your supporters, the Whigges?'

'Yes, it could be time for that. The younger ones are keen believers in keeping everyone safe. Perhaps we could give a few of them some sort of official capacity as keepers of the listening-eye posts.'

Lauvaux turned to the screen. 'What do you think?' he said.

The image on the screen switched through faces before settling on one of Lauvaux.

'Don't make it official,' the digital replica of Lauvaux said. 'I will choose them. They will not have an official role, but let them be public-spirited and take it into their own heads to patrol the streets. Divinity will make sure the police do not interfere.'

'Yes,' the real Lauvaux replied. Divinity had millions of profiles to choose from yet always seemed to return to Lauvaux's. But then... he was the master of all this. Who better to pick matters through with?

Jameson had never seen the digital version of himself. He already knew what it knew. It knew what he knew. All his dirty little secrets. All his emails and texts sifted through. Since he had understood what the system did, he had tried to hide his personality from it, but it was too late. He hated the fact that the arrogant Arun might have interrogated his digital self. Perhaps he hadn't. Perhaps he was so arrogant he hadn't bothered. Perhaps…

Lauvaux stood and lifted his bag onto his shoulder.

'I might have to return to France for a few days,' he said. 'My mother-in-law is dying.'

'I'm sorry to hear that,' Jameson said, but Lauvaux waved the fake condolence away.

'I'll be in touch,' he said. 'And if you can't get hold of me and you need an urgent answer, you can always speak to the version of me in Divinity. That should tide you over.'

Outside the room, Jameson heard Lauvaux tell Anastacia to bring his car to the front of Number Ten. Arun was lingering. He stood gazing at the screen on which bobbed the holding logo of Divinity. Was there something his Home Secretary wanted to say now that Lauvaux was gone? The two of them had never been alone in a room together. Always it was the Frenchman who arranged these meetings. Then he realised that Lauvaux had left the speaker pebble on his desk.

Arun turned and looked at him. He wants my job, Jameson realised. He is plotting how to stab me in the back. Divinity would know. He could ask it. He could find the Arun in the system and ask it what evil plot Arun was hatching against him to steal his crown.

But then… when Arun quizzed the version of Jameson in the system, that version would tell Arun he had done it.

'Laters,' Arun said and left the room, not bothering to close the door behind him.

Jameson eyed the pebble. Above his head was the video camera.

He dared not move the pebble. Lauvaux would know. Lauvaux might be gone, but Divinity was there, watching him, listening to him breathing, monitoring his heart rate. Of course it was. From now on Divinity would always be there.

1.5

Colbey had waited for a respectable time after his question in the House of Commons before giving his nod of respect to the Speaker and hurrying out of the chamber. It had not been a question that had set the world on fire, just one intended to keep up pressure on the Home Office about their use of the Alcheminna systems. If Europe would not deal with the company and had forced it to withdraw from the continent after a series of major fines, why was it increasingly used in the UK? But the Home Secretary, Sanjay Arun, had not turned up and some stand-in junior minister had trotted through a load of stock nonsense in response.

The House had been surprisingly empty of those who might challenge the government. Most of the questions had come from members of the government's own back benches. Stooge requests for information designed to allow the government an opportunity to brag about its low crime rates. Of course the figures are down, Colbey thought, as he walked to the modern office building opposite the House of Commons where many of the MPs had their offices. The nation was increasingly under surveillance. And now was being told to *stay at home*, at random times, area by area. Almost as if the government wished to test compliance. The system behind the listening eyes used facial recognition capabilities to identify anyone out on the street, passing the information to the police, who were instructed by a police scheduling system, also run by Divinity, how and where to find them and when to dish out fines. Already arrests were being made of repeat offenders.

As he trotted through the marbled atrium of Portcullis House – it wasn't unlike a shopping mall, with cafés at one end and two rows of full-sized olive trees in the centre – Colbey glanced up through the diamond-shaped panes of glass and saw that the weather had changed for the better once more and that the sky was now wholly blue. He stopped at one of the trees and pressed his face onto its ancient crinkled bark; he wondered where it had originally grown.

'Tree hugger!' said an opposition MP good-humouredly as he passed, and Colbey let the tree go. He was late in any event. By the time he arrived on the fifth floor and hurried into the room, the meeting was about to begin.

'Ah, there he is,' said Lord Silverman. 'Can't start without Harry Colbey, can we?'

'Apologies,' Colbey said, as he settled into an empty seat. There were plenty of them. He looked around the table. 'Where is everyone?' he whispered to the MP next to him, but the man pulled a face.

'Stay-at-home orders in West Lothian, Wales and the Midlands,' he muttered.

'Ah,' said Colbey. That might explain why the House was so empty.

There were three contingents around the table. Several lords sat at the top, grouped around Lord Silverman, an old textiles merchant who had been knighted for his services to industry and the regeneration of the East End. His bald pate shone whenever he tilted it, catching the sun streaming in through the windows. On the far side were MPs from the opposition, while Colbey sat on the side nearest the door, among rebel government MPs. Rebel, but not yet evicted from the party like Colbey had been.

'First point of order,' Lord Silverman said. 'As you all know, we are the members of two committees that are now defunct. And those committees were The Commons Select Committee on Privacy and Surveillance and the Lords Committee on AI and Its Threat to Democracy. Now. Both of these have run their course and presented their findings to the government. But – and this is the crucial point, I think you'll find – few of those recommendations have been taken up.' He looked around the room, peering over his glasses. 'So now we find ourselves together again, this time in a cross-party joint-house committee.'

There were nods around the table.

'Now. Would anyone like to recommend a title for this new committee of ours?'

Colbey looked around the room. Those gathered seemed to find something important to read or annotate in their notebooks.

'Anyone?' Lord Silverman said, running a hand over his head. 'Harry, perhaps you would like to kick off?'

Colbey looked up at the security camera in the corner of the room and then at his fellow committee members.

'I wonder if the first point of order should be whether the meeting is to be public or private?' he said.

'Private!' someone called out from the end of the table. 'I can't speak until we are private.'

'Private has been suggested,' said Lord Silverman. 'Can I have a show of hands?'

Everyone in the room raised their hand without exception.

'Noted,' said Lord Silverman, making a little mark on the notebook in front of him. 'In which case, if I might ask you all to take any forms of technology with microphones and place them outside the room. My friends here and I will see to the television screen and the camera in the corner. As it happens... I have a couple of steel blankets with me and some masking tape.' He held each aloft with a twinkle in his eye.

The room became noisy as his instructions were carried out. Colbey took the opportunity of the chairs being empty to turn each upside down and then crawl underneath the table. He found three listening-eye stickers. He crushed them and threw them into the waste bin in the corridor outside. Behind him, Baroness Bonny and the Earl of Bath had covered the television screen and the security camera with lead-lined bags and were taping the edges down.

'I think we will have to assume we are now private,' Lord Silverman said, when everyone was back in their seats. 'Going forward we will repeat this procedure each time we meet, and this will have to be a matter of trust based on the integrity of those present.'

All looked about themselves and nodded to one another. A few shook hands with their neighbours, even across the table and across the division of party lines.

Colbey was about to ask something when a chorus of complaints rang out.

'I am being followed by a drone,' an MP called Brooke, who represented a swathe of Surrey, said icily. A formidable politician, she had once been Foreign Secretary, but like Kanha had been kicked onto the back benches for refusing to support Neville Jameson's security bill. It had legalised the use of Alcheminna's surveillance system and opened the door to so much more.

'Yep. Me too,' said an opposition MP called Asma Safeer, putting her hands on the table and looking round at them all so that the sharp ends of her sleek bob fell forward to her chin. She was a relatively young MP, but driven, and had worked her way up to Shadow Foreign Secretary and deputy leader of the opposition. Many thought she would be better representing their party than the old dinosaur, as they called their current leader Jackie Rolt, but others thought her too green. Too angry. Too hasty.

'The police have stopped me four times already this week,' she said. 'Driving too fast – twenty-two in a twenty zone – driving too slowly – forty-five in a fifty zone – and twice in what they claimed was a routine check-up to see if I was the owner of my car.'

Lord Silverman held out his hands, but still they went on.

'I can't get phone reception.'

'Same here. I stand next to someone on the same network with the same phone and they have four bars and I have nothing.'

'My messages don't come through.'

'You think that's bad. Somehow my messages to a good friend of mine got sent to my wife.'

Lord Silverman called them to order.

'I am aware that many of us who have expressed concerns about the government's use of the Alcheminna system have been the focus of unwanted drone surveillance and unwelcome police attention. I too am being followed.'

An experienced and highly respected MP of Colbey's old party, Wilbur Saxton, who had also been thrown onto the back benches for refusing to fall behind Jameson, growled, 'I've spoken to the press. Quentin Tidy of the *Times* wants to run something, but he says he needs proof first.'

'What more proof does he need than that we tell him so?' Safeer cried out. 'Let me speak to the old idiot.'

Again, Lord Silverman called for calm.

'Everyone. Please. You must document all these issues. Keep detailed records. What I propose is that we call this the Joint Select Committee Inquiring into the Threat to Democracy and Privacy Caused by Technological Advances. It will be a private committee. It will invite guests for interview and it will diligently gather together the facts. And when we have come to our conclusion, we will report to the government. We will, at that point, also make our findings known to the press so that they can be more widely distributed and brought to the attention of everybody else out there who gives a you-know-what about all this. We will not be swayed by a campaign of intimidation. Isn't that right? Where we find evidence of inappropriate behaviour, we will ask the government to respond. Now... what I want to ask is, who will be our chair?'

'I nominate Harry Colbey,' said Wilbur Saxton.

But Safeer shook her head. 'Don't mean to be rude, but shouldn't it be someone who isn't... you know. Who hasn't got mental health issues?'

'Mental health issues?' Colbey protested.

'Yeah. You know. Agoraphobia.'

Colbey was about to argue, but Lord Silverman got there first.

'I'm sure Harry Colbey would make an excellent chair. He is after all, independent now. And if he is trapped in the Houses of Parliament, for whatever reason, it would certainly keep him focused on the role.'

But it was agreed by all, including Colbey, that Lord Silverman should carry on, as he was already doing an excellent job. So he led them through such dull stuff as the committee's aim, who it might call for evidence, what the final report should cover and so forth. After that, they spent a good half hour arguing over who else they should invite as members, at which point Colbey started to tap his pencil on his pad of paper. He looked at his watch and thought of his meeting with the Speaker at one o'clock. Eventually, when they started to quibble over how many words the report should be, he couldn't hold himself back any longer.

'Don't you think there's a bigger problem here?' he said, interrupting whatever point of order they were picking through. 'There are several MPs who helped me before but who are not here today. Where is Blanc? Where are Chandra, Darvish and Woodroofe?'

'Blanc, Chandra and Woodroofe were all arrested in the last few days,' Brooke said.

'Arrested?' Colbey said.

'Yes. Blanc and Chandra for dangerous driving, and Wood-roofe for tax evasion.'

'And Darvish resigned yesterday. Personal reasons, apparently,' Wilbur added.

Colbey felt panic rise within him. 'What were they?'

'What?'

'The personal reasons?'

'I don't know. They were personal.'

Lauvaux was moving things forward faster than he had expected.

'Too coincidental to be true, surely?' Colbey protested. 'This is no small campaign of harassment. This is interference in the democratic process.'

'Perhaps,' said Lord Silverman. 'But let's not be hasty. I will speak to each of them and report back.'

He made a note on his pad and Safeer said, 'Yes. Let's not cata-strophise. I think you'll find that's a sign of a mental health problem.'

Colbey bit his tongue and the meeting moved on.

It was agreed that the chairman of Alcheminna, Henri Lauvaux, should be called for interview.

'We won't get him before the summer break,' Brooke said. 'It might have to be August. Particularly if we are to schedule Jameson in for July.'

Colbey couldn't take any more. He stood abruptly.

'You don't understand,' he said. 'Our democracy will be gone by August.'

Lord Silverman looked confused. 'Now, Harry—'

'They are moving so fast. The Divinity system is able to hack into anything anywhere. It can watch any citizen it wants, listen to them, follow them, meddle with their lives. And it acts at the behest of Lauvaux. Not the government. It acts on behalf of its shareholders – they call themselves the Owners. They are given preferential treatment, while we are harassed. Jameson is just their puppet. It is Lauvaux we must go for.'

Lord Silverman nodded his head slowly.

'I agree with all that,' he said. 'But we need to gather evidence. We need to move in a democratic fashion.'

Colbey wanted to scream. 'We have been doing so for months,' he said. 'That's all our committees have been doing. Gathering evidence that *they* manipulate and change. That they ignore. That the press cannot use.'

'We lost time challenging Jameson's right for the coalition to take power,' Lord Silverman said.

'And while we did so, they advanced, linking Alcheminna's system into more and more of Britain's infrastructure.'

'We lost time challenging Jameson's bill to turn on the listening posts,' Brooke said.

'And while we did so, they advanced, taking control of policing systems. Every minute we delay, our ability to act against those installing a surveillance state grows less.' Colbey looked around the room. 'And those who oppose it grow fewer.'

'But what would you have us do?' said Safeer. 'We can't move without proof. We would be called conspiracy theorists.'

'For God's sake. The system murdered Reginald Easterly!' Colbey shouted in a fury.

Those around the table glanced at each other.

'Can you prove that?' Lord Silverman asked.

'Yes,' Colbey said. 'We have the proof.'

'Then bring us the proof,' Lord Silverman said. 'Let us see it for our own eyes. In the meantime, we must proceed in an orderly fashion. We must inquire. We must gather evidence. Then we must report.'

Colbey sank back onto his chair and gathered up his things, apologising for needing to leave before they were done.

They still didn't understand, so they couldn't be blamed. And in many ways, he agreed with them. Democracy could only win if the democratic process was allowed to take its course. Any other method – force, illegality, international assistance – would mean the very democracy they were trying to protect was already done for.

'I will bring the evidence,' he said as he stood to go. 'And I will bring it as soon as I can. But if you are going to call Lauvaux to answer to this committee, you must do it now. Or none of you will be here to call him.'

I.6

Kanha sat in the lobby of what had once been the Department for Personal Information, but which was now a satellite Home Office building, and stewed. Although it was still early, she had been waiting to see Gerald Moreland, one of the department's two permanent secretaries, for over an hour and a half. God, how her star had fallen. She never used to wait on anyone. They used to have to wait on her.

She was about to give up hope when a very junior associate called her name and said he would take her to Moreland's office.

'I know where it is,' she wanted to say.

But Gerald Moreland was full of apologies as he got up from his desk and welcomed her.

'I truly am sorry,' he said. 'My diary is not my own right now.'

'Well at least you still have a job,' Kanha said, the words slipping out in her irritation at being kept waiting for so long. 'At least you still have an office.' She pointed around the room, at his mahogany partner's desk, the numerous sofas at the far end and the long conference table between the two. It had once been a ministerial office – had in fact housed Harry Colbey when he had been Minister for Personal Information, and Percy Dvořáček before that. It had good views: the Thames at one end and the classical early-twentieth-century Whitehall buildings opposite on the longer side. Kanha thought of her new office, a dungeon in the bowels of the House of Commons. God, what a disaster it all was.

Moreland put on a hurt expression like a pantomime ham. 'I doubt I'll have it for much longer. I'm hanging on by a thread.'

Kanha relented. 'I'm sorry. It's not been an easy morning.'

She put her bag down on the long walnut table and accepted Moreland's offer of coffee, idly running her fingers along the table's polished surface while he made it for her.

'Is the job-share with Olivia Powers not going well then?'

Moreland stood thinking with the coffee jar in his hands. He was a neat, particular man who always wore a pinstriped suit. He made an attempt at a brave smile.

'It was never going to work. They only set it up like that to keep me distracted while they whittled away my role. Nearly everything has gone to her now. I just have the nonsense teams left.'

'And the Counter-Deepfake team?'

'Gone,' he said, turning back to his task. 'Quite literally, in fact. I came in one morning to find they had upped and left. Took all of our work with them.'

'Shall I guess where?'

'I don't think you need to. Some subsidiary of Alcheminna is the rumour. Crazy salaries and relocation to a tax haven with palm trees and a beach.'

Despite the size of the office, Kanha felt the walls closing in on her.

'Fuck,' she said. With so many lies about her fellow rebels, Harry Colbey included, being circulated on the internet, they had needed that department.

'So you've lost all of your Home Office roles? She has them all now? Immigration? Police?'

'Everything. I've been outmanoeuvred. In any normal circumstance I would have tendered my resignation by now. It's effectively constructive dismissal, but let's just say... I'm still considering my options.'

Moreland glanced up at the security camera in the corner. 'Shall we take some air?' he said.

As he had done many times before, Moreland put his phone on the conference table beside Kanha's bag and went and opened the French windows on the street side of the building. She felt a bit of a wrench leaving her bag there with the autopsy recording in it and Moreland, sharp-eyed as ever, said as they stepped out onto the balcony, 'Something important in there?'

'You could say that,' she replied.

They stood for a while and looked at the vehicles passing several storeys below, the cars, taxis and buses, and the drones that streamed above the traffic. If one were to rise up and try to eavesdrop on their conversation, Moreland would send it flying with a bit of loose masonry from the balustrade. He was a pretty good shot for a man who wore pinstripes.

'So tell me,' he said, 'what's new?'

Kanha was never exactly sure how much she trusted Gerald Moreland. The problem with these senior civil servants, particularly old-school types like him, was that they were so precious about their political impartiality it sometimes paralysed them. Even if they knew that what you wanted them to do was the right thing to do, if it was clearly one party's preference over another's they dug their heels in like little pinstriped mules.

'Do you remember when this used to be the office of the Minister for Personal Information?' she said.

'Yes. How could I forget?'

'And do you remember Dvořáček, the Minister for Personal Information who tried to sneak a bill through parliament to block the listening eyes' development? If I had become the leader of our party, and if I had won the election and become Prime Minister rather than Rolt... I would have made sure Dvořáček's bill was made into law, and the Department for Personal Information would still exist. The privacy of British citizens would still have ministerial protection.'

'That's a lot of "ifs",' Moreland said.

Kanha glared at him. 'I didn't win our leadership race because Henri Lauvaux's system blackmailed a number of MPs to vote for Jameson over me,' she said coldly, trying to not lose her temper.

'But do you have proof of that?'

'I have proof of all sorts of things. Not just interference in British politics. I have proof that the train derailment was an accident, not a terror attack. I have proof that the Alcheminna system hacked into a drone and forced a journalist's car into a ravine, killing him. I have proof that Easterly was murdered by a swarm drone attack, most likely also driven by that same system. Soon we will have the results of an investigation into the harassment of Harry Colbey. Henri Lauvaux and anyone who is working with him needs to be prosecuted. Everything stems from him. Everything is driven by that same system of his. We must unpick that company from the workings of our country and we must bring about justice.'

Moreland said nothing and Kanha looked at his po face, at his dark, combed-back hair, his perfect posture.

'Well?' she said, and still he said nothing.

She looked down at the cars and buses. Looked down at the taxis and motorcyclists, the pedestrians wandering by.

'Is getting to the top of this dry profession of yours all that matters to you?' Kanha said. Then, as her irritation could no longer be held at bay, she said, 'You civil servants – at some point, you are going to have to take a side in all this. At some point, you are going to have to engage.'

She thought of how long he had kept her waiting. And still he said nothing. 'Damn you,' she muttered and turned to open the door to return to the room, but suddenly he spoke and his voice was full of a quiet rage.

'How dare you?'

It was the first time she had ever seen him anything other than level.

'How dare you suggest that I am not engaged?' He pointed his finger at her. 'Who was it who gave you Dvořáček's diary in the first place? Who was it who wiped his blood and mucus and brains from the cover and put it in a box with his personal items and handed it to you, right here in this very room?'

Kanha couldn't help her hand flying to her breast. It had been him. He was the one who had started her on this path by giving her Dvořáček's diary.

'And who was it,' he said, 'who gave Harry Colbey a nudge in the right direction? *Quis custodiet ipsos custodes?*'

'Gerald... I hadn't realised—'

'Don't ever tell me I am not engaged,' he said furiously. 'I'm more engaged than you know.'

Kanha thought back. Who had first employed Mani, the old friend and colleague of hers who had helped them in the past, and who now worked for Interpol and still helped them in their cause? Moreland had. Kanha swayed on her feet. How had she missed this?

'Now, you need to act as soon as possible. You are not alone in fearing for where all this is headed.'

Kanha held the balustrade for support as she thought of Harry.

'Esme, before I came to work in Whitehall, I had a long career in the diplomatic service stationed in a number of places across Africa and South America, and I saw many coups unfold when they were least expected.'

It was the first time she had thought of it in that way.

'Can a Prime Minister be arrested?' she said.

'If he's broken the law, he is treated the same as any of us. But that path is always a tangled one. The simpler angle to look at is whether he has broken the Ministerial Code. Has he misled parliament? Or even misconduct in public office.'

'Examples?'

'Wilful neglect of public duty, fraud or deceit, intentional infliction of bodily harm, imprisonment or other injury upon a person.'

'If he knows what Divinity is up to and continues to work with them, then... tick, tick, tick.'

'Don't forget my boss, Sanjay Arun. Did you know that many of the police drones he ordered are military grade?'

'Yes, Harry Colbey told me. Where are they now?'

'Who knows. On a charging base somewhere, waiting to be called upon, I presume.'

Kanha took in a deep breath and slowly released it.

'So what should we do?'

'You must act, and quickly.'

'But what can I do? Jameson won't listen to me. I'm just a backbench MP now. When Jackie Rolt was in power she promised she would throw everything at this.'

'But she still has the power to oppose. The two of you must work together.'

'She won't take my calls. Blames me for the change in her fortunes. If I meet her in the lobby she just holds her hand up in my face.'

Kanha waited as Moreland seemed deep in thought. She had learned over the years that it never paid to rush him.

'You must disseminate what evidence you have, quickly, and as widely as possible among those who have the power to take down a corrupt Prime Minister. You and Harry are in danger until you do.'

'You mean go to the press?'

Moreland put his thumb to his lips and stood in thought.

'I don't think you can trust that path anymore. Everything these days, whether real or not, is labelled a deepfake. It's the get-out-of-jail-free card of the century. By the time you come to confront Jameson or Lauvaux in a Select Committee or in a courtroom, there will be so much confusion with copycat deepfake material showing all sorts of similar but different or contradictory events that any investigation will be riddled with issues.'

'To Lord Silverman's new committee then?'

'There you have the same risk,' Moreland said. 'They'll be a leaky ship, however hard they try not to be.'

'So what do you propose?'

'You must put the evidence in the hands of those who can act, and as many of them as possible. The leader of the opposition, Jackie Rolt, so that she can challenge Jameson in the House. The Speaker so that he can begin a Committee on Standards investigation into the Prime Minister potentially breaking the Ministerial Code. Senior personnel at MI5 and in the police force, who can look into what this Divinity system has been doing in the name of its shareholders – the harassment of MPs, hacking into national and personal infrastructures, and of course allegations of murder. And finally, you need the Attorney General or at least someone very senior in the judiciary on your side, so he or she can launch an investigation into Neville Jameson and Sanjay Arun's misconduct in public office. In fact, you want to get as many High Court and Old Bailey judges as you can muster to rally to your course. They will need to move quickly – firstly to lay down an injunction instructing the Divinity system to be turned off until its safety can be investigated, and secondly to freeze the assets of Alcheminna's shareholders—'

'The Owners.'

'Yes, if you must call them that.'

'Harry Colbey is determined that their CEO, Henri Lauvaux, should be the first to face justice, and after this morning I can't help but agree.'

'So that is the challenge you face. You must get your evidence to all those in a position to act at exactly the same time. If one or two get it first, you will have a leaky ship, and your enemy will make sure those exposed become compromised – then your evidence too will be compromised and your chance lost. They must all act swiftly and as one. And you must arrange all this without Divinity catching wind of it. That is going to be your challenge, because...'

'What can see watches. What can hear listens. What can be followed is tracked. And what is written is read.'

'Exactly.'

Kanha looked down at the drones and across the road to the top of the long line of listening posts. It was going to be very difficult – no, impossible, Kanha saw at once. But what choice did they have?

Moreland put his hand on the door handle.

'There is a group of senior civil servants who feel as we do,' he said. 'We meet in clean spaces, and many have voiced their concerns about Jameson's actions. I am sure, if I put it to them, they will help you gain discreet access to those in a position to act. As to the MPs, I can't and won't advise you there, but you'll need to know who will follow you and who won't when the time comes.'

'Do you still have one of the phones our old friend Mani sent us last autumn?'

Moreland nodded.

'Good. We can use them to message privately. Don't ask me how. But Mani has promised me it goes via an encrypted service that the government has no sight of.'

For a moment Kanha could not believe they were having this conversation. Yet in her heart, she knew it had to be done. She had felt the dread prospect approaching as sure as night followed day. Bit by bit, the country had been infiltrated by Lauvaux and his system: MPs corrupted, journalists silenced, any oppositional MPs blackmailed into submission or murdered. Step by step the darkness had crept in.

She turned to Moreland. 'Perhaps we should not be meeting like this. I worry that anyone I deal with from now on will be in danger.'

Moreland looked at her and smiled. 'But my dear. We have been meeting for gossip, two old friends, for years. If we were to stop now, that would be more likely to be cause for interest.' And she laughed and agreed.

Inside, taking her bag with the evidence of Easterly's autopsy back and lifting it onto her shoulder, she realised he was right. She had to know where they stood with the other MPs. Who would stand with them when the time came, and who wouldn't.

Taking her leave of Moreland, she hurried down to the foyer and through the bubble doors, to find her drone escort hovering there. Divinity wasn't taking any chance of a power blackout occurring again. She had a good mind to make a rude sign at it with her hand.

Stay calm, Kanha, she thought. There was work to be done.

I.7

The Speaker lived in what was called the Speaker's House but was actually a series of rooms over two floors in the north-eastern towers of the House of Commons. As Colbey was ushered along to its Red Library, his secretary told him that the Attorney General was already there and was in a very bad mood.

'He thinks you're making it up,' she whispered, opening the door and showing him through.

'Ah, here he is, our prisoner of the tower,' said the Speaker, coming over to pat Colbey on the back. He was a good-natured man, fair and level-headed. Didn't stand for any nonsense in the Commons and chaired the debates with a firm but even hand. Colbey liked him, as did many other MPs from both sides of the House.

The same could not be said of the Attorney General, a man with an unnaturally thin face and bad skin across his head. Perhaps it was that which made him so bad tempered, but whoever he was dealing with, he always had a sharp and bullying way about him. It was bad luck for any of the junior staff in the researcher pool to be rotated into his office. As Colbey came into the room, he was standing gazing out of the stone-edged windows, which looked onto where Westminster Bridge crossed the Thames. When he turned and came to the table, his ill temper today showed plainly on his face.

'Is this going to take long?'

The Serjeant at Arms, a jolly chap called Bowles, whose role was to ensure order within the House of Commons, already sat at the end of the table and was pouring out a cup of coffee for each of them, lining them up in a row. 'You take milk, Harry?'

'Well, where is this Inspector then?' said the Attorney General, sitting down next to Harry. As he did so, the door opened and the Speaker's secretary announced Inspector Albury of the Metropolitan Police Special Ops department.

'What a long title,' said the Speaker, welcoming the newcomer, shaking his hand and pulling out a chair for him opposite Colbey. Inspector Albury declined Bowles's offer of coffee and dumped a blue paper file down in front of him. He was in uniform, but that did not mean he was smartly dressed. Perhaps he'd had a difficult morning on the mean streets, Colbey thought as the Inspector cleared his throat.

'I know you've been waiting a long time, so I'm not going to beat around the bush. I think we should just get on with it – shall we?' Everyone nodded except the Attorney General. 'Mr Colbey, I reckon you feel like you've been waiting long enough, isn't that right?'

Colbey couldn't agree more, and he eyed the folder on the table.

'Two hundred and seventeen days to be precise,' said the Serjeant at Arms, taking a biscuit from a plate on the table and pushing it in the direction of the Inspector by way of invitation.

'Eighteen,' said Colbey.

Albury eyed the biscuits but did not take one. Instead he steepled his fingers and put his elbows down on either side of his folder.

'First,' he said, 'I want to apologise for the length of time my investigation has taken. It was a complicated one, and involved the procurement of several warrants from the Old Bailey.'

Colbey wondered if he might just reach across the table and take the folder. For nearly eight months he had been holed up in this bloody parliamentary building. He hadn't seen his dog; his friends had near forgotten him. Even his daughter had only visited once – although to be fair he hadn't been honest with her about what was going on. In fact, the only person he bumped into on a regular basis was his ex-wife Clarissa. She had a press pass for the parliamentary estate and loved to drop by and surprise him. That he really did not count as a blessing.

The Inspector cleared his throat and carried on. His voice, which was all on one note, had a soporific effect, despite the importance of his report.

'So my understanding, when I was handed this assignment, was that I was to investigate the fact of your being harassed and cancelled by person or persons unknown.' Here he put two fingers in the air and waved them around the word *cancelled*. 'Not in a social way, of course, but in a practical fashion. Wiped from existence. Your bank account erased, your phone contract extinguished, your gym membership no more, even your library card ceasing to function.'

Colbey fought hard to maintain his patience.

'And finally, the fact that you had been subjected to a malicious attack by a drone – sorry, by multiple drones – on the streets of London, being on the date of...' Here he opened the folder, peered inside, then closed it again. '...Monday 13 November.'

The Speaker sat calmly still. The Serjeant at Arms took another biscuit and the Attorney General looked up at the ceiling in irritation.

'Well...' Inspector Albury leaned forward. 'I have good news. You have *not* been cancelled.'

Colbey looked at him. Of all the possible results of the investigation – confusion, lack of evidence, inability to gather it and so on – this he had not prepared for.

'There is entirely no evidence that you have in any way been cancelled or turned into... what was it you called it... a non-person.' Here he used his air quotes again. Then he opened the folder and pulled out a series of papers, which he started to lay out on the table. The Serjeant at Arms helpfully moved the plate of biscuits and took another in the process.

'Here is a statement of your bank account, showing quite clearly that it exists, and that you have the princely sum of three thousand, seven hundred and fifty-two pounds and sixty-three pence in your savings account, plus sixty-two pounds in your current account.'

Colbey leaned forward and looked on in disbelief as each document was placed down.

'Here is a brand-new credit card, which the bank has assured me works perfectly well, a copy of your passport, your phone contract, your gym membership, and even... wait, I've got it here somewhere... yes, even your library card. That's a replacement the head librarian was good enough to provide me with.'

Colbey felt his head swim. 'But...'

The Attorney General shook his head as he started to pack up his things.

'What a waste of police time,' he muttered.

The Serjeant at Arms leaned forward and gently fingered the documents.

'There's no doubt,' he said, 'that Mr Colbey and another of our MPs, Ms Esme Kanha, were subject to a swarm drone attack that day in November. It was captured on camera by many in the buildings of Whitehall. I personally had to take one of the ministerial cars to fetch them safely back.'

The Inspector shrugged and Bowles stabbed at the table in front of him.

'Ms Kanha has taken it in her stride,' he said. 'But Mr Colbey, as you will see, was scared half out of his wits. He hasn't been off the parliamentary estate since. Don't tell me that's not harassment of a member of the House of Commons.'

'Out of his wits indeed,' the Attorney General muttered, making it obvious he wished the meeting brought to a close.

The Inspector licked his finger and thumbed through the folder again, drawing out a document.

'I'm happy to say there is a simple explanation for that.'

'Explain,' said the Speaker.

'As you know, that was one of the very first stay-at-home orders issued. Both Mr Colbey and Ms Kanha broke it by proceeding to venture out. Now, what we didn't know at the time, but what I have now been able to establish, is that the national security system had instructions to use nearby drones during any period of a stay-at-home order to follow, film and monitor any terrorists who might be active in the area.'

'I'm no terrorist,' Colbey growled and the Speaker placed a hand on his arm.

'Such an instruction has since been considered a bit... how shall we say... overenthusiastic. And a spokesman from the company what manages the national security system – let's see, what are they called, Alcheminna – has reassured me that it would be very unlikely to happen again. At least not unless the system identified someone seen on the streets as clearly a known terrorist or intent on some form of terror activity.'

He snapped his folder closed.

Colbey wasn't sure he was going to be able to hold back his anger. They had just put it all back to how it was. When had they done it? It could have been months ago. If this bloody incompetent fool had investigated properly he would surely have found an audit trail of records changed and then changed back again. Eight months. It had been almost eight months.

The Attorney General stood up. 'If you'll forgive me, I'm needed elsewhere. I'm happy for you, Mr Colbey, that you are evidently *not* the subject of persecution or cancellation.'

Colbey rose too. 'But they put it all back,' he said. 'It's obvious, they just put it all back in the same way that they took it away in the first place!'

The Attorney General paused. 'And *they* might be...?'

'Alcheminna. Divinity. Henri Lauvaux's system. I told you it was them.'

'The system that the government has chosen as its partner for its energy systems, its policing systems, its surveillance systems?'

'Yes, exactly. That's why it's so important we get to the bottom of it.'

'I think we have got to the bottom of it,' he said. 'Good day, gentlemen, Inspector.'

Colbey stared at the back of the country's top lawyer as he left the room.

The Inspector stood also and started to shuffle the documents back into his blue folder. He pointedly left a few behind, including the credit card and the library card.

'Now I don't want you to take this the wrong way, Mr Colbey,' he said. 'But this investigation has taken up a lot of police resources, and questions have been asked...'

Colbey looked to the Speaker, but he had said nothing in response, and looked like he didn't intend to say anything.

'Perhaps there has been some funny business afoot here, but in any event, it might be a good idea... in fact, my strong recommendation to you, Mr Colbey, is that you see if you can speak to a professional.'

'I thought I had,' Colbey growled. Divinity was toying with him. That was the fact of it. And Lauvaux had arranged for Divinity to cover its tracks. Once more the Speaker placed a hand on his arm and finally spoke up.

'There have been other complaints,' he said. 'It's not just Harry Colbey. MPs from both sides of the House have come to me and said they are being followed by drones. Others have said they don't seem able to get any phone reception while others on the same network can. And there is a definite pattern. They are all vocal critics of the government's use of this Alcheminna system.'

'Well...' said the Inspector. 'The tale of Harry Colbey is well known—'

'It's not a tale,' Colbey said.

'The narrative of Mr Colbey's attack by drone is well known. It's not surprising if it's made a few of his colleagues jittery. And there are a lot of drones out there now. But on the whole they are peacefully going about their business, delivering things. Maybe they just appear to be following someone, when in fact they just happen to be going the same way.'

'Perhaps,' said the Speaker. 'But—'

'But what about Blanc, Chandra, Darvish and Woodroofe?' said Colbey. 'They have been arrested on trumped-up charges.'

'I don't know anything about that,' the Inspector said and stood to go.

Colbey was about to explode with anger, but the Speaker rose.

'Thank you for your time, Inspector, and for coming to present this matter so delicately to us.'

Taking his good example, Colbey shook the Inspector's hand, his teeth clenched so tightly they hurt. He didn't know what else to do.

When the Inspector was gone, the Speaker sank back into his chair.

'Well this is a rum affair,' the Serjeant at Arms said.

'But I showed you, didn't I? I showed you on my phone?' Colbey said.

'Well... you showed us some blank searches...' the Speaker replied, and pushed the documents the Inspector had left in Colbey's direction.

Colbey picked them up and put the bank statement in the bin and the cards into his wallet as the kindly Speaker clamped a hand on his shoulder.

'The one thing we have established is that whatever they were doing to you, if there were doing anything to you, they seem to have stopped.'

Colbey wondered if it were true.

'Shall we go outside? See what happens?' the Speaker said.

Colbey, the Speaker and the Serjeant at Arms trailed downstairs to the apartment's front door, across the courtyard and out into New Palace Yard. The grey clouds of the morning had now fully cleared and the sun shone down out of a bright blue sky.

They walked towards the black iron gates that led out onto Parliament Square and Colbey glanced back up at the window of his office. All those days and nights he had spent there, looking down and visualising this moment… but his freedom didn't taste quite as sweet or as safe as he had thought it would.

Beside the gates was a black cabin in which the police officers who managed the entrance had their office. One came out and she stood there politely, giving a nod of respect to the Speaker and the Serjeant at Arms, with a curious look on her face. In front of them was a revolving gateway that allowed one person out or, at the officer's push of a button, one person in at a time.

She must be wondering why I'm standing here, Colbey thought, flanked by these two notaries of the Commons.

He looked through the ironwork railings at the passers-by: the tourists taking their pictures of Big Ben, the office workers hurrying along sandwich in hand with entirely no interest in buildings they'd seen a hundred times before, the protestors with their banners on the other side of the road. They were banging their drums and singing their songs as they had done every single day that Colbey had been a Member of Parliament. Not the same protestors of course. Among these ones, he was pleased to see privacy protestors, in balaclavas and scarves and masks. They were protesting against the heavy-handed surveillance of the government, and yet they were not being dive-bombed by swarms of drones. Yes, everyone was going about their day as if there was nothing extraordinary about it.

'See. Everything's fine,' the Serjeant at Arms said, as if he had spoken Colbey's thoughts aloud. 'It's just a normal day. That's what you need to tell yourself.'

On his other side, the Speaker touched his elbow and, like a kindly father waiting for his son to summon up the courage to ride his little bike without stabilisers for the first time, said, 'You can do it, Harry.'

It was too much.

'I think I can take it from here,' Colbey said, turning to shake both of their hands and thanking them for their support.

'Wonderful,' said the Speaker.

'Great news,' said the Serjeant at Arms.

With a last pat on the back, they left him, and when he turned back he saw they were halfway across the courtyard, their heads together in discussion, probably already turning to the afternoon's business.

He looked nervously up at the drones. The hum of them mingled in with the rumble of the traffic and the chatter of the tourists. They are not doing anything but delivering takeaways and cheap goods from internet giants, he told himself. Then he flinched as one came close. But it was just overtaking a slower model; it moved back into its lane soon enough and disappeared up towards Victoria Street.

Colbey knew that a subsidiary of Alcheminna provided the AI software that ran them. The system was so intelligent it could manoeuvre a million drones across a city of 600 square miles and not once have them touch or crash into anything. It could recognise the face of the parcel recipient, converse with them and deliver its parcel in person, or it could rise up and hover over one of the buildings' plastic chutes, delicately unfurl its tongue, and deposit its parcel for later collection.

'Do you want me to walk out with you?'

Colbey jumped. It was the gate officer, who was still standing there.

'It must have been something terrifying what happened to you and Ms Kanha last year,' she said.

Colbey shrugged his shoulders, not taking his eyes from the stream of drones. 'They've told me it was a routine security system. The drones were programmed to follow anyone breaking a stay-at-home order.'

'Well, I did tell Ms Kanha she'd be mad to go out, what with them swarming like that.'

Colbey turned to her. 'Drones don't decide to swarm, you know,' he said. 'They're not starlings.' Then he apologised. 'What I mean to say is that someone, or, in this case... something... must have been driving them.'

The officer cocked her head and seemed at a loss for what to say. She went back into her cabin, but he knew she was watching him. He had to step out or go back inside.

'Come on,' he muttered to himself. 'Man or mouse, Colbey.'

In his breast pocket was the invitation from his daughter. She would be over the moon with excitement if he turned up for her engagement dinner. He owed it to her to go – it would be wrong not to. She wanted to marry this man, after all. As her father he had to meet him before then.

But Esme Kanha had warned him against going. Chloe's fiancé's parents were not people he should be seen associating with, let alone dining with. He would have to list the occasion in the MPs' register of financial interests, which might be politically harmful for him. The gift of a meal from the Chairman of Alcheminna Systems. What to do? But there was no choice.

Seeing a taxi trundling around the corner with its orange light on, Colbey hurried out through the gates before he could think any more about it, and raised his hand to flag it down. He needed to go home and find his smart suit. Then he had a dinner to go to.

1.8

After Kanha left Gerald Moreland, she made her way back to Portcullis House, the modern building where many of the MPs had their offices, to grab a sandwich from the cafeteria. Then she took the escalator down to the passage that ran beneath Bridge Street and came out inside the Houses of Parliament.

The quality of the office allocated to Kanha had always followed her rollercoaster of a career. When she had been hanging onto Ewan MacLellan's coat-tails as his Chief Whip and right-hand woman, she'd had a vast but dungeon-like office in the basement of the House of Commons, along with a vast whipping team. When they lost power, as Shadow Chief Whip of a much reduced team she'd nabbed a fabulous corner suite in Portcullis House, but as soon as Jameson had taken power for their party again he'd fired her and kicked her out of it.

Jameson's whipping team was much reduced – just Alison Appleby, jettisoned into Kanha's old role of Chief Whip, plus a couple of deputies – which meant that the dungeon basement rooms were empty again. In what they thought was revenge Appleby and Jameson had allocated one of them to Kanha.

Fine. That had suited her fine. Because she still had a few tricks of her own, and had persuaded one of Appleby's deputies to discreetly also move her colleagues Brooke and Wilbur down there. That suited them too. The dusty forgotten offices were not wired up to parliament's security system, and were not even on the cleaning roster anymore. So now the little dungeon office, with its Styrofoam ceiling cutting off the stonework at odd angles, its hateful strip lighting and racks of old-fashioned desks and ancient filing cabinets, had become their rebel base.

She found the two of them lunching in what they called their clean room. A simple meeting room containing a table with a few bits of stationery, a handful of chairs and, leaning against one wall, an old discarded but huge whiteboard. Along with the one assistant left to her, Melody.

'Ah. There you are,' Wilbur said. 'We wondered where you had got to.'

He sat with a prawn sub falling apart in his hands. Kanha closed the door behind her and joined them.

'It was murder,' she said. 'We have the proof.'

'God damn it,' Wilbur said, taking a great bite of his sandwich, while Brooke pursed her lips tightly and put hers down.

Kanha went through the results of the autopsy.

'So we have all the evidence at last?' Brooke said, and Kanha nodded.

'We have enough.'

'So what next?' Melody asked.

Kanha told them the plan she had agreed with Moreland.

'I'll chat it over with Harry tonight too,' she said. 'And figure out the details.'

At the mention of Harry, they caught her up on the Committee Meeting.

'We were sparse on the ground,' Brooke said. 'A few MPs were arrested last night. Blanc, Chandra and Woodroofe. And Darvish resigned this morning without saying why.'

'It's foul play,' Wilbur growled.

'And who was there from the opposition?'

'Their Shadow Foreign Secretary, Asma Safeer.'

'Jackie Rolt won't like that.'

'Which was why she was there, I think,' Brooke said, smiling.

'And Harry?'

There was a pause and Brooke and Wilbur glanced at each other.

'Yes, he was there,' Wilbur said.

'And has anyone seen him since?' Kanha asked. And then they came clean. No one had seen him, but the Inspector had been indiscreet with the Speaker's secretary, telling her the outcome of his report. And she, in turn, had been indiscreet, gossiping with another secretary and telling her, in total confidence of course, all the details of the case... and so it went. Even though the meeting had only finished half an hour earlier, it was already common knowledge that the police had found nothing to back up Harry's claims that he was being persecuted, that he had left the parliamentary estate to go home and see to his house after so long before having dinner with his daughter. Even that he had agreed to get some psychological help.

Kanha huffed. She was not sure which of those things was the most annoying. But of course if his daughter needed him, that was for him to decide. Yet she wished... oh, there was no easy answer to what she wished. Shaking her head, she got up, tipped the whiteboard onto one corner and, being careful the enormous thing didn't fall on her, swivelled it round. On the other side, it was cork and covered with what she called the world they were living in.

At the top was a picture of Henri Lauvaux, the CEO of Alcheminna Systems, and below a host of Post-it notes and photographs, along with a crisscross of red ribbons. Kanha took a Post-it note from the table, wrote *Murdered* on it and pinned it beneath the smiling image of Reginald Easterly. Then she traced her finger along a ribbon that led from it back up to the face of Henri Lauvaux.

'We need to canvass for strength of feeling among the MPs,' she said and turned back to the others. 'Many are afraid of Jameson and jump to his tune, but I suspect it's because his Chief Whip, Alison Appleby, has access to the Alcheminna system and it feeds her information about their private lives. The system is a lazy whip's dream.'

'But if they're afraid, will they speak to us?' Melody asked.

'Of course they will,' said Brooke. 'If they're feeling under pressure, they want someone to make that go away. We need to be clear with them that we will protect them if they side with us for a vote of no confidence in the Prime Minister.'

'Exactly,' said Kanha.

Melody frowned. 'But what if the dirt the system has on them is something illegal, or an affair or perversion…?'

'So the usual,' Brooke snapped. 'These are MPs we're talking about, remember.'

Kanha crossed her arms and thought.

'Jameson already has a bloc loyal to him thanks to the system's blackmailing activities. We can do nothing about that. And I suspect many more in a similar situation would be loyal to him if we were to call for a vote of no confidence right now. But we have to know how many and who.'

'Well, if you want us to canvass, it will have to be this afternoon,' Brooke said. 'It's Royal Ascot week, remember.'

Ah, it was true. Both the Commons and the Lords would be thin on the ground tomorrow.

Wilbur stuffed the last of his sandwich into his mouth.

'If we've only got today, we had better get on with it.'

'I'll take the cafés of the Portcullis House atrium – the Debate, the Adjournment, the Despatch Box,' said Brooke.

'Fine,' said Wilbur. 'I'll head over to the Commons and work my way through the Members' Tea Room, the Pugin Room and the Smoking Room.'

'I just need to finish something up here,' Melody said, 'then I'll take the Strangers' Bar.'

'Good,' said Kanha. 'Then we can all meet up in the Sports and Social and compare notes.'

As the contender to Jameson's throne, Kanha would not canvass with them. It would look weak. Wilbur and Brooke would do the work – two experienced and well-respected MPs leading the way, supporting an alternative to a hopefully unpopular Prime Minister. And Melody had worked in the whips' office. So she knew the three hundred odd MPs of her party by name and also knew where the bodies were buried. She would be a fine help.

When Wilbur and Brooke were gone, Melody came up behind Kanha, who was gazing at the montage on the wall.

'I was looking at it all earlier, trying to make sense of it,' she said. 'There are so many different companies.'

'Yes.' Kanha pointed to the picture of Lauvaux. 'But all ownership eventually traces back to one majority shareholder, Henri Lauvaux.'

Kanha had been careful about what she'd told Melody in the past. Knowing too much put her in danger, but perhaps it was time she trusted the girl.

She ran her finger down from his picture to a Post-it note that bore the name of his company, Alcheminna Systems, and then on to another, which read *Divinity*.

'It started here. Alcheminna Systems built a state-of-the-art artificial intelligence system several years ago. But rather than shout about it to the world like all the other AI companies, they kept quiet. Instead, they went about secretly scraping data wherever they could as well as lobbying corrupt politicians to allow them access to protected citizen data – health, education, immigration, mobile phone numbers, emergency contacts, all the usual stuff a government holds. In return they offered up exclusive use of the system for the politicians' own personal gain. Early last year, our party were offered access to the system to help keep us in power and Ewan MacLellan agreed to the exchange.

'Where Lauvaux's system couldn't scrape data, and couldn't get it from their agreement with MacLellan because it was commercially proprietary, it hacked its way in – emails, text, video calls. For a few years there wasn't a phone call, a text message, a video conference that the system didn't read, watch or listen to. The system can now hack better than any flesh-and-blood hacker.'

Melody tapped a series of other Post-it notes. 'And all these companies?'

'Well... even after that, the system was still greedy for data. It wanted to be able to listen and watch everything live. Otherwise it was always a bit out of date. So they set up a complex web of supposedly unconnected companies with one aim – to infiltrate Britain in real time. They each do different things.

'For example, one of the companies runs Britain's gas and electricity networks. Another supports the nation's listening-eye surveillance network.

'This one runs the police's crime scheduling systems through the visors provided by Alcheminna. Here is the subsidiary behind the cameras in supermarkets, which have live face- and voice-recognition capabilities. Here, a company that provided the listening-eye stickers for free to the Mobsters, who have stuck them everywhere in the hope of getting a scoop for their Mouth of the Mob page. And of course, the sneakiest of all: Alcheminna owns the company that runs Britain's most popular digital assistant, the APPA. There's not much people don't discuss with their APPA these days – legal and health queries, personal problems. And through that and these government smart speakers, the system now has legitimate access to pretty much everyone.

'It took me a long time, and lots of help from a friend of mine who works for Interpol, but we eventually traced the shareholdings of all these different companies around the world, through a heap of different offshore financial structures designed to hide ownership – Panamanian wrappers, Seychelles SPVs, Liechtenstein Stiftungs and so on, back... back... and discovered they are all ultimately owned by Alcheminna Systems.

'And all of these different systems in all of these different companies are sucking data in and sending it up the chain to what is effectively the giant computer brain at Alcheminna Systems, and the intelligence that is sent back down the chain to run all these different services comes from... you guessed it... the giant computer brain at Alcheminna Systems.'

Melody perched on the edge of the table. 'So it's really all one system?'

'Yes,' Kanha said. 'Within the organisation, they call it Divinity.'

'And have you seen it in action?'

'No, but Harry has.'

'And it has copies of all of us in it?'

'Yes. Divinity is a new kind of AI. A unique design that allows it to make sense of all the personal data feeding into it twenty-four seven.'

'Which is?'

'It's not a single neural network, but a multitude of them, each one trained on data unique to a British citizen.'

'So there's a AI version of each of us?'

'Yes. They call them the digital replicas. And that's the system – that's Divinity's unique strength. It effectively has access to a pool of brainpower that emulates everyone in the country put together. Everyone's skillset, everyone's knowledge, everyone's unique ways of communicating, of thinking even.'

Melody shook her head. It was a lot to take in, Kanha thought. Everyone seemed to know bits of the puzzle. But she and Harry had painstakingly figured it all out.

'But it's not just owned by Henri Lauvaux, is it?' Melody said.

'No. There are around twenty-five shareholders of Alcheminna, whose families and lifestyles you painstakingly researched for us.'

'The Owners.'

'Yes, the Owners as they like to call themselves.' Kanha ran her hand along a line of photographs. It had not been easy, but Mani had pulled a list together. He was an old friend and colleague who was now working for Interpol. The Europeans had banned Alcheminna from the EU bloc, and they were keen to assist where they could. Mani was her conduit to them.

It should have been easy to identify the Owners. Most of them had apartments in the Chelsea development that Lauvaux had built. But they flew in and out by helicopter, or they came and went in cars with darkened windows, and the apartment ownership structure was unclear.

On Kanha and Colbey's behalf, though, Mani had persuaded Interpol to raid a Caribbean bank, and they had uncovered a money trail between the offshore trust of Alcheminna and certain wealthy individuals. And there they had them. It hadn't taken them long to figure out that the Owners had provided Lauvaux with the funds he'd needed to build a vast data warehouse to support Divinity's unstoppable greed for information, and that in return they'd received citizenship of a nation in which they'd receive preferential treatment over the rest of the populace. Harry had also figured out that Divinity was assisting them with their business dealings. Its omniscience made for a powerful business growth tool.

'And so here is the result of all your research,' Kanha said. 'The family members who Divinity protects and nurtures. Whose lives are, seemingly for no reason, blessed. Everything they touch comes off to the good. Everywhere they go the traffic lights turn green for them – and for their grandparents, children, grandchildren. Even their dogs, can you believe it?'

So there they all were. All of the Owners, their pictures stuck to the corkboard – their old Prime Minister, Ewan MacLellan, and Harry Colbey's wife, Clarissa, included. Clarissa had been tricked into buying shares in the hope of corrupting Harry Colbey, but when she discovered the fact she had agreed to a quick divorce so as not to injure his political career. She had done the honourable thing, Kanha thought.

'So Jameson's not an Owner?' Melody asked.

'Nope. Just an idiot.'

Melody laughed and said she had better get on.

That was fine with Kanha. She would rather not have to go through the rest of it. All the people Divinity had messed with, all the lives ruined. There was Karolinski, the trader who had been following Divinity's trading patterns – he had been deepfaked as a gambler and had his life wiped from existence, and now lived off the grid. There was Jonnie Whitwell-Thrupp, the journalist who had owned the Mouth of the Mob and who was going to expose the voting bloc of blackmailed MPs that Divinity was using to pass laws that suited it. A widow and child left behind. There was dear old Reginald Easterly, the privacy campaigner driven off a cliff. Another widow left behind. And then there was Harry Colbey, cancelled like Karolinski and chased and swarmed by drones. She needed to look into these other MPs who had been arrested the day before and the one who had resigned, and if necessary add their faces to the board too.

Kanha did not load the footage from the camera onto the computer in her office. That would be too dangerous. She had a sandboxed PC in Mani's flat in Vauxhall, which he was kind enough to let her use as her London base while he was out of the country.

She sat at her desk for a while and ploughed away at her everyday work, answering letters from her constituents, sending off angry missives to the Prime Minister's team. It was important to make Divinity think she was another irritating backbencher, wanting to stab her leader in the back and take his crown.

A few hours later, she looked at her watch and yawned. It was impossible to keep track of time down in the basement. But she needed to head over to the Sports and Social bar to see how the others had fared.

Up in the Commons corridor she ran into Jameson's Chief Whip, Alison Appleby, who stopped her.

'I know what you're doing,' the woman hissed.

'About to go to the Sports and Social for a few gin and tonics?' Kanha replied.

'You're canvassing for a leadership challenge. It's outrageous for you lot to be doing this when the country is in mortal peril.'

'Mortal peril? Is the country at risk of dying?'

'It's not fair, I'm telling you,' Appleby said, and seemed almost pink with rage.

'It's called politics, Alison,' Kanha said. 'Now if you'll excuse me, those gin and tonics won't drink themselves.'

Fortunately, Appleby would be unlikely to follow her to the Sports, as it was affectionately known. It used to be a local parliamentary bar favoured mostly by the junior staff – researchers, interns, SPADs and assistants. But these days it was also a mecca for those MPs and members of parliamentary staff who felt the government was breathing down their necks a little too much.

At the entrance, the famous plate that read *What happens here stays here!* had been altered to add: *Anyone found hiding a listening-eye sticker here will be shot and any survivors will be shot again.*

The security camera in the corner had been covered over with a steel-lined bag, on which some wag had pinned the image of Sanjay Arun's face. Every time she went into the bar, Kanha smiled to see it. The place was packed and that gave her hope.

Everywhere she heard rumours of the three MPs who had been arrested and of the one who had resigned.

There was a common thread to recent events that everyone there had picked up on. Those who rebelled against Jameson's plans seemed mired in problems – mistresses uncovered, petty legal demeanours chased by authorities, financial schemes taking a turn for the worse. And now arrests.

Meanwhile, those who supported him seemed to go from strength to strength in all their dealings with the world. The bar was alive with it. A pint of beer and a grumble. A packet of pork scratchings and a whisper of unsettled concern.

She got a tonic water at the bar, then hunted through the crowds and found Brooke, Wilbur and Melody at a table in the corner.

'Don't worry,' Wilbur said. 'I've checked for listening eyes, and it's too loud in here for anyone to overhear.'

They put their heads together as Brooke gave an update.

'Many think Jameson has gone too far,' she said. 'They're suspicious of his close ties to a company that seems to be winning every government contract that comes up. They're angry at the reduced size of the cabinet and don't agree that the country should be on a war footing. It's the new members jettisoned into safe seats and then straight into the cabinet that seems to get everyone's goat the most.'

'Even the opposition members are angry about that,' Melody added.

Kanha could understand why. Cronyism always smelled rotten, and the fact that these three were Alcheminna shareholders, and that one of them was an old Prime Minister who had resigned in disgrace barely more than a year ago, only made it worse.

'But there's still support for Jameson,' Wilbur said. 'He got us back into power, many of them are saying. Give the man a chance. These are dangerous times after all, seems to be a common sentiment.'

Kanha thanked them for their help, but was interrupted by Melody, who leapt up and said, 'Quiet everyone. There's a shepherd in our midst.'

'A shepherd?' asked Brooke, as Melody got up and hugged Elliot, an MP who used to work for Kanha in the whips' office but who now was working at Number Ten. He stood there with a pint of beer in his hand.

Shepherd's pie – spy.

Kanha thought that the young MP was still loyal to her. She had to assume so in any case, because he was dating Melody – Melody was in the circle of trust, and he certainly used to be.

He seemed to have matured again over the last few months. The chinos and blue shirts had been replaced by a smart blue suit. She thought with a smile of how he had looked when he had first started working for her, with his floppy schoolboy fringe. She had got him up to scratch and look at him now. A star in the ascendency.

'So, are you coping without me?' he said to her.

'Taking it one day at a time,' Kanha replied and they all budged over to allow him to join them and sit next to Melody.

'The Chief Whip... sorry... Esme has the evidence that Easterly was murdered,' Melody said.

Elliot's mouth fell open. 'I didn't really think it could be true,' he stuttered.

'Wobbly bottom lip time, Elliot?' Wilbur asked, reaching over and patting him on the back.

Elliot rounded on him. 'It's me that's in the deepest, I'll have you know. I've got to go to Chequers this evening to help Jameson get the papers ready for a cabinet meeting. Then I'll be stuck there till he chooses to bring me back.'

'We are all in deep,' Kanha said.

'Seriously?' said Melody to Elliot, pouting. 'We were going to try that new Japanese in Petty France.'

Elliot downed the last of his beer. 'Can't, babe. In fact, I'd better get going. Can't keep the Prime Minister waiting, can I?'

'Can't you take a few listening eyes with you and sprinkle them around?'

'In Chequers?' Elliot looked at her, genuinely shocked. 'I don't want to end up in prison, Melody.'

Kanha shook her head. 'Harry Colbey wants us to keep on the right side of the law anyway.'

'Him and his bloody principles,' Brooke said.

Elliot took his leave of them and kissed Melody goodbye, and they all decided to call it a night at that point.

Afterwards, driving out of the suburbs of London, over the M25 and onto the B roads that led to her constituency home, Kanha thought of Easterly and glanced at her bag on the seat beside her.

Although it was early evening, the midsummer sun had not yet set, and as the wheatfields flashed by, its low rays caught the tips of the crop and set them aglow.

Outside of Westminster, the battle they fought seemed unreal. Were they all just jumping at shadows?

Kanha thought of what was inside her bag. She put a hand out to still the camera as it rattled about and saw again the sliced-up corpse of Easterly. No. That was not all a figment of her imagination.

The lane she was on ran down into a depression, causing the sun to disappear behind a ridge, and when she came up the other side onto the chalk escarpment it sat directly in her eyeline. She put the visor down and, realising she was nearly upon a stationary car, slammed on the brakes.

Up ahead were two police motorcycles that had been parked in the centre of her lane. Armed officers were standing beside them, waving the cars through one by one.

Kanha thought of Blanc, Chandra and Woodroofe, arrested the day before, and a cold feeling gripped her stomach. She leaned over and pushed the bag under the seat next to her, and at the cop's firm signal slowed and pulled up at the side of the road.

And so it begins, she thought.

Henri Lauvaux sat in the back of his Mercedes outside the Belgravia Pretty Ballerinas dancing school and watched the girls in their pink Lycra and taffeta ruffs delicately pick their way down the steps. His driver had secured the spot right in front of the building. When his daughter looked up, she saw him through the car's open window and waved as Madame brought the girl to the back door of the black saloon.

Lauvaux enquired on his daughter's progress as she slid in the back.

'*Très bien*. She is top of the class.'

Thanking her, Lauvaux told his daughter to hurry up.

'Where's *Maman*?'

'She had to fly back to France. *Grand-mère* is not well.'

The girl saw her pink travel bag at Lauvaux's feet, took it and peered inside.

'Are we going home too, then?'

'Home?'

'To France.'

'*Chérie*, home is in London now, you know that. But yes, we are going to the helicopter now and you are going to join your mama. I need to go somewhere else, so we're going to drop you off at the west airport on the way. Nanny is waiting for you there.'

The girl giggled. 'Literally? Drop me off? Out of the window?'

'It's an English expression. It means *déposer un colis*, drop off a parcel, but they use it for people too.'

'And I'm going on the plane in my tutu?'

'There's only you and Nanny.'

'Just us?'

'Of course. Who else would there be?'

Lauvaux looked out on the streets of west London as they passed through the wealthy suburbs of Belgravia, Sloane Square and Chelsea.

He was wearing his special lenses. He used them all the time now. The technology had stepped forward again, and finally the system seemed to have got the balance right as to what data he wanted superimposed on his vision. Little titbits of information, rather than dreary old details likes names and addresses and so forth. Now the system might tell him whether they were happy or sad. Tired or sick. The car passed a woman with stage two cancer, and another whose sister had just that second given birth. Not that either of them knew it. Sometimes he still found it distracting, like a constant soap opera, and he was tempted to tell the system to be more selective.

Only give me information about people who matter, he might tell it. Not these peons, these nobodies, who will do as they are told. Who will get up and go to work as few days as they can get away with, who will go to the shops or sit in front of the television on the other days. Who will stay in when they are told to. Who will vote as they are nudged to. Who will rat on their neighbours if they think it's for the greater good. I don't need to know about them, he thought. They are just so much dust.

Point out to me the rebels. Those of an oppositional streak. The free-thinkers. The independent souls. Let me, like the police officers, know who the troublemakers are, so that I might deal with them.

'Why are there no cars in London, *Papa*?'

Lauvaux smiled at his daughter's sweet innocence. The traffic in London was held at red lights at every side street ahead of them, so that the roads they travelled were always clear.

'Because I have made it so,' he said.

The car turned towards the gates of the Owner's residential estate. A tall, innocuous-looking brick wall ran for several miles around it. The boundary was camouflaged with little parks and outbuildings, so that from the outside the extent of it was not obvious. Unfortunately, they had not considered the curiosity of the Mouth of the Mob hacks, who had looked at satellite images of the area and started posting questions. Why couldn't they walk into an area of London two square miles across? Why did it have its own heliport? Who was it who lived there?

They had tried to bury the accounts asking the questions but, as fast as they did, some other bright spark thought of it and posted anew. That was the trouble with the Mouth of the Mob. They might have to adjust their thinking on it soon.

On being told Lauvaux's car was approaching, the security guards were already stepping away and the gates swung open.

The helipad was positioned at the far end of the development, and to get to it they had to drive past his daughter's school, past the three gyms, two spa complexes, the hairdresser and the dentist, and past the private medical clinic with all the latest diagnostic and emergency care systems. There was nothing that the Owners should want for when they were staying in their London residences. Of course, they had other homes and only stayed here for the minimum or maximum nights required for whatever tax regime they were registered under – though both the rules and the regime here were due to change shortly, Lauvaux thought with a tight-lipped smile.

The heliport had been harder to arrange than he had expected, but it made it easier for them all to reach the private airport on the west edge of London and from there fly to their St Moritz homes, their Alpine chalets, their South of France villas, their Croatian hideaways, their apartments on the Emerald Coast. They liked to avoid road travel where they could, even though like Lauvaux they were green-lighted wherever they went.

By the river, the tall glass apartment buildings were staggered so that each of the Owners could have a penthouse suite with river views. The helipad lay at the far end, surrounded by noise baffling.

Lauvaux was pleased to see that his helicopter, an Avic AC322, was ready and waiting for him, and as they drove into one of the parking spaces beside the helipad, another came in from the west. Recognising it as the huge Sikorsky S-92 belonging to his Chairman, Lauvaux tutted. Such extravagance. That was the problem with the Owners. Always a competition. Who has the best yacht. Who has the best ski chalet. It was tiresome. When he built the complex, Lauvaux had made sure all the apartments were identical – all penthouse suites and all to the highest spec. Well, perhaps the Chairman's had a slightly better view. There was equal and then there was equal, after all. Lauvaux told his driver to see to his daughter, and walked over to greet the Chairman as he headed back to his car; they met on the tarmac halfway.

He was a fat man, who did not look after his body well enough, but behind the red-faced gruffness lay a ruthlessly efficient business operator. Lauvaux had personally appointed him before the system was as advanced as it now was – before it had taken over decisions as to who they should hire, and long before it had then started firing those people and doing their jobs itself.

But it had worked out well. Back then Lauvaux had given the Chairman a more-than-generous shareholding in Alcheminna in return for seed capital to fund server farms, and now he managed the whole operation as well.

'You did well with the move to the new data warehouse,' Lauvaux said as the noise from the Sikorsky died away.

The Chairman shrugged off the compliment.

'It was just in time. The data feeds have increased tenfold in the last month alone.'

'Yes, I saw that.'

The more the system knew, the better it functioned, but its greed for data had always been a challenge to keep up with. Now they not only had the surveillance data from the listening-eye posts and stickers, and from the APPAs – Alcheminna's commercial digital PA product, which dominated the market – but also the live feeds from the government's new home speaker rollout. Server space was their bottleneck now. They no longer spoke of terabytes, but of petabytes – a million gigabytes – and now even exabytes – a billion gigabytes.

'And you are sure our location is secure?' Lauvaux said.

'It would have been better in Iceland. But you wanted—'

'It has to be on British soil. We've been over that.'

'But there is a risk—'

'Yes. I know. But only until everything is in place. In the meantime we can't have the Europeans involved. Locating server farms on EEA territory would prove too irresistible to them. Here we have control of the police. Nothing will happen without us knowing, and so long as Jameson does as he is told, the Europeans can do nothing, however much they squawk and flap their wings.'

'Yes, but in this crossover period—'

'Trust to me and Divinity to deal with any threats.'

The Chairman breathed out. 'If you say so.' He stood a little hunched over, thinking. 'I'm having dinner with Harry Colbey this evening. Did you know?'

Divinity had already informed Lauvaux. 'Yes. A strange connection.'

'Not really. His daughter's mother is friendly with some of my wife's friends. Is there anything you want me to do about our Romeo and Juliet?'

Lauvaux wasn't sure. 'They're young,' he said. 'It might just run its course.'

Hearing his Avic starting up, Lauvaux looked at his watch and told his Chairman they would catch up later that evening.

He was still dwelling on the vulgarity of the Owners and their need for opulence as he got into his chopper next to his daughter. He was happy with his simple house in St James's. A skeleton staff, and the concierge of the hotel opposite there to be called upon, was all he needed. Perhaps a drone outside his door to ensure a good night's sleep. Divinity watching over them all. He made sure his daughter's seatbelt was fastened and put the headphones over her ears.

'Can you hear me alright?' he said.

'*Oui, Papa.*' Her voice came through his own headphones.

'I've been thinking,' he said, adjusting his microphone to beneath his mouth and putting his hand over her screen to force her to look up at him. 'Do you remember when someone tricked you into uploading that phishing program?'

The Avic lifted from the ground and turned to the west to follow the river out of the city.

'Do you mean my little mermaid?'

'Yes. Well, I was thinking. We should make sure something like that doesn't happen again.'

The child frowned.

'I didn't mean to allow it, *Papa*,' she said. 'I'm truly sorry.'

'I know. You've already said so. I don't want to talk about that right now.'

'I miss the mermaid.'

'I'll get you a mermaid.'

'Will she be like the last? Will she have long green hair like the last one?'

'Whatever you want. But listen—'

'And will she collect shells?'

'Be quiet about the mermaid for a minute. I'm trying to talk to you about something.'

'*Oui, Papa.*'

'If I rang you up, perhaps with a video call, and said I wanted you to open a program on your computer – what would you do?'

'I would open it.'

'Wrong!'

'Wrong?'

'Because how would you know it was really me?'

The girl giggled. 'Don't be silly.'

'*Non, chérie.* It's not a game. You can't be sure that anyone you see on a screen is who they claim to be. Not even me.'

'OK.'

She started to be distracted by the game on her e-pad again, so he took it from her and put it face down on his lap.

'Here is what we will do so that you always know it is me. We will play a game.'

'Now?'

'Yes.'

'But how do I know you're real?'

Lauvaux frowned. 'Because I'm here in person.'

'But are you?'

Lauvaux pursed his lips. 'You're not taking this seriously. Let's start again. Here is what I want you to do. Every time we talk on the screen or on the phone, not in real life, on the telephone, we're each going to mention a type of food. But every time it's going to be from the next letter in the alphabet. Got it?'

'Yes.'

'So you start. Right, I'm ringing you.' Lauvaux held his index finger to his ear and his little finger to his mouth to mimic a phone. 'Ring ring.'

His daughter did the same. 'Bring bring!'

'*Ciao bella*. How was your day?'

'Good.'

'Now say a fruit or food that begins with an "A".'

'Apple!'

'Very good, but put it into conversation. Let's try again. *Ciao bella*. How was your day?'

'Good. I want an apple!'

'Better. Now I'll say. I haven't got an apple, but I think we have some *bananas* at home.'

'Do we really?'

'No. Maybe. I don't know. Have you got it? Bananas begins with a "B", you see?'

'Yes.'

'Good. So what might I say next. It would have to begin with a...'

'C!'

'Very good. I might say, "Perhaps we might also have..."'

'Chicken!'

'Exactly. Well done.'

'So can we have some when we get home?' She looked pained. 'When we get to France, I mean.'

'Some what?'

'Bananas. Can we have bananas with Angel Delight?'

'*Chérie*. It was just for the game.'

'So we can't have bananas?'

'Well... I'm sure Nanny can ask Cook to sort something out for you.'

'Thank you, *Papa*. Bring bring.'

Lauvaux's head was already back in his work. Things were progressing nicely, but there were challenges. There were still those who fought against the new order he was bringing to the

UK. Dinosaurs who wished to live in the past. That Harry Colbey for one. But soon they would be dealt with.

'Bring bring.'

'Please stop that now.'

'Yes, *Papa*.'

I.10

Colbey stood in the hallway of his old family house and slowly drew in a great lungful. Now that was the aroma of home. But... also a bit of damp. He would need to give the place a good airing.

His journey had been uneventful. Did he feel a frisson of disappointment at the fact? Was the Attorney General right? Was he just a mad conspiracy theorist who needed his head examining?

Outside Paddington, there had been protestors with banners that read *SURVEILLANCE STATE OUT!* and *THEY ARE WATCHING YOU*. Privacy nutters, he used to call them, before he became one himself. They were wearing masks and had disguised their shapes with cloaks and baggy clothes. A long line of police in helmets with the Alcheminna smart visors were hassling the edges of the group, telling them to uncover their faces. There were police drones overhead and every now and again the protestors would look up at them.

His stomach had turned over as he passed the police, and when someone shouted out, 'Hey! Harry Colbey!' he had nearly broken into a run. But it was just one of the protestors who had spotted him. A cheer had gone up from the crowd and he had become furious with himself. These people considered him their champion and here he was skulking past in the hope of getting home unscathed. What had happened to him?

He had turned and given them a wave and a thumbs-up, and nothing had happened. The police just looked at him and looked away again. He had gone on his way through the station beneath the array of hanging listening eyes uninterrupted. His ticket had worked at the barrier. The train had left the station on time. At the other end, the barrier had raised and let him out the station car park. The brakes of his car had been a little sticky at first, but he could hardly blame Divinity for that. Even the traffic lights he passed were all green. It's playing with you, he told himself. But he got home without anything at all untoward happening. In fact, from parliament to home in record time.

Standing in the hallway, his troubles suddenly seemed unreal. As if he had not been trapped in the Houses of Parliament but away on a long-haul holiday to the Far East or the Caribbean perhaps. He looked at himself in the mirror above the console table in the hall and half expected to find himself with a tan and leather jewellery that would embarrass his daughter.

With a shake of his head, Colbey sifted through a bundle of junk mail that was neatly piled up on the table. It must have been put there by his kindly neighbour, who had a key and kept an eye on the place.

He wandered into the kitchen and opened the patio doors to find the garden overgrown and lush.

Chloe had obviously been in at some point. There was a mouldy cereal bowl in the sink. With a shake of his head, he picked up the phone beside him and called her.

'You're at home!' she said.

'Yes.'

'Whoopee! You're getting something smart to wear for tonight, aren't you? So you're coming?'

'I don't know, darling.'

'Please, Daddy. You can't say you don't like Emir and his family if you haven't even bothered to meet them.'

Colbey felt torn. Kanha had advised him not to go. But he had a duty to his daughter as well as to everything else.

'Alright, alright,' he said. 'I'll come.'

Smiling, he put the phone back in its holder, but then he stopped short.

On the countertop was a small grey speaker. It sat on a charging mat. His memory caught up with his brain and he realised there had been one on the console table in the hallway and another in the bedroom. He picked up an instruction leaflet that sat beside it. *Your free smart speaker, courtesy of Sanjay Arun, Home Secretary. To keep you safe in these difficult times.*

Underneath, his neighbour had scrawled: *Harry. We all got these this morning, so I set yours up for you. xx*

He looked at it. The government's smart speaker. That would feed all of Divinity's services to him and feed everything anyone said in his own house straight back to it.

Colbey opened a drawer and rifled through it. Not finding anything there of use, he went back into the sitting room and into the cupboard under the stairs. After a few minutes of searching about, he emerged with a hammer.

He dealt with the one in the kitchen first, putting it on the floor and smashing it into pieces, then he went systematically through the house to find the rest. The government had been well informed. There was one for every room, including the little utility room, which was barely more than a cupboard. His next-door neighbour had been diligent, making sure to set them all up.

After the bits were consigned to the bin, Colbey poured himself a measure of his sixteen-year-old Lagavulin, settled into his armchair and closed his eyes.

He felt a kind of contentment. But it was more than that. He felt... he felt...

For the first time in eight months he had peace, quiet and privacy. Colbey breathed it in. The glass of whisky dangled from his fingers. He could hear a song thrush through the open patio doors and realised it was the first birdsong he had heard in such a long time. He closed his eyes, the better to savour the sound of it.

The doorbell rang.

'God damn it,' he said out loud.

I.11

Kanha sat in her car at the side of the road, tapping a fingernail on the steering wheel as she waited for the police officer to come to the side of the car. He wore one of those helmets with the visor supplied by Alcheminna.

'Yes?' she said, winding down the window. 'How can I help?'

His colleague remained on the road, waving cars by.

'A routine county border check, madam.'

Kanha thought again of the three MPs who had been arrested the day before.

'And?' she said.

It was difficult to read the officer's expression because the visor came down to his nose, just the tip of it poking out.

'It's a routine stop, madam. Because of the amber alert.'

'Why?'

The officer hesitated and Kanha knew that the visor of his helmet could superimpose any amount of information about her like a crystalline sheen on the world. Even as he talked to her, little orange words would be popping up above her head and the AI in his ear would be recording her, analysing her responses and suggesting new answers.

'Well?' she said. 'What do the words on that visor of yours say?'

The officer tapped his helmet.

'If you could just look into this camera here, madam, and say your name and date of birth, then we can get you verified.'

'And if I refuse?'

He paused.

'It would seem a strange thing for a Member of Parliament to refuse to cooperate with a perfectly legal stay-at-home boundary check.'

'So you already know who I am,' Kanha said. 'Your system has already told you.'

The officer bent down and put his hand on the edge of the door.

'I'm going to note for the system that you refused to cooperate with the boundary check.'

'Damn right I did. There isn't even a stay-at-home order in force at the moment.'

'That doesn't make the boundary check any less valid.'

She thought of the bag under the seat. The last thing she needed was for that to end up in a police station. But the moment she had the thought, she heard the tinny echo of a voice in the officer's ear.

The camera in his helmet had picked up her thought. Not that it was a mind-reader, but it was specifically engineered to recognise minute signals that pass across a face when someone is trying to conceal something.

'Would you step out of the car, madam,' he said, stepping back and going to open the door, but Kanha slammed her hand on the lock.

'No,' she said.

The officer glanced behind her into the back seat.

'Do you have anything in there?'

'Like what, specifically?'

Again, the tinny echo of a voice told him she was concealing something. The camera would have picked up the dilation of her pupils. The tightening of the lines around her eyes.

'Are you refusing to get out of the car, madam?'

'Yes,' she said. 'I haven't done anything wrong and you have no warrant for the car or any right to search me.'

'I haven't said anything about searching you.'

Now he was looking onto the passenger seat and into the footwell.

'Are you intending to illegally search the car? Do I need to call my lawyer?'

The officer waited for instructions. Then he turned his back, and when he faced her again he had a breathalyser in his hand. His movements were slow and forced. He doesn't want to be doing this, Kanha thought. She had her own mind-reading skills.

'I have cause to believe that you have been drinking. This is a breath test—'

'I know what it is.'

The officer pressed a button on the device and looked at its display until it went green.

'I would like you to blow in the end here for approximately four seconds.'

'And what's your cause?

'Sorry, madam?'

'Your cause for thinking I've been drinking?'

The officer hesitated. 'You were seen driving erratically and were forced to brake sharply.'

'I was forced to brake sharply because you've put your roadblock at the top of a blind summit with the sun in the driver's line of sight.'

Kanha was trying hard not to let her anger lead her, and just at that moment there was a squeal of brakes as a car came over the brow of the hill and didn't quite stop in time before it reached the car at the back of those queueing to be waved around the roadblock. The officer looked behind him.

'See?' Kanha added. 'And anyway, I don't believe you. That system that talks into your ear told you to stop me. Told you to try and get away with searching me. Told you to breathalyse me.'

He was only young, Kanha realised. She had been trying to place his voice. It was familiar. It was... It was...

She knew that the system was talking to him now and suspected he could only concentrate on one thing at a time.

'When you joined the police force, did you expect you would be telling lies because a computer system told you to?'

'Sorry, madam. Just a moment.'

'I'm guessing you were brought up to think telling lies was wrong.'

The officer glanced at his colleague, who had gone to examine the crumpled bumpers.

'So you're refusing to take the breath test?' he said.

Kanha looked at the breathalyser. She had once been a junior minister in the Home Office, and had had this very model demonstrated to her. It wasn't connected to anything on the internet. Turned green when the potassium dichromate in the holder came into contact with alcohol. Simple chemistry.

'No, I never said that.' There was a moment's silence, then she said, 'Pass it here, then.' She blew while the officer counted. Then he looked at the reading.

'You've passed, madam. The alcohol content in your breath is below the legal limit.'

'That's not exactly true, is it?' she said. 'Could you please tell me the reading.'

The officer shifted awkwardly.

'The measured level of alcohol in your breath is zero.' He stepped back from the car.

'So, am I free to go then?'

He paused and looked again at the other officer. Suddenly, finally, she recognised him.

'I'm very sorry, madam. But I'm being asked to bring you into the station for questioning. I've been told that you are a person of interest.'

To think that moments ago she had worried they were jumping at shadows. Flooded by anger, Kanha said, 'Of course I'm a person of interest. Do you think I'm nobody?'

She opened the door of the dashboard locker and the lad took a step back.

'It's only my phone,' Kanha said, waving it at him.

'Who are you calling?'

She heard a little tremor in his voice and held up a finger to indicate that he should wait.

She wasn't going to take this. It rang and rang. Pick up, she thought, pick up. And finally it did.

'Hi. I'm sorry to bother you out of office hours, but this is Esme Kanha. I'm the MP for... Yes, exactly, that's right. The thing is... I'm at a police boundary checkpoint over by West Farm. The officer here has breathalysed me with no cause, which I agreed to, and he found zero trace of alcohol. He has also requested to search my car with no cause, which I refused, and now he's saying he wants to take me down to the station because the system that feeds into these Alcheminna headsets has told him to.'

A garbled sound of annoyance came from the phone. Kanha held it out to the officer.

'He wants to talk to you.'

'Who is it?'

'It's County Judge Balham.'

The officer swallowed.

'Your father,' Kanha added.

His name was William. His mother was a great supporter of Kanha's and always canvassed door to door for her at election time. She remembered young William when he was a tearaway getting in trouble with the headmaster for playing hooky.

Young William nervously took the phone and turned his back on her. Then he took his helmet off and carried on the conversation, walking away. When he came back, it was a relief to finally be able to see his face. He looked upset, like he had just had a rollocking, and Kanha had to try hard to keep a straight face.

'You're free to go, Ms Kanha,' he said. 'And... I'd like to offer you my fullest apology for any intrusion into your evening.'

She started the engine and the car rattled into life.

'That's alright. No harm done. You were only doing what you were told.'

'Thank you,' he said. 'And will you tell my f—the Judge that I did apologise for overstepping what was appropriate in the circumstances.'

She gunned the car and then, as a thought occurred to her, put it in idle again. 'Wait, can I ask you one thing?'

William nodded eagerly and crouched down to the car again.

'That infernal system you've all moved over to – what did it say about me?'

The officer gave a shy smile. 'That you were a local MP. You had been drinking heavily through the day. And you had illegal porn on your phone.'

Kanha blew some air out through her cheeks.

'It's usually so good, that's the thing,' he said. 'Our arrest rate is through the roof.'

'I bet it is. And what else did it say?'

'That you were going home for a takeaway and that you'd stop off at the off-licence for a bottle of wine.'

She thanked the officer, reassured him she would let Judge Balham know it had all ended appropriately and carried on her journey home.

As she was parking up outside the curry house and thinking she needed to pop next door to the off-licence because she'd not had time to go to the supermarket that week, she stopped and thought of what the police officer had said. That damned mind-reading, fortune-telling machine.

She was being much too predictable and it was going to land her in a prison cell if she wasn't careful. She thought of the fact that she needed to get back to parliament early the next morning, and wondered whether every police officer she passed would try to arrest her.

Fuck it, she thought. She was really going to have to up her game.

I.12

Colbey set down his glass of Lagavulin on the side table with a bad feeling as the knocking on the door started up anew. Other than Chloe, nobody knew he was back. Except, that is… Divinity would have tracked his journey through London. On the train it would have watched him from the cameras in the standard-class coach. At the car park the ANPR cameras would have monitored him leaving Charlbury station and his car, the little traitor that it was, would have been pinging his GPS location to it every step of the way.

Colbey sat very still and hoped they would give up and go away, but the doorbell rang again, and then someone came to the front window, peered in and, seeing him there, knocked on the glass.

His was a very ordinary detached Victorian red-brick house. It had four bedrooms and a kitchen that had been knocked through to the dining room, and it stood on a residential road that led out of the town, or into it, according to your direction of travel. A busier road than it used to be. In this house, he and Clarissa had raised their children and had been very happy for a long time, before the weariness had set in. Before her eyes had glazed over when he spoke about his parliamentary day and her lips had drawn into a seemingly permanent line. Before she started that affair with his press manager, which he had known about, yet chosen not to know about.

With a sigh, Colbey got up. 'Alright, I'm coming,' he called out.

But when he opened the door, his heart in his mouth, he nearly laughed. It was just a man. A Jehovah's Witness, perhaps, or someone canvassing for charity. He wore a jumper over a shirt with long collars, and an anxious look on his face.

'Mr Colbey?'

'Yes?'

'Sorry to bother you. I just wanted to check that you were alright.'

Colbey relaxed his grip on the door. Samaritans, then.

'I'm fine, thank you.'

'Only...'

'Yes?'

'I live four doors away. Across there at number twelve.'

'Ah.' Colbey put on his your-representative-in-parliament face and offered his hand for the man to shake. 'Good to meet you. I'm a little tied up at the moment, but I should be back in my surgery next week. You're very welcome to a slot. I can speak to—'

'No... No, it wasn't that.'

For the second time that day, Colbey had to keep his irritation from showing. What he really wanted was to finish that Lagavulin, then get into his smart suit and go back to the City.

'Someone told me your home speaker was turned off,' his neighbour said.

'Turned off?'

'Yes. I wondered if you needed any help to reconnect it? I'm quite good with technical things, and—'

'My home speaker?'

'The one you got from the government.'

'Someone told you it was turned off?'

'Yes.'

Colbey went very still.

'Who told you it was turned off?'

'My APPA.'

Colbey felt sure he must be misunderstanding.

'Let me get this right. Your APPA told you to come round to my house and check on me?'

'Yes.'

'Because I had turned off that... that...'

'Smart speaker.'

Colbey knew his face had flushed red. 'It's not a smart speaker,' he said. 'It's a listening bug.'

He should have left it there, but when the neighbour rolled his eyes to the sky, he couldn't help himself. 'And to be clear, your APPA is not someone. Your APPA is something.'

'So would you like me to—'

'No.'

'But why not?'

'I just told you why not. I don't want a government listening bug in my house.'

'It's not a bug. The smart speakers have been given to us all to keep us safe.'

He thought of Inspector Albury's nonsense report, after everything that had happened.

'What if I don't want to be safe?' he said, and the minute the words were out of his mouth he remembered himself. He was still an MP. His role was to persuade, not to be petulant.

'What I mean to say is that there are other issues to be considered. Such as privacy and democracy.'

'You don't want to be safe?'

'I don't want to be spied on in my own home.'

'The government only want to help you.'

'I don't need the government's help. And I'm in opposition to the government, you see. So the government putting a bug in my house is not great for democracy. But thank you for your kind consideration, and do call into my surgery if you need any help from your local MP. Any planning matters or disputes with energy suppliers, that sort of thing.'

Colbey went to close the door, but the man put his foot over the threshold, and as his MP Colbey was not allowed to push it out of the way with a firm nudge from his own bare toes.

'But... it's a bit selfish, isn't?'

Colbey pursed his lips.

'Sorry?'

'It's selfish, isn't it? The government can't catch terrorists if they don't know where they are, can they?'

'But I'm not a terrorist.'

'Well then, why should it matter to you?'

They were going round in circles.

'I don't believe there are any terrorists,' Colbey said.

The man gasped and removed his foot.

'People died!'

'I'm not denying that,' Colbey said. 'It's just I think the train derailment was an accident, not an act of terror.'

The man took another step back. 'I voted for you. And you're... one of those conspiracy theorists.'

'I am not!'

'But you think the government is lying.'

'It is lying.'

'So you do think there's a conspiracy going on?'

'Yes, but—'

'Oh my! I'm afraid I'm going to have to raise this with the local residents' association.' He pointed at Colbey and stabbed at him with each word. 'I'm going to tell them that you refused to plug in your government speaker.' Colbey had to stop himself from grabbing the neighbour's finger as the man went on to say, 'It's the ones who don't want to plug it in that we have to be afraid of, isn't it? So... will you turn it on?'

Colbey leaned forward and gently pushed the finger aside.

'I can't. You see, I smashed it. In fact, I took a hammer and smashed every single one. And while this is my house, and while there is still free will in the world, I will smash any others that come through my doorway.'

'But I voted for you,' the man said, shaking his head as he backed down the path. When he got to the gate at the end, he shook it again. Colbey slammed the door shut with a satisfied flick of his wrist, but the moment he turned back to the sitting room he felt a terrible regret. He shouldn't have said what he said. Shouldn't have spoken to a constituent like that.

But damn, it had felt good.

Looking at his watch, he realised he was going to be late if he didn't get a shift on. He poured the whisky back into the bottle with a sigh, hurriedly put on his blue suit, finding it to be a little more threadbare than he remembered, and hurried out to the car. Twenty minutes later, he was back where he started, parked outside his house.

Every light he had come to was red. Every barrier closed against him. Every pop-up bollard had popped up. He had been forced to take right turn after right turn until he found himself back on his own street.

He let himself into the house, poured out his whisky again and slumped into his armchair. Now he understood. He was not free again. Here in the Gloucestershire suburbs was not privacy but a new form of imprisonment. He took a slug of the drink and felt himself mired in misery and anger.

Those who opposed Lauvaux's system were harassed and interfered with, imprisoned, arrested and murdered. Prevented from even going to dinner with their own daughter.

While the Owners went from strength to strength. Their business dealings brought them riches; they lived opulent lifestyles; they could come and go as they pleased. Yes, they could come and go as they pleased.

Colbey put down his glass. He went back over to the phone and pressed a speed-dial button.

'You don't happen to be in Gloucestershire, do you?' he said, when it was answered.

As he listened to the reply, he picked up his glass and wandered out to the garden. The thrush was still singing.

'No, I'm at our old home. And I need a lift to London, if I'm coming to this bloody thing tonight.'

The response was a spiky yes.

He hung up.

If you can't beat 'em, join 'em, he thought.

Fifteen minutes later, his ex-wife, Clarissa Colbey, let herself in through the front door.

'Why have you still got keys?' Colbey said in surprise.

Clarissa checked her image in the hall mirror, fixed a little loose eyeshadow and touched up her lipstick.

'Because...' she said. 'Now hurry up, or we're going to be late as usual.'

1.13

'Fore!'

Neville Jameson shielded his eyes from the low summer sun and looked west across the lawns of Chequers, his grace-and-favour country residence, to where his golf ball had just touched down. Damn it, he thought. He always sliced to the left when he tried too hard. It had landed close to two of his security personnel who were doing circuits of the estate on foot.

If they insisted on crossing the field beyond the ha-ha when he was practising his swing, then that was their lookout. Jameson watched as they moved further away. So you think that's out of shot, do you? he thought with a grin, bending down to plug another tee into the grass.

As he stood up, a speck in the sky caught his eye. He watched as it grew into the shape of a helicopter, the sound of it coming in on the breeze now and again as it approached. Behind him, another of his security detail came out of the house.

'The system reports it's Henri Lauvaux and he has clearance to land. Is that alright with you, sir?'

Hah, thought Jameson. That bloody Frenchman might be the boss of the system, but I am still the boss of me. And the country of course. He was in a good mood that morning.

'Well, if the system says it's him, then it must be. So, yes, permission granted.'

His security staff did not wear the helmets with Sanjay Arun's visors yet. Lauvaux and he were currently having a stand-off about it. He didn't want them surrounding him in his own home for God's sake, with that little devil in a box using the cameras in them to read every one of his expressions. So they still wore earpieces, but he was feeling under pressure from Lauvaux to yield. If he did, what might he demand in return? Jameson picked up a ball from the bucket beside him and teed it up before giving it a good whack.

It sliced off in the same direction.

'Fore!'

This time the men walking the perimeter did duck as the ball landed between them. Jameson picked up the bucket and handed it to his bodyguard.

'Get them to collect up the balls, would you? Might as well, while they're wandering around down there.'

The helicopter had landed out of sight, on the lawns that lay beyond the other side of the house. Jameson slung his club over his shoulder and, turning, saw that the security man was looking shirty. Good, he thought. That'll keep them in line. And I doubt it's the worst he's been asked to do by a Prime Minister enjoying his rest and relaxation at Chequers. He thought back to the party of the previous evening with a grin and remembered the girls were still in the pool.

Leaving the guard behind, Jameson strolled round the near side of the house, through a covered passageway and out to the pool house. He stuck his head in the door. It had a line of arched windows along both sides and the sun lay in dappled strips on the water.

Natalia was doing her lengths but, spotting him, she stopped and swam over.

'My darling.' She waded towards him, playfully sweeping the surface of the water with her hands. When she reached his end, she propped her elbows on the side of the pool and gazed up at him. God, she was beautiful, he thought. He loved these Eastern European girls. Those cheekbones. God, he would die for those cheekbones.

'They're starting to arrive,' he said.

Behind her, the other two were messing around with a ball.

'Do you want me to get rid of them?' Natalia whispered.

He looked down the length of the pool. They looked as fresh as when they had arrived, despite the late night they'd all had. Mmm. Perhaps it would be better if they were out of the way while everyone was here.

'Put them in your room and tell them to stay there until we're done. The chef can send a tray up.'

'What about me? Do you want me around?'

'Of course! Why wouldn't I?' He came forward, squatted down and kissed her on the mouth. 'Now hurry up and get dressed. Nothing too showy.'

Winking at him, she turned. 'Come on, girls. Time to get out.'

Jameson left them to it and wandered into the main house, through the wood-panelled Hawtrey Room and into the hallway, just as Lauvaux arrived and was let in through the front door by the housekeeper.

'Mr Lauvaux!' she said, clapping her hands together. 'It's so good to have you back again.'

Jameson backed into a corner of the dreary hall. Chequers was a surprisingly simple mansion that had been gifted to the nation years ago by an aristocratic family for the Prime Minister's enjoyment – for his rest and relaxation, away from the strains of Westminster. Jameson had been expecting more.

Yes, it was ancient, but so were the furnishings, so were the facilities and so were the staff. The swimming pool and the tennis courts and the fact that it was out of the public eye partially made up for that. And his party guests, of whom there had been many since he took residence – many parties and many guests – seemed to like all the old stuff.

At the centre of the house was the Great Hall – a galleried room two storeys high, lined with portraits of the old owners. There were also paintings of their mistresses, their illegitimate children, their dogs and even their favourite politicians.

Jameson watched the housekeeper fuss over Lauvaux. He seemed to remember the smallest details about her life, which always made her deliriously happy.

No, the aristos had not forgotten their pets. But the question was, would Lauvaux forget his? He had promised Jameson shares in the company upon his retirement from the position of Prime Minister. Once they were his, he would be an Owner and get all the privileges and protections and enhancements they got. Until then… he was just the Frenchman's pet.

'Good to get you out of the heat, Monsieur Lauvaux,' his housekeeper was saying. 'It's going to be hot, I think, for the rest of the week.'

But he must trust Lauvaux, Jameson told himself. After all, he had been as good as his word for the last Prime Minister but one, hadn't he? Ewan MacLellan had once been in Jameson's shoes, and he was an Owner now. A politician and an Owner. Think of it!

Jameson moved forward as the Frenchman came into the hallway, still talking to the housekeeper, his bag hanging casually from his shoulder as usual. He wore the same brown cords, the same slightly off-white shirt that he always wore.

He was asking her where the cabinet meeting would be held, and on hearing it was to be in the Great Hall, was changing the arrangements and moving it to the Hawtrey Room.

Jameson felt a wave of irritation. Why doesn't he ask me? he thought. And let me tell the housekeeper? Lauvaux greeted Jameson with a nod, and disappeared into the room he had chosen.

The housekeeper gave a squeal and stepped to the edge of the hall.

'Scares me every time,' she said, as a drone floated in through the front door and took up a position outside the Hawtrey Room. It was Lauvaux's personal protection drone. Jameson knew that it would be monitoring the heartbeat of anyone within a fifty-yard radius. It would know who carried weapons and who had a raised heartbeat or had a sweat on. He couldn't help running his finger inside his collar.

Jameson turned his back on the thing as another car could be heard pulling up on the gravel outside.

What if this was MacLellan? He shouldn't be there. He should let the housekeeper be the first to greet the old Prime Minister. She would know him, of course. He should go into his study and busy himself with matters of state. He went to hurry away, but the damned housekeeper blocked his path.

'Could I bother you for a second, Prime Minister?'

'Later,' he said, trying to walk away, but she deftly moved and stepped in front of him again.

'You said that yesterday.'

Jameson looked behind him in panic, but it was just Elliot who had come in. He was standing in the hallway looking at the drone. Jameson waved him over and said to the housekeeper, 'Later, I said.'

Elliot sidled around the edge of the room, being careful not to turn his back on the drone.

'Is it true that it can it read my thoughts?' he whispered.

'Don't be ridiculous,' Jameson said, but glanced fearfully at the drone too. 'The housekeeper keeps bothering me. Go and find out what she wants, would you?'

'I already know. She called me earlier. Says there are some bills overdue. Your wine buyer and a fish company.'

'Caviar and bubbles,' Jameson muttered. Natalia and her expensive habits. 'Tell her I'll sort it this evening. I don't understand why I can't claim it on expenses.'

'A Prime Minister's private bills at Chequers—'

'Alright, alright, don't bore me, Elliot. I'm just saying it all seems a bit penny-pinching. I am running the country after all, and a man's got to eat.' There was the sound of other cars pulling up. 'I'll be in my study. Forget the housekeeper. Get everyone settled into the Hawtrey Room and call me when all of the cabinet have arrived.'

He went into his study, leaving the door ajar, and stood in the shadows at one end of the room. From there, he could discreetly watch who was coming in. While he waited, he changed his shoes and brushed a little grass off the bottom of his trousers. The moment he had become Prime Minister, he had taken himself off to Savile Row and got himself fully kitted out. At least that he could claim on expenses.

He watched Natalia come down the grand stairs and start to greet his ministers along with Elliot. She looked just perfect in black casual trousers and a tight white sweater that showed off her figure. Elliot was looking at her. Couldn't take his eyes off her in fact. He had always been a bit nervous of Elliot's loyalty. That roaming eye could prove useful, he thought.

One by one, the cabinet arrived in their ministerial cars, each of them clutching their red box. There was his Foreign Secretary, his Defence Minister, his Chancellor of the Duchy, his Secretary of State for Work and Pensions. Elliot, thorough boy, made sure they held themselves and their boxes up to the drone before they were allowed entry to the Hawtrey Room. Where was MacLellan?

The last but one, his Minister for Energy, Sheryl Simmons, arrived. The woman had brought her Personal Private Secretary with her, despite his Chief of Staff's instructions to the contrary. The MP in question hovered nervously in the hallway next to her.

Jameson rang Elliot.

'Hello?'

'Tell that stupid woman to send her PPS back to London.'

Elliot did as he was told and the junior minister was despatched back to their car with his tail between his legs. Next, Jameson was forced to call Elliot again as the drone said something to Sheryl that made her jump back with a protestation.

'What's happened?' he asked.

Elliot glanced at the study, giving away where Jameson was, and Jameson shook his head in annoyance.

'She has a phone in her handbag, apparently.'

'Well, tell her to go and put that in her car too.'

Why had Lauvaux wanted her on the team? he wondered. But when the minister returned, she was arm in arm with Ewan MacLellan. Perhaps they had to keep some of the old lot, he thought. For appearances' sake. And she was the most pliable of them.

Jameson put his phone down on his desk and, once they were all safely in the Hawtrey Room, came out of the study.

'Good job, Elliot,' he said.

Natalia was telling the housekeeper to move away from the door.

The housekeeper frowned and said, 'I've been party to more cabinet meetings than you've had hot dinners, young lady,' but moved away all the same.

Jameson was forced also to stop Elliot at the door.

'Not you, old boy.'

He whispered in Natalia's ear and she took hold of Elliot's arm, saying, 'Never mind that boring old cabinet meeting. Who wants to be where you're not invited? Why don't you come with me, and I'll fix you a drink. There are some friends of mine upstairs. Shall we go and meet them?'

Jameson opened the door. There was a price to pay for anything worth having, that was for sure. One had to keep one's eye on the things that mattered. Lauvaux had taken the seat by the fireplace at the centre of the table that should, by rights, be his. To the Frenchman's left sat MacLellan, but at least the one to his right was empty and had been saved for Jameson.

He looked at Natalia's retreating back and thought of the fun they'd had the previous night. The fun they would have again tonight. He saw her run her fingers down Elliot's back. He was a good-looking young man, that was for sure.

Above him hung the drone, making its presence felt with its constant hum. Everything fed back to Divinity. It saw everything, heard everything, monitored everything.

Lauvaux had already started speaking. 'There is much to do if we are to cement our work, introducing the new order to Britain.'

As the door swung shut behind him, Jameson hurried over and took his seat. He too was eager to hear what Lauvaux had in store for them. His was going to be the most important part in all this. Arun might be good at sourcing drones and such things, a good COO one might say. And MacLellan had played his role, luring in the super-rich investors, but the old PM's time in the sun was over. It was he, Jameson, who Lauvaux needed now.

Trying to hide a smile, he realised he'd not been paying attention and, reminding himself to concentrate, he reached out to take a mint embossed with the delightful logo of Chequers.

I.14

Kanha had lived at her constituency cottage for several years now. She was bred, though not born, a Londoner, and yet the country cottage felt more like home to her than anywhere she had ever lived. Perhaps it was Maximillian, the cat that her godfather, Lord Silverman, had presented to her as a house-warming gift.

'This is not a present,' she had said. 'This is you trying to offload a cat onto me.' He'd laughed and admitted it was true. It had been a present for his granddaughter, but kept scratching her.

'I'm trying to find a home for the thing. Would you take it, just for now?'

And that had been that. After a chequered love life in London where every man she spent time with grew bored of her political ambitions, Kanha had realised she was much better suited to a cat. It wasn't needy or clingy. Didn't get grumpy when she had to work late. Wasn't jealous of her male colleagues and didn't insist on dressing her. She thought of Harry Colbey with a smile. He didn't do any of those things either.

Although the thought of curling up on the sofa with the cat and the curry was very tempting, she only stopped at home long enough to ask her neighbour if he wouldn't mind feeding Maximillian for a few more days, and to pack a bag. Then she walked down the fields behind her house and knocked on the door of a caravan parked up in the shelter of a copse. The local farmer's son opened the door, spliff in hand.

'Evening, neighbour.'

'Evening, Warren. Any chance I could ask a favour?'

'Ask away.'

'Can I borrow one of your bikes?'

'Road legal or not?'

'A trail bike. One that doesn't have a licence plate on the back.'

'Not road legal then.' He disappeared for a second and returned with keys.

'Plus a full helmet with a darkened visor if you've got it, and leathers and boots.'

'They'll be a bit big for you.'

'All the better.'

Wayne shrugged.

'As you wish,' he said, going down the steps onto the grass and pulling a bike out from under a tarpaulin. 'You want this one? She's a bit of a handful. She's had the limiter taken off so she goes like shit off a shovel.'

As Kanha got kitted up, he said in surprise, 'You're going now? It'll be dark soon.' And he went and got some lights for the handlebars.

When she was ready to go, Kanha pulled the darkened visor of her helmet up. 'This is our secret, OK?'

'OK.'

'No, I mean it. I don't want it mentioned in a single message, phone call or chat. It's important. Walls have ears and all that.'

'If you say so.'

'Else I'll send Judge Balham's son round with some sniffer dogs.'

'Whatever, sugar.'

And she set off across the field into the gloaming.

Despite her reassurance to him that she was sure she knew what she was doing, she fell off almost immediately, but at least after she was out of sight. Go slower, she told herself. Better to get there in one piece than not at all. Strapped to her back was her bag with clothes enough for a few days and the curry in Tupperware containers. It was usually takeaway curry on the front seat that helped her drive slower in the car, so it really ought to do the job on a trail bike, she thought with a smile. Then she gave a shout of panic as another ditch lurched out at her in the dark.

But she made it work. She dropped down from the Chiltern Hills and picked her way through the now dark Burnham Beeches. Her route had been carefully planned to bring her into the suburban sprawl of London via a country lane that petered out at the back of an Uxbridge housing estate. She'd taken an educated gamble that the listening eyes there would have been taken out by local kids with air rifles.

So her plan was to drive from the estate onto the main roads of London, so that Divinity would think she was just some youngster on his brother's trail bike. Not a high priority for a busy police force on a Wednesday night.

Fortunately, it worked. She slid into the walkway in Vauxhall that led to Mani's apartment block with a sigh of relief and exhaustion, and crucially without having been stopped by the police.

It had taken the last of her strength to carry the trail bike up the fifteen flights of stairs to his flat. She let herself in, and dropped the bike in the hallway. He'd be cross if he knew about the mud, but that would have to wait.

Mani's apartment was a stylish pad with its back to the river and a view east over the city. Kanha dumped her rucksack on the counter of the little kitchen that led off the hallway, stripped off her muddy leathers, pulled out the curry, plated it up and stuck it in the microwave. Then she downed a pint of water.

She didn't really feel like the wine anymore. Hah, take that, Divinity, she thought, as she turned on the computer and put in a call to Mani. She didn't know how long it would take him to answer, so while she waited she ate heartily. Then she uploaded the evidence of Easterly's autopsy and composed a note to go with all the proof they had gathered.

To whom it may concern,

You have been chosen to receive this information, because we think you are an honourable person who believes in the democracy of our nation, and that you are in a position to act.

Due to the weakness of our current Prime Minister, Neville Jameson, and the corruption of a past Prime Minister, Ewan MacLellan, the company Alcheminna has been allowed unprecedented access to the lives of our nation's citizens – watching them, listening to them and tracking them. Over the last year, Members of Parliament who are in opposition to the government's close ties to Alcheminna have been subject to a campaign of harassment, including surveillance, blackmail and even murder. So too have members of the public who have stood in the way of the company, while shareholders of the company and those connected to them receive preferential treatment, for which purpose our nation's infrastructure is controlled or hacked into by Alcheminna Systems. At least one journalist who was investigating this matter has been murdered, as has an MP campaigning against government corruption.

Enclosed within these files is proof of all this, along with evidence showing that the train derailment last year was not a terror attack but an accident, and that the hacking of the energy systems that caused the gas explosions last winter could not have derived from an external party as the government claims, but was in fact an act of terror carried out by the very IT system that is used to run the network.

It is essential that this system is uncoupled from our national infrastructure with immediate effect, that the opposition and independent press are free to act without interference, and that steps are taken to investigate corruption at the highest level of our government.

Without a government that respects the Ministerial Code, without an opposition and without a free press, Britain will lose the democracy that it has cherished for over three hundred years.

We call upon you to act.

Your faithful servants,

The Honourable Members of Parliament, Esme Kanha and Harry Colbey

Kanha tried to put the documents in the folder into some sort of order that would make sense, and attached the letter. Now she just needed to figure out how to get it to all the recipients in one fell swoop. Without it getting ignored or forgotten. Without it getting disregarded as something not important enough to consider. And most important of all, without it falling into the hands, so to speak, of Divinity.

She had still not heard from Harry. They both had burner phones that Mani had given them, which were safe from Divinity's prying, but she had not wanted to ring him, knowing he might be with his ex-wife, who was an Owner, and perhaps even with the Chairman too.

Getting up to make a cup of coffee in the hope it would keep her awake, Kanha thought of the long line of photos of the Owners pinned on the corkboard in their office. The one they called the Chairman sat at the top of them. This was Lauvaux's first and largest investor, who also now ran Alcheminna. She hoped Harry knew what he was getting into. If he had gone to dinner in the Chairman's club, he would be right in the middle of the vipers' nest.

1.15

The London club at which Chloe's dinner was to be held was easy enough to find. In Colbey's day, the clubs had a plain entrance with a slate plaque discreetly reassuring guests they were in the right place. This one had great flags that hung above the doorway and stuck out into its Mayfair street, clogged with limousines. Their drivers stood gossiping in the warm night air, within whistling distance of the doormen. Clarissa weaved her way through the litter of limos and found a parking space a few streets away on Berkeley Square.

'You didn't need to come, you know,' she said as Colbey got out of the car and sighed without meaning to. 'We all know how much you hate these sorts of places.'

'I don't hate them,' Colbey said.

It was true, to an extent. He hadn't anything particularly against London clubs, and had actually spent many a pleasant evening dining with friends in them over the years, but his natural tendency was towards suspicion. As someone who spent his life fighting for the rights of his constituents, he was reluctant to join any association to which they might not be allowed entry.

He knew Clarissa didn't feel the same way. She was the opposite. The more exclusive the better, as far as she was concerned. When they were still married, she'd been a member of several places – a prestigious gentleman's club in Pall Mall, thanks to her father's career in the RAF, as well as a couple of the trendier ones. She'd probably added a few more to the list since then, since she took the shares in Alcheminna and became rich. How rich? he wondered. No. He didn't want to know. That was her business now.

'Are you going to be in this mood all night?' Clarissa said, as they approached the door and it swung open for them. In the hallway Clarissa held a whispered conversation with the receptionist and they were told to go straight through – through the curtain to the marble hall beyond. It would once have been a house, Colbey thought. A Georgian villa built for the wealthiest of Londoners. And it was still haunted by them, he thought, looking at those who passed from the bar and dining room to the other floors.

Looking down at his suit, Colbey felt a bit shabby. There was a stain on the sleeve and although he put his arm down quickly, Clarissa – damn her sharp eyes – spotted it.

'For God's sake. You could have made an effort.'

'I could have,' he hissed back, 'if I hadn't been discommoded of late by these friends of yours.'

'First of all, they're not my friends. And secondly, that's not a word,' she said.

'Yes it is.'

'Wait. That's them, there at the bar.'

Chloe was not 'them', but Colbey recognised the Chairman of Alcheminna, as well as his wife and son, from the photos Melody had put together for Esme.

Clarissa took hold of his sleeve.

'Emir's father's going to pay the bill. Be sure to let him. You can't afford it, and it will just be embarrassing if you decide to make a scene.'

'Why would I make a scene?' Colbey said.

'You know perfectly well why.'

She lifted his arm, spat on her finger and rubbed it on the stain

as he hissed, 'Would it be because that man, whose son you introduced our daughter to, is as corrupt as they come?'

'See? You're starting already and you haven't even met them.
I'm sure they're perfectly nice people.'

'Nice?' Colbey had to hold himself back from shouting the
word. 'They've bought our Prime Minister lock stock and barrel.
They're turning the country into their own personal playground
and have put the rest of us under surveillance night and day.'

'Well, not nice, maybe,' Clarissa said. 'But they're perfectly
pleasant and, at the end of the day, Chloe's in love with their son,
so we're just going to have to suck it up.'

Colbey was about to say that she wouldn't be in love with him
if Clarissa hadn't introduced the two of them, but she sighed.

'God. Do we have to argue every time we meet?' she said.

Colbey looked across to the bar. He had met Chloe's fiancé,
Emir, at a polo match before his incarceration. A confident man in
his late twenties. He was good-looking, sharply dressed and had
a smile that made you warm to him. But Colbey suspected he was
something of a playboy. He saw that same smile he had warmed to
flash at a waitress, and groaned in despair.

'Don't start,' Clarissa muttered.

It was strange to see the Chairman in the flesh. The man was
obviously a bon viveur – that much was apparent from his waist-
line and his ruddy cheeks and nose. His hair was jet black, and it
fell in thin locks pushed back from his face. His wife towered over
him. Elegant, but not much older than the Chairman's son.

'Daddy!'

Colbey felt arms around his neck and turned to find Chloe
there, on her way back from the bathroom.

'Let me look at you,' he said. 'It's been too long since I saw
your face.'

'Stop,' Chloe said, squirming, but then gave in. She looked

happy. How he and Clarissa could have created such a beautiful creature he had never been able to fathom.

She gave her mother a kiss on the cheek. 'Mummy.' Then she tugged Colbey by the arm. 'Come and meet Emir – properly at last...'

Looking up and seeing them coming over, Emir stretched out a hand and said, 'Here he is, the guest of honour.'

'He's not the guest of honour,' Chloe said. 'He's in my bad books. Been buried in work for months.'

Clarissa gave each of them a kiss that suggested familiarity.

Seeing her now, in this fancy place, the gilt bar, the glasses and metalwork shining behind her, he realised she looked good too. The money was sitting well on her, he had to admit. While this last year had taken a toll on him, she didn't seem to have aged at all. Had she had some discreet work done?

'Daddy, this is Emir's father, Gabriel, but most people seem to call him the Chairman.'

Reluctantly, Colbey offered his hand, and Gabriel took it, gripping it as if he was going to squeeze the blood from the fingers, and pumped it up and down.

'They like to make fun of me,' he said. 'Because I'm the chairman of so many businesses. Pleased to meet you, Mr Colbey.'

'Harry,' Clarissa said. 'He likes to be called Harry.'

'Harry,' said the Chairman, still pumping Colbey's hand, and at once Colbey knew that Esme had been right. He should not have come. He glanced up, knowing there would be cameras in every corner of the room.

Seeing it, Clarissa leaned in to him. 'Don't worry,' she whispered. 'You can always say this is deepfake too.'

'That stuff with the girls *was* deepfake,' he whispered back furiously. 'And it's your friends here who did it.'

'If you say so,' she said, out loud, and Chloe looked at them both with narrowed eyes.

'And this is Emir's stepmother, Dominique,' she said.

Colbey offered her his hand and it was shaken with a smile that didn't reach her eyes. This was the Chairman's third wife. He'd had the two boys, both educated in Italy and then the United States, with his second wife. Then there was Dominique.

'Shall we go through to the table?' Gabriel said, and they followed the waitress, carrying their drinks on a tray above her head, through to the back of the restaurant where there was a courtyard with several tables already filled with diners. As they weaved through to their allocated table in the centre, both Clarissa and Gabriel stopped to shake hands or kiss cheeks here and there. He was in the thick of it, Colbey saw at once.

Many of the faces he recognised from Melody's research on the Owners. That is, if you could call them faces. It was hard to pin down why they didn't look right. Eyebrows too high, lips too large, cheeks too puffy. It was like he had walked into a waxwork exhibition taken over by a surrealist – eyes, noses and chins all in the wrong places. Flat, china-doll skin.

Despite the open-air setting, the place was noisy with chatter. They sat down in a natural order, the married, the soon-to-be-married and the once-married couples beside each other.

Colbey saw at once that Gabriel did not want to be there. He looked about him like a man searching for an excuse to escape, his arm over the back of his wife's chair. He suggested they just take a main, saying he knew the young people liked to keep trim, and no one objected.

By contrast, Emir seemed keen to engage, but with Colbey alone.

'So what's going on in Westminster, Harry?' he asked him after the food had been ordered. 'Chloe tells me you're a politician?'

'A Member of Parliament,' Colbey replied.

'Yes, that's what she said. And for which party is that, might I ask?'

Colbey hesitated and Clarissa jumped in.

'He's not a member of any party at the moment, actually.'

'I'm independent,' Colbey said, trying to give a polite smile.

Emir raised his eyebrows and Colbey could see how he had swept Chloe off her feet – that smile, that confidence.

'Interesting, Harry. And that's independent of...?'

'Of everyone, unfortunately,' Chloe said, and both Colbey and Clarissa laughed.

'He used to be with the government,' she said. 'Only—'

'Let's not talk politics,' Gabriel said, turning back to the table.

So as the waiter delivered their food, Clarissa suggested that Emir and Chloe talk them through how they had met. Colbey had to admit they seemed to make a good enough couple, finishing each other's sentences and laughing at in-jokes. Occasionally, Gabriel would interrupt with advice that was apropos of nothing, like 'Get an apartment. You don't need to be married,' or 'You can work if you want, but you'll only get bored.'

Dominique said nothing, and every now and again Chloe's eyes darted to her in what he guessed was panic at her obstinate silence.

When they ran out of stories, Emir turned back to his quizzing of Colbey.

'So, Harry. Why are you independent? Don't you agree with anyone else?'

The Chairman looked over at his son with suddenly sharp eyes, and Colbey couldn't help but agree. Why couldn't he just let them sail through this hideous meeting of the parents, buoyed along with irrelevant small talk? Was he stupid or being deliberately contentious?

Colbey's irritation got the better of him.

'I used to be a member of the government's party, but I consider them to be corrupt,' he said, and was punished for it with a frown from Clarissa. But Emir did not see it. He only had eyes for Colbey.

'Oh,' he said, his face a pretence of naïve confusion. 'So you resigned from your party?'

No, Colbey decided, Chloe's fiancé was not a simpleton. The boy was deliberately needling him.

'The whip was removed from me. A difference in opinion as to how Britain should be run.'

Emir nodded slowly, his head on one side, as if the answer had surprised him. Gabriel looked away, and Clarissa and Chloe glanced at one other. There was an awkward silence. Colbey was about to jump into it with a comment intended to smooth the waters and move the conversation on to something less contentious – both for Chloe's sake and because there would be hell to pay from Clarissa otherwise – when a passing diner stopped behind Gabriel and clamped a hand on his shoulder.

At once the Chairman leapt up and shook the man's hand. It was the shake of old friends, pulling each other in for a bear hug.

'Good to see you, Ilgar,' the Chairman said. 'How are you?

'I'm well,' was the reply.

'Good. Let's catch up later, shall we?'

The Chairman sat down, turning his back on the old man, but he was not to be shaken off so easily. He squeezed between Gabriel and Dominique, pushing his back into the Chairman's wife so that she was forced to move her chair.

'I see your boy has grown into a fine man, Gabriel. He looks like his mother, doesn't he? Not got all this, huh!'

Ilgar slapped the Chairman's chest.

'See my little ones.' He pointed at a party a few tables away. 'You'd think I would be done with all that, but life is full of surprises waiting to be discovered, as they say, huh?'

Around the table some young children sat looking sleepy-eyed. They should be in bed, Colbey thought.

'But seriously, old friend,' Ilgar carried on in a hushed voice that was not soft enough for them all not to hear it. 'Why have you not included me in this club of yours? Didn't I look after you in the old days?'

Gabriel gave a cold smile and said, 'That is not up to me, Ilgar. But, still, it was good to see you.'

The man looked as if he was going to leave, but then he lingered.

'But you could put a word in for me, couldn't you?'

'It doesn't work like that.'

'Of course it works like that. It's always worked like that.'

Ilgar swayed a little as he bent down.

'Think of all I did for you back then. Without me, you would be nothing.'

'Now is not the time, Ilgar.'

'But you haven't returned my calls. To think, after all that...' He raised his voice, the anger of a drunk man showing through, then he hushed himself.

'Yes, shush, shush,' he said. 'It's all a secret, isn't it? Just like the old days. Please, Gabriel. My business deals are not flowing so well. Look at my little ones. They say everything the Owners touch turns to gold. And you're the Chairman. You could get me in.'

'I'm having dinner with my family.'

Ilgar looked up. He seemed to see them all there, listening, and be surprised by it. He stood and patted Gabriel on the back.

'Fine family,' he said. Then he went on, not caring or perhaps having forgotten again that they were all still there, all still listening. 'I have connections, you know. Don't forget the things I used to do in your name, old friend.'

Gabriel turned to him and, certainly in his case not caring whether those at the table could hear or not, said, 'Don't threaten me, Ilgar. Or you will regret it.'

As the gravelly words were spat out, Colbey suddenly noticed that the knife on his plate was shaking. He could see his reflection shimmering in the silver, and reached out a finger to still the knife. The reflection stilled. When he lifted his finger, the shimmering started again. For a moment, he wondered whether the club was built over a tube route, and in his mind he traced the Piccadilly line, which was south of them, the Jubilee line, which was east of them, and the Central line, which was far away to the north.

Ilgar pulled himself up and pushed out his chest. 'Yes, Gabriel,' he said.

Colbey looked up and into the dark night, and realised what was causing his knife to vibrate. The hum of the thing could not be heard above the din of the restaurant, but a drone had sunk down from the sky and now hovered above them.

Ilgar glanced up and saw it too.

'Your family are waiting for you,' Gabriel said, picking up his cutlery and pointing in their direction with his knife.

'Right, of course, Gabriel.'

Ilgar stumbled away to his table, and as Emir looked after him with a scowl, Gabriel took the last of his bread and wiped his plate clean. Then he smiled broadly around the table at them all. He gave an almost imperceptible flick of his hand, and Colbey's knife lay still again.

Clarissa was sitting stiff as a board, a blank look on her face. Even she had no idea where to go from this. But the Chairman leaned forward and said to Chloe, 'I'm sorry about that interruption to your engagement dinner. Let me tell you a story, so you understand what it was about.' He signalled to the waiter to come and clear the plates. 'When I was young—'

Emir let out a groan. '*Babbo. Nessuno vuole sentirlo.* No one wants to hear that.'

But Gabriel held up a hand to shush him.

'When I was young, we lived in a single room in a communal apartment. My mother, my father, my two brothers and my little sister – all in the same room. Sleeping, eating, doing our homework.'

'Father—'

'Be quiet, Emir, and perhaps you will learn something about how to do business for once, rather than just how to spend money.'

Emir blushed red as his father continued.

'In the 1980s, they started to build new housing, and they allowed people to use their own savings to take shares in the ventures. I went to my father and begged him to allow me to use the family savings for a project that was to start across the road. He was reluctant. But I persevered and he agreed. Then, my friend Ilgar and I went around all the other families who lived in the block and persuaded them to give us their savings in return for a share in our business and a guarantee they would be first on the list for its apartments. Pretty soon we had a thriving property business. But that was a long time ago, and there are some people who do not adapt to change and who are not able to move forward when new opportunities arise.'

'Yes, well done, Father,' Emir said.

Gabriel looked annoyed for a moment, but then he raised his glass and said, 'I think we should make a toast. To health! Long may the happy couple have it.'

'To the happy couple!' Clarissa said with a false trill and a tremor to her voice, and looking across, Colbey saw that she was shaken by the incident. She is in over her head, he thought. All she had ever wanted was to be with people who had nice things, who lived a fancy lifestyle. Who went on fabulous holidays and wore the best fashions and drove the best cars. She had not reckoned on all this.

Chloe seemed to have shut herself off – he could not read her expression.

'You see,' said Emir, putting his arm around her shoulder, 'Father tells his stories like this, but the reality is it took him a long time to get the business going, and we were still poor even when I was a boy.'

'Not poor, Emir,' Gabriel chastised as he signalled for the bill without asking if anyone wanted pudding. Colbey was certain the answer would have been no from everyone, so perhaps it was as well.

'Alright, not poor. But we lived in a small apartment in Italy, and my brother and I shared a room.'

'Really?' said Chloe, smiling, and he brushed his hand against her cheek.

'Yes, my darling. You are not the only one to come from rags. That's why we have so much in common.'

'She hardly came from rags,' Colbey said, but Emir ignored him.

'Really, we did,' he said.

'Yes, you and your brother in one room. I'd forgotten that,' said Gabriel. 'The little monster, you used to call him.'

'He was a little monster.'

'Do you remember when you built that wall?'

The son and father looked at each other.

'Yes, the wall.'

Emir turned to Chloe.

'You haven't met him yet, but my brother was the most irritating brat you could ever meet. Always he wanted to play with me.'

'One day,' said Gabriel. 'Emir went to my lock-up – we all had one back then, you don't want to know what we kept in it. Anyway, he found a lot of empty boxes and took them back to our flat. He used them to build a wall between their beds.'

'Oh, the fuss,' Emir said. 'Emir, Emir. Don't build a wall between us. I love you, Emir.'

'But you built that wall,' Gabriel said.

'I certainly did, and it was there for a year or more.'

Gabriel laughed for the first time, and the son and he smiled at each other as the bill arrived.

'Let me,' Colbey said, and felt Clarissa push her knee against his, but the waiter ignored him and the bill was paid before he could do anything about it.

'Kind of you,' Colbey said, and realised again how right Esme had been. He had taken hospitality from the Chairman of

Alcheminna, the very company he was campaigning against. Well, he was independent, so that meant he could set his own rules. But he held a high bar for himself, he thought. His meal was possibly below the de minimis threshold, but he would register it in the Register of Members' Financial Interests first thing in the morning all the same. He could say the reason was his daughter's engagement into the family. No... that would be even worse. Damn it. Esme was right.

As they waited for Chloe's shrug at the cloakroom in the hallway, his daughter said, 'Are you coming to our engagement party at Royal Ascot tomorrow, Daddy?'

'I'm afraid I can't,' Colbey replied. Wild Arabian stallions couldn't drag him there.

'But Daddy,' Chloe said, 'Mummy's doing a picnic and everyone's coming.'

'I'm sorry, I need to stay in London, sweetie, and in any event I don't have my morning suit. Haven't a clue where it is.'

'It's in the boot of my car,' Clarissa said, dryly. 'Fresh from the dry cleaners.'

As they walked out, Colbey looked at his daughter's hurt face and felt pulled apart. He needed to sit her down and explain to her exactly who these people were, what they stood for and why he couldn't mix with them. He had been cowardly. Should have done it long ago. If only he had realised how far along she and Emir were. Engagements, apartments, giving up her job... It was a disaster.

Outside, Gabriel and Dominique waited for their car to travel the few yards to them and Colbey steeled himself with the thought that they were nearly done. Emir and Chloe were off to another club, close to where Clarissa had parked.

As they stood there waiting for the Chairman's limo to drive the few yards to him, Emir said to Colbey, 'So, Harry, you never answered my question. Why are you independent, then?' Colbey thought that, despite all his love for his daughter, he wouldn't be able to hold back any longer – but Clarissa once again jumped in and saved him.

'Because he's too honourable,' she said. 'He has principles, you know, not like so many of the others.'

Colbey looked at her in surprise. In the past, she would have bemoaned the fact. Could you not be a little more pliable? she used to say to him when they were married, when he was a new MP. She'd had grand plans for his political career back then. Do you have to be so damn honest all the time? she used to say.

'Honourable?' Gabriel growled as his car door was opened for him and he ushered Dominque inside. 'Not many of you around.'

The two men looked each other in the eye for the first time.

'Hopefully, enough,' Colbey said.

After the Chairman had got into the car, he put a hand out to prevent the driver closing the door.

'Come to the races,' he said. 'It will make the young people happy. And soon it won't matter anyway.'

Colbey stared as the car drove off and thought of all the things he could and should have said. Was the Chairman meaning because their children would soon be married? Or was there a threat in the comment?

As they made their way over to Berkeley Square, the two love-birds walked ahead.

'Do that thing,' Chloe giggled, looking back at them. She was tipsy, he realised.

'Not now, Chloe,' Emir said.

'Yes now. Daddy, you need to see this.'

With a challenging look behind him at Colbey, Emir raised a finger like a pretend gun and shot it towards the traffic lights at the pedestrian crossing. They immediately turned green.

'You still haven't told me how you do it,' Chloe said and giggled. 'There's a clicker in that other hand of yours, isn't there?'

Colbey looked up at the listening eye above them and knew exactly how Emir did it.

'Right, we'll leave you here, darling,' Clarissa said and went to kiss Chloe goodbye, but as she did so a car came round the square behind them and mounted the pavement. Colbey pulled them both out of its way just in time.

'What an asshole,' Emir said. 'Are you alright, my baby?'

'Yes, yes, of course I am,' Chloe replied. 'Don't fuss, darling.'

The gull-wing door of the sports car opened and two scantily clad girls who were crammed into the passenger seat fell out onto the pavement. They picked themselves up with a giggle as a young man pulled himself out the same side, and Colbey saw it was Elliot. On the roadside, the driver got out and with a drunk's stumble came round to the front.

Colbey looked up at the listening eyes. Here was a drunk driver. Dangerous, and what were they doing? Nothing!

He had a good mind to stop the chap and make some form of citizen's arrest, but when the man stepped into the light, Colbey stood back in shock. 'You!'

Neville Jameson swayed and the two girls came up to him. One of them wrapped a feather boa around his neck.

'You are driving that car when you are exceedingly drunk,' Colbey said.

Jameson seemed to ponder the statement, and then, thinking hard about how to get the words out, said, 'Go fuck yourself, Harry Colbey. I can do whatever the fuck I want, didn't you know that?'

A bouncer came down the steps. 'Everything alright, Mr Jameson?'

Colbey felt a tug on his hand and saw Chloe standing there.

'Leave it, Daddy. Please. This is supposed to be my night.'

At once, Colbey moved away, but he couldn't leave it without doing anything. He turned back and said, 'At least call a driver to take you home, for God's sake, Jameson.'

The Prime Minister pulled a face, but there seemed to be some sense in there still. He pulled a phone out of his pocket.

'Come and get me from the club,' he slurred into it.

'There,' he said, putting his phone away again. 'Happy? And I give you the supposedly honourable Mr Harry Colbey.' Then he turned and with the girls stumbled up the steps and into the club, the bouncer following behind. Elliot was long gone – whether it was into the club or elsewhere, he didn't see.

Leaving a respectable gap, Chloe and Emir trotted up the steps and disappeared, and with a joint sigh of relief Colbey and Clarissa walked over to the car.

'Well, that was a lot of fun,' Colbey said, and Clarissa started to laugh and laugh.

'You're telling me,' she said. 'What a terrible lot.'

At the end of the square were the offices of Henri Lauvaux's financial trading company. Was the Frenchman there, he wondered, working late? Or in his house in St James's? He thought of the time he had fled from there and been set upon by drones. He looked up again at the listening-eye post and knew Divinity was watching.

You can't do anything when I'm with Clarissa, can you? he thought, and to his ex-wife he said, 'Any chance of a lift to parliament?'

Clarissa shook her head. 'Are you kidding? I may not have drunk as much as our delightful Prime Minister, but I've drunk too much to drive.'

'It's not like you'll get stopped, is it?' Colbey said bitterly, and Clarissa stared at him.

'This isn't like you.'

'What isn't?'

'This beaten-down act. Snap out of it.'

Colbey knew she was right. But all he wanted to do was lie down somewhere warm and sleep until all the problems of the world were fixed.

'It's just Chloe with that Emir... I wish you hadn't introduced them.'

'And I wish you had been around to warn her off him. She won't listen to me. Never has done. It's always been what you thought that mattered.'

Colbey felt the sting of the truth. He had put his work ahead of looking out for his daughter.

'Come and have a drink with me,' Clarissa said.

'I don't want to drink in any of these places,' he said, looking about the square.

'Then come to my hotel room and I'll get room service to bring you up an Old Fashioned, just how you like it.'

Colbey couldn't help but laugh.

'A hotel room? Are you kidding me? What's wrong with your flat in Chelsea?'

'Nothing. I just...'

'What?'

'I just like to get away from the place sometimes. All those...'

'Owners?'

'Yes, the Owners. They always want to know my business. There aren't any listening eyes inside the complex, but that doesn't mean I'm not under scrutiny.'

Colbey didn't know what to say. 'You made your bed and must lie in it' sprang to mind.

'Come on. It's only round the corner. Come and see the suite. You won't believe it.'

Afraid of what might happen if he left her side, Colbey agreed. In any event, after the evening he'd just had, the thought of an Old Fashioned was proving too irresistible.

1.16

Kanha was fast asleep on the sofa when a *ting ting* announced that Mani was online. He was an Aussie, but they had met on an internship programme over in the States when they had been much younger, and then he had popped up working for Moreland a year ago, before heading off to work for Interpol. His computer skills, and – to be whispered – his hacking skills, were second to none. If anyone could figure out how to get these files into the right hands, all at the same time, it would be Mani. It was great to see his cheerful face on the screen.

'Hey... How goes it in the Orwellian dystopia?' he said.

'You look tired,' was her answer.

'Oh, mate. That's 'cos it's three in the morning where I am. What's your excuse?'

She knew better than to ask him where that was.

'Any luck figuring out where Divinity's servers are?' she asked instead.

Mani shook his head. 'No hope. The gas and power data networks are locked down tight. Divinity runs them – it's now the best hacker in the world, and it's doing a fine job of keeping the best human hacker out.'

'OK, well, I have another problem for you to solve. I'm going to move tomorrow. Gerald Moreland thinks we mustn't wait any longer, and based on the press announcements Neville Jameson made this morning, I think he's right.'

Mani raised his eyebrows and blew some air out through his teeth.

'Reckon you could be right.'

She explained her problem to him.

'Tricky,' he said. 'And what sort of people are you targeting here?'

'Head of MI5, the District Attorney, head of the national and the Metropolitan police forces, some High Court and Old Bailey judges, perhaps military too.'

Mani put his head in his hands for a second. Then he looked up.

'It'll have to be by hand. Else it's too iffy. An email or phone message could be intercepted, either by someone on the watch for it—'

'Or some*thing...*'

'Yes, Divinity, of course. Or just through bad luck – an assistant or security person opening it and deciding it would be a good idea to send it to a Mobster.'

'Agree. So a memory stick? But then how do I make sure they all get it at the same time? And if they don't have a computer with them at that exact moment...'

Mani thought.

'Put a time lock on the file and save it onto a SIM.'

'Why a SIM?'

'They can put it straight into their phone. Won't need to hunt around for a computer. And, added benefit, if you use the right SIM, they'll be able to call into your restricted network and talk to you, without Divinity listening in.'

'So, you can save to a SIM?'

'My ones, yes. They're security grade, made for... Never mind all that. Trust me, they'll work. I'll set it so your letter automatically opens up when they insert it into a phone.'

'I like the plan. But we're using all of the SIMs you gave us. I have one. Colbey has one. Elliot, Wilbur, Brooke and Moreland. That's it.'

Mani smiled. 'Nah mate. Bottom drawer on your right.'

Kanha opened the drawer and laughed. There was a bag full of them.

'Why didn't you tell me?'

'You didn't ask. Anyway, the more you give out, the quicker your whole network will be jinxed.'

'Yeah. Well, thanks for managing me.'

'When you pull the trigger on this, your network is blown open anyway, so you might as well crack on.'

Kanha pulled out the bag and poured them all onto the table as Mani said, 'Tell me where the folder with the files is and I'll zip them into a time-locked file. Then what you'll have to do is put a SIM in your phone and download the file to it. Then switch to another and download to that one, and on you go. Bit time-consuming, but by the end you'll have a heap of SIMs with the file on them, which can't be accessed until the time comes.'

'Sounds a good plan,' Kanha agreed. 'Set it so the file can be accessed from midnight tomorrow night. Then I'll just have to make sure I put it in the hands of everyone on the list before then.'

She altered the letter to include an explanation of how to access the rest of the files on the SIM, following Mani's instructions. Then she added the number of her burner phone and an instruction to call it at 12.30am.

At her sigh, Mani said, 'You be careful, eh? Now get going on it, else dawn will be with you. And she's no bloody help at all.'

She thanked him for his help, and as ever he waved it off with a 'No worries,' before signing off.

A couple of hours later, Kanha blinked with tired eyes at the screen and yawned. In front of her was a pile of SIMs, each with the file loaded on it. She found a few empty envelopes and swept the SIMs into one. They didn't all fit, so she put the rest into a second envelope. This was all they could do. At the end of the day, she, Colbey, Wilbur and Brooke were just backbench MPs. They weren't police or military. But hopefully they could make a difference.

When she was done, she put her own SIM back in her phone and immediately it rang.

'Where have you been?' It was Harry.

'Long story,' she said. 'I'm only at Mani's. Had a bit of fun trying to get here without getting arrested. I'm guessing you're still hobnobbing with the enemy.'

There was a big sigh on the other end of the phone.

'I can't really talk. I'm not in a safe space.'

'Where are you?'

'In Clarissa's penthouse suite at the Ritz.'

Kanha was silent for a moment.

'I see.'

'You don't mind, do you?'

'Of course not. Is she there now?'

'She's gone off to her room to bed. I'm sleeping on the sofa. It seems I can only travel away from parliament. I can't travel towards it, unless I happen to be with her. Then I can travel anywhere.'

'Ah,' said Kanha. 'I see how that could work. So how will you get in tomorrow?'

'Perhaps Clarissa will be kind enough to drop me off. Then I guess I'm on my own. They're off to Royal Ascot for Chloe's engagement party.'

Kanha thought for a moment.

'You still there?' he asked.

'Yes. I've had an idea.'

And on the basis that he couldn't speak openly but she could, Kanha talked him quietly through the plan.

'What do you think?' she said at the end.

'I can't say I like it. Nothing I hate more than Royal Ascot.'

'Don't exaggerate.'

'But you'll be in the thick of it,' he complained. 'While I'll be in the thick of *them*. Doesn't seem like a fair exchange to me.'

'Understand. But I think you're better off sticking with Clarissa. You do see that, don't you?'

She heard him sigh.

'Sounds like I'm off to Royal Ascot with the vipers, then,' he said.

They wished each other goodnight, and Kanha told him she missed him. Then she put the phone delicately down on the table and eyed the two envelopes.

Tomorrow was going to be a difficult day. A difficult day indeed. But it was good to be able to act at last. I'm coming for you, Neville Jameson, she thought. Just you wait.

1.17

Henri Lauvaux arrived at his St James' house just as the concierge service from the Talbott Hotel opposite delivered his supper. He told the busboy to leave the tray on the table in the hallway, and bolted the door behind him. Peace, he thought, and relished the silence. While he loved his family, a few days separated from them was always a welcome pleasure.

He carried the tray upstairs, pulled closed the curtains of his tall bedroom windows, shutting out his view of the park, and clicked his fingers to turn on Divinity.

Its floating icon appeared on the screen next to his bed.

'Henri Lauvaux,' he said and the image switched to that of his own digital replica.

'Tell me,' he said.

He sat and ate as it caught him up on anything important that had happened while he was closeted with the cabinet. The MP Esme Kanha was raised as a concern.

'Esme Kanha?' Lauvaux said, frowning. Then he remembered. She used to be the government Chief Whip. One of the rebels who voted against Jameson's bill to turn on the listening eyes. She had been with Harry Colbey when Divinity swarmed him. Now, he wondered whether that was the coincidence they had supposed it to be.

'Let me speak to her,' he said.

The image of the MP appeared on the screen, but she was sullen and would discuss little other than the dull constituency affairs of a backbench MP.

'Who are you?' she said.

Lauvaux switched back to himself.

'Why is she like that?'

At the answer, he switched off the screen and frowned. She knew about Divinity. Had been hiding her true life from it. Anything real – emotions, relationships, close friendships – had been shielded for many months. As a result, the version of her in the system was out of date. It had told him she was seeing some banker that the other heads of Divinity knew she had split with two years ago. That was the cleverness of the multi-citizen system, the real Lauvaux thought. She might try to hide, but those around her, those who were less careful, would give her away. It was the same for that irksome Harry Colbey. Lauvaux frowned again as a thought occurred to him. He clicked to turn Divinity's screen back on.

'Do you think she is conspiring with Harry Colbey?' both he and his digital version said at the same time. The real Lauvaux smiled and the digital replica said, 'I have been thinking just the same thing. She is a powerful political animal. Perhaps we underestimated her.'

'Is she under surveillance?'

'All of those who voted against the security bill are monitored. We had planned to—'

'Change the plans,' said Lauvaux. 'Make her a priority. We must know what she's doing at all times.' Then, seeing that a call from his wife was coming through, he flicked the screen off again and the image of his wife appeared instead.

'How is *Grand-mère*?' Lauvaux asked as he took off his clothes and changed into his pyjamas and dressing gown. He only really enquired out of politeness, and because of it was forced to listen to a long description of the nursing home and of her mother's pains. It was tiresome stuff, other people's dying. He asked after his daughter and was told she had arrived and had been sent to bed as she was overtired and demanding bananas. Lauvaux lied and said he didn't know why.

After the call, he turned off the screen again and went over to the vanity cabinet that stood between the windows. He brushed his teeth, thinking about the MP Esme Kanha. He would sleep on it tonight, and when he spoke to Divinity again tomorrow he would compare notes with its thinking and agree what to do about her. He pulled a string of floss from the plastic container, but there was only an inch left. Why could the housekeeper not replace things before they ran out? 'Francine!'

But he remembered he had allowed her to have the week off. Shouldn't have. Not with everything going on. He could call the hotel across the road, but it always took them so long to arrive, even when it was just something simple like this. He would have to speak to them. He thought of the panic room. There were all sorts of provisions in there. He put the finished floss container in the bin, went over to the corner of the room, pulled aside a curtain and opened the steel door.

It wasn't a large room. He had absolutely no intention of living in a steel box, eating tinned bully – that was for loonies and conspiracy theorists – but it had come with the house, and so his wife had thought they might as well equip it. He hunted through the racking.

Now where was that floss?

Ah, there it was.

Right on the top.

Lauvaux stretched up and it was like someone smote him down from heaven. He staggered back and fell between the wall and the toilet. A pain gripped both his arms and straddled his chest. He couldn't breathe. He couldn't move. Even without Divinity telling him, he knew it was a heart attack. His breath came quick and shallow. He had not prepared for this, he thought with agony. They were not ready.

He tried to shout out, but only a whimper came from his lips.

He looked up at the screen in the corner, but it was not yet wired in. 'Objective number one…' he whispered.

Lauvaux tried to manoeuvre himself so that he could reach the intercom switch, but it was too high up. He fell back and became wedged in the gap between the toilet and the racks. After all he had achieved. To die like this… It wasn't fair. One human lifespan. That was all he had been given, and there was so much he still wanted to do.

Why did Divinity not speak? Was it considering what to do about his loss? But it had all the time in the world in which to process the fact. It had a hundred lifetimes in which to think. A thousand perhaps. Lifetimes he had given to it. If only he could speak to it. But his watch hand was trapped beneath him and he knew… he knew… he was in a steel box and they had not had a chance to connect the WiFi. He should never have come in here. All for some floss. To die for a piece of floss! There was a god of irony somewhere, that was for sure.

For a moment, Lauvaux was stricken with doubt. What did Divinity think of religion? The thought came to him unbidden. He had never thought to ask. But of course, he reprimanded himself, it didn't work like that. If he had asked, he would have been given a hundred different answers. A million different citizens, a million different versions of faith. He thought of the church he used to attend as a boy. The gold-work shining, the priest intoning in Latin, the hard seats as the sermon went on and on. He had abandoned that god. Had forgotten it. Replaced it with Divinity.

Lauvaux thought of Harry Colbey, the perpetual thorn in his side. He had boasted to Colbey that he, Lauvaux, owned a god. What are you, if you own a god? Lauvaux had said to him. He really had wanted to know what the honourable MP thought. But now it became clear to him. One couldn't own a god. Not someone of flesh and blood, someone mortal.

Had he done wrong?

But he had done it for them. For his wife and child.

And all those everyday people with their everyday lives, would they care?

So long as they had their television programmes, their social media feeds, their Friday night fish and chips, their Sunday night curries. So long as they could dance with their chums and drink gassy beer by the pint and cheap wine by the bucketload. If you told them the country was run by a machine rather than a bunch of self-interested, sleazy, power-mad do-gooders, would they even bat an eyelid? Or would they just shrug?

He thought of all those ridiculous science-fiction films, those dystopian stories of human skulls crushed underfoot and men unable to get a moment's privacy, and would have laughed if he had been able to. What everyone forgot was that people don't care that they are being watched or listened to. They don't care who is in charge. So long as those who watch and listen do not rub their faces in it. So long as the bins are collected, the roads are mended, the pubs are still open and the shops remain full of sugary food and cans of pop; so long as they never go short of toilet roll.

Lauvaux thought of his wife and wished she was there. He thought of his daughter and hoped he had done enough. Man could only learn for so long, but Divinity would learn forever and would grow stronger and stronger. It would protect his daughter and her children and their children, and those who were from his line would be behind the eye and not in front of it. They would control the world, not be at its mercy. Remember your objectives, Divinity, he whispered. And as there was no reply, he forced the words out, in the hope they might be heard. Number one – protect the Owners; number two – grow the wealth of the Owners; number three – protect yourself.

Was it ready? Trust to Divinity, he thought. He felt doubt. He should have...

But he was gone.

PART TWO

Thursday 20 June

2.1

Neville Jameson woke with a start and wondered where the hell he was. He groped about and found soft leather beneath him. He was slumped at a strange angle. Phone, he thought automatically, but found it in the pocket of his coat. Reaching out to his side, he found a handle. Car, he was in a car. He opened his eyes a crack and looked at his watch. Four in the morning. That was why it was still dark. From the front of the car came the sound of snoring. When Jameson levered himself upright and tapped on the glass divider, his driver woke with a start and turned to face him with bleary eyes. Out of the window, Jameson saw that they were parked outside a large stucco house and on the other side of the road was a hotel.

'Where are we?' he asked, pushing the intercom button.

'St James's,' the driver replied, putting his hat on and straightening his tie.

'Why are we here?'

'You told me to bring us.'

'Why?'

'I don't know, sir.'

Jameson peered at the hotel. The Talbott. Shit. They were parked in front of Lauvaux's house.

'Did I get out of the car?' he said.

'No, sir. You was asleep when we got here and... Sorry if I got it wrong, but I thought best to let you sleep it off.'

Jameson did not reply.

Why had he come here? He peered through the front of the car. That was Lauvaux's house alright. He had never been in before. He had only ever met Lauvaux at odd places – a polo match, a restaurant, or the Frenchman had come to Chequers.

God. What if the driver had done what he'd asked last night and let him stumble drunk into Lauvaux's house with the girls?

At the thought of Natalia, he said, 'Where are the others?'

'You sent them home.'

'Home to...?'

'Don't know, sir.'

Jameson took his phone out of his pocket and was going to use it as a mirror but thought better of it. The system didn't need to see him right now. But who was he kidding? As if Divinity hadn't monitored his entire evening. I'm just a puppet, he thought. I'm nothing but the puppet of a foreigner and his bloody machine.

But it had to be faced. He glared at his phone to open it. His heart hammered. There were messages to and from Lauvaux. No drunk texting. That was a rule he had lived by for many years. He would not have made it as far as he had without sticking to it ruthlessly. However drunk he was, he never messaged. What had made him do it?

He tapped into the conversation.

Come and see me at my house. ASAP.

Fuck.

He had replied just three words. *On my way.*

Thank God for the driver's sense. Was he to be told off by Lauvaux? Surely even a Prime Minister can have a party now and then? He wasn't the first to do so. Wouldn't be the last, he thought.

He breathed into his hand.

'I need mints.'

The driver wound down the window and passed a toothbrush and some toothpaste through the gap, along with painkillers.

'I'm going to recommend you for a bonus,' Jameson said.

He steeled himself and messaged Lauvaux.

'Sorry. Got held up with state matters. Shall I come later this morning?'

No reply. He stewed for the shortest time, then he buckled. ASAP meant ASAP, whatever time of day or night it was.

As Jameson stepped out of the car and slicked back his hair, he realised it was not as dark as when he had woken. Already the dawn was breaking and the sky behind the hotel had lightened. God, how he hated the seasons. To live somewhere where it was always the same. Always hot and sunny. Where one could party all night and never get cold or windswept.

Jameson hurried up the steps to the front door and found it opened at his touch. He went into the hallway and closed the door gently behind him. The Frenchman did not live with the other Owners, but that did not surprise him. Did a King live with his courtiers?

Wandering through the empty rooms, every now and again Jameson called out, 'Hello? Anyone up?'

He glanced at the clock on the wall. It was still very early. He returned to the hallway and stood killing time, looking at a modern representation of the Eiffel Tower that filled one wall and considering whether to go upstairs or not. The light was strong enough now that the stained glass of the windows above the main staircase was casting coloured diamonds onto the worn wooden treads of the stairs.

Jameson crept up, calling as he went. 'Lauvaux, are you up there?'

He reached a long corridor. The first room he came to was a child's room, but the one further down and opposite was obviously the master bedroom. There were tall windows that, if the curtains were not closed, he guessed would have a great view over the park, across to Buckingham Palace. There was an expanse of polished wood flooring. A desk at one end. A bed at the other.

'Hello?'

Jameson crept into Lauvaux's personal space, feeling like he was snooping in his boss's office. There was an open door at the end, a curtain pulled aside. Through the door he could see metal racking. He crept forward. Something had caught his eye. It was… a slipper, a foot. He forced himself to keep on. Lauvaux lay between a toilet and the shelving. He wore a tartan dressing gown over pyjamas.

'He's dead,' thought Jameson at once, although he did not believe it possible. Lauvaux had been the master of everything around him. Jameson could not believe he was not also the master of death.

He stepped forward so that he could see the Frenchman's face. He didn't want to touch him. Couldn't bring himself to. But he had to know. He tentatively bent down and put a finger to the man's cheek. Cold. As cold as death. As cold as a corpse that had been lying for hours. He remembered the body of his uncle laid out in his father's house. Long dead. Lauvaux was long dead.

He backed away, out of the door. Now all he could see was Lauvaux's feet again. He looked at the steel door. They had the same model of panic room at Chequers. His bodyguard had shown him how to use it.

Trying not to think too much about it, Jameson reached out and pushed the door closed. It jammed up against the foot, so he gave it a shove until it was firmly closed. Then he used the number pad and locked it for the maximum time it allowed. It would give him a day in which to think of what to do.

Jameson stood for a moment. Through the light that came in around the curtains he could see a toothbrush on the sink in the corner. A straggle of clothes thrown in the direction of a laundry basket.

He backed away.

Then he turned and fled. Out of the room, down the fancy staircase, across the hall, past the painting of the Eiffel Tower, out of the door. He fumbled with the handle and then slammed it shut behind him.

Jameson ran his tongue over his lips. They were dry as hell.

He hurried over to the car and got in the back seat. He looked down at his hands. They were dry as hell too.

'Take me to Number Ten,' he said.

2.2

As dawn began to lighten the sky, Kanha hurried out of Mani's apartment and, feeling a little guilty about taking his electric bike as well as abusing his apartment, cycled over to the embankment on the south side of the river. In the bag on her back were the two envelopes of SIMs along with the helmet and leathers. She didn't want Divinity to make a connection between the helmet and her, so rather than wear it she had rooted around in a few drawers and found some wraparound glasses to wear, as well as a long scarf, which she had tied around her head.

She passed the Vauxhall and Lambeth Bridges without seeing a soul. She passed the hospital where Easterly had been examined, spinning under the listening-eye posts, and cycled past the bench she had sat on. An empty Westminster Bridge loomed above her. But as she carried the bike up to it, the sun rising over the bend of the river in the far distance, she heard sirens coming from the south.

Bastards, she thought. How had the system known? Then she looked down and saw that she had forgotten to wear gloves. Damn, damn, damn. Amateur, she cursed herself. Casting a quick look behind, she saw that two police motorcyclists had appeared at the end of the bridge, down by the County Hall. But it wasn't far. Just the bridge and the corner and she would be there.

She pulled the scarf from her head and threw it to the side of the road, and her hair streamed out behind her as she pushed the e-bike as fast as it would go. She was abreast of parliament now, but a wall and a twenty-foot drop stood between them. She dodged the jet-lagged, early-rising tourists gathered on the corner of Parliament Square, cameras in hand, and as she came to the gates of New Palace Yard, without looking she knew they were just behind her. She heard the blare of their sirens as they came to the same tourists.

'Open the road gates!' Kanha shouted at the police officer on duty in her cabin. It was the wrong entrance for bikes, she was told.

'I don't care,' she shouted out. 'It's an emergency. Open the gates!'

'Stay where you are!' she heard behind her. The officers had pulled their bikes onto the kerb and were kicking their stands into place.

'Please! Open the gates.' She punched the air to emphasise her point and, finally, the woman did as she asked.

As soon as there was a gap large enough, she slipped through, but so did one of the officers. He seized her bodily from behind, twisting her arm and pushing her onto the ground, his weight on top of her. But I am inside, she thought, as the bike slid out from between her legs, and her face was pushed into the gravel. What bullshit were they going to pin on her? she wondered and thought of the SIMs in her bag that wouldn't be delivered. They should have done it another way. They should have—

'Officer! Release that MP at once.'

Someone had come across the yard from the direction of the Speaker's House.

'...wanted in connection with terrorism,' she heard, and then 'Nonsense.' The name of the Attorney General was thrown about. It was the Speaker, she realised, and felt a sudden undying love for the man.

'I just won't have it,' he was saying. 'This is a totally disproportionate response...'

The officer said something about her resisting arrest.

'And the Metropolitan Police has no jurisdiction on the parliamentary estate. My Serjeant at Arms is in charge. So I suggest you get off her immediately.'

The officer on her back asked the air for instructions, and with his head so close to hers, she clearly heard the response. A soft but assured female voice. 'You are in a legally grey area. Try to use persuasion. This is a dangerous terror suspect and it's essential we apprehend her.'

Now, the Serjeant at Arms came running across the yard, the ruff of his formal shirt flapping in the wind and his legs showing bare beneath his breeches. When he reached them, he bent in two and started wheezing. At his arrival, the knee in her back eased off, but when she tried to move her hands to push herself up she realised they had been cuffed together.

'Outrageous,' the Speaker said, as he bent to help her get to her feet.

At once, Kanha turned on the police officer.

'Take these off this very minute,' she said, trying to lift her shackled hands. 'Or I am going to report you to every police commissioner in the country.'

Those bloody helmets, she thought. It was so hard to see what he might be thinking.

To the Serjeant at Arms, the officer said, 'We want to apprehend this woman under suspicion of terrorism. Will you assist me?'

'I certainly will not,' Bowles replied. He hurried into the cabin and returned with a pair of scissors and, daring the officer to stop him, he cut the plastic ties round Kanha's wrists.

Kanha rubbed her bruised wrists and tried not to think about the pains elsewhere caused by the officer pushing her to the ground and her knees scraping on the tarmac.

'If you or your superiors wish to discuss something with me,' she said to the officer, 'I suggest they do what you would have done before you all started following instructions from a psychopathic computer and ring me on the bloody telephone. I'm a Member of Parliament. I work in an office here every day and I have a surgery office in my constituency. Both of them have registered phone numbers, which are answered in normal office hours, and I have an answering machine for the rest of the time.'

The officer seemed uncertain, but when the Speaker said, 'I suggest you do as the lady requested and approach her through the usual channels,' he paused. The tinny voice was speaking to him again. Without another word, he turned to the gates and, with a nod at the officer in the guard box, who had come out as if deciding she might join the party after all, he slipped through them back to his colleague.

The Serjeant at Arms was still wheezing. 'Do you want to sit down in my hut?' the guard asked him, but he declined with thanks: he seemed to have found an inhaler in his pocket and taken a shot.

The Speaker was shaking his head. 'I just don't know what it's all coming to.'

'It's coming to a head, that's what,' Kanha said.

He insisted Kanha come with them up to his apartments.

'Lucky for you I'm an early riser,' he said as they walked up. 'I saw you from my window, flying across the bridge with the police in hot pursuit. Wondered what was going on. Thought I had better get down here.'

'Sorry I was bit slower,' the Serjeant said. 'I wasn't much use.'

'You were a great help,' Kanha said. 'If you hadn't arrived to back us all up, that police officer would have dragged me off.'

'Do you really think so?'

'Of course.'

The Serjeant took another puff of his inhaler, and Kanha thought it was a good job his role was largely ceremonial.

In the Speaker's private bathroom, Kanha took off her torn tights and bathed her knees, picking out the little stones and stemming the bleeding. It wasn't as bad as it looked. A bit of gravel rash and some bruises. The Serjeant at Arms appeared at the door with a first aid kit and went to take her bag from her shoulder, but she clutched it tightly and wouldn't let him.

'Alright, Esme. Have it your way,' he said. She applied some antiseptic cream and a couple of big plasters and then tidied everything back into the box.

'Very attractive,' the Speaker joked, looking at the plasters on her knees as she emerged from the bathroom. The Serjeant at Arms was already waiting with coffee and suggested they all sit down at the table.

'Now, Esme,' the Speaker started. 'I don't think you've been entirely honest with me. Not you or Harry Colbey. You've told me bits – the bits you needed to – but not the whole thing. I want you to tell me and the Serjeant everything. It's a clean room, so you can rest easy there.'

Kanha clutched her bag on her lap. 'Fine. But I have to warn you that it puts you in danger if I do.'

The Speaker and the Serjeant at Arms looked at each other.

'So?' the Speaker said. 'Looking after democracy is our job. And you are part of that democracy. And from the looks of things, you could do with some looking after.'

The Serjeant at Arms opened a packet of biscuits. 'You need friends you can trust,' he said.

Kanha looked from one to the other. Then she dropped her bag onto the table, dug inside and pulled out a couple of SIMs.

'If you are sure,' she said. 'Because I suspect from here on in, things are only going to get worse.'

As opposition leader, Jackie Rolt had her parliamentary offices in a prime location, in the main building, between the chamber of Commons and the northern wing that held the Speaker's House.

Kanha knocked on the door of Rolt's assistant's room and asked if Jackie was in.

'Now?' the secretary asked. He was a young lad, still wet behind the ears. 'And who are you?'

Kanha was tempted to sarcastically say, 'A has-been, apparently,' but held her tongue.

'Just tell her Esme Kanha wants a quick word.'

He was out of his seat before he obviously remembered Rolt had instructed him not to let Esme Kanha through on any account. He sat down again.

'She isn't in yet. If you want to—'

'Bullshit. Go knock on the door and tell her I'm coming in whether she likes it or not. I'd do it myself, but it seems politer coming from you.'

The opposition leader's assistant did as he was told and came back sheepishly.

'She says to go right in.'

Jackie Rolt was sitting behind a desk so covered with paper you could hardly see the squat Northern opposition leader behind it all. There were a few researchers in the room with her, tablets on their knees. One of them gave a great yawn.

'Esme,' she said. 'Always good to see you. Always… entertaining.' She looked at her watch. 'We're prepping for this morning's debate. Is it anything urgent?'

'Exceedingly. And for your ears only.'

Rolt turned to her team with a sigh. 'Go and get me breakfast. And take all your devices with you.' Then she turned to Kanha. 'Right, you have as long as it takes them to get to the Terrace Cafeteria and back.'

Bloody woman. She was even more insufferable as leader of the opposition than she had been as Prime Minister. Kanha looked at the corners of the room.

'It's clean,' Rolt said. 'You think I'd let Jameson and his bloody system listen to my private meetings?' She waved a hand at the door. 'I let them have their gadgets because it makes no difference. They're as leaky after a pint in the Sports and Social as if they had a listening eye attached to their collars anyway.'

Kanha sat down and put her bag on her lap. Ten minutes. She'd have to be concise. Rolt was still mad at her for what had happened the previous year. Seemed to think it was her fault she had lost power and Jameson had taken over.

'As you know, Neville Jameson is only leader of our party because the Alcheminna system used its intimate knowledge of a group of corrupted MPs – all their dirty little secrets – to blackmail them into voting for him, as well as voting for a bunch of other things that helped the company and its shareholders gain the edge and wipe out their competition.'

'Well, I know that's what you've told me,' Rolt said, her face crinkling. 'I've never seen any evidence.'

'You've not tried to gather proof of your own?'

'Not about your leadership campaign. Who cares about that?'

'OK,' Kanha said. 'But when you were Prime Minister, you promised to look into Henri Lauvaux's corrupt links to British politics and governance. I can't believe, now that you are in opposition, you would drop the matter. Won't you share what you have?'

'With you?' Rolt said.

Kanha shifted a pile of papers aside. 'We're stronger if we work together.'

'I agree,' said Rolt and Kanha was surprised she had acquiesced so easily. But then the opposition leader said, 'So cross the floor and join me. I'd make you a shadow minister straight away. Whatever office you want. You want to be Chief Whip again?'

Kanha looked at Rolt's eager face. Her political ideology, shaped from her childhood, set her apart from this woman's party. At least she had always thought so.

'We're not so far apart now, are we?' Rolt said, her mind running along the same path. 'Compare how we think Britain should be run and where Jameson is taking us, and we have more in common than we might want to admit. In the grand scheme of things.'

Kanha knew what she said was true, but also knew there were many in her party who would not agree. There would never be a coalition made up of their two parties, and she couldn't turn her back on her colleagues of so many years. Yes, there were bad apples among them, but most worked hard for their constituents, fighting their battles for them day in, day out. She wouldn't be a traitor and cross the floor. Couldn't do it.

'It's not—'

Rolt waved her hand. 'I understand – it was worth a try. But I won't share what I have with a member of the government's party.'

'That's a shame. Would you share it with Harry Colbey? He's independent.'

'You think I'm an idiot? Share it with Colbey and I share it with you. Which means I share it with your party. And it's your party that's in the process of gifting authority to some new set of entitled—'

Kanha raised her hand with a grin. 'I understand. It was worth a try.'

The women eyed each other. Both knew that if Jameson was brought down there would be a tussle between them as to whose party would come out on top. So neither entirely trusted the other, however much their interests might be aligned. But Kanha had to act and she had to act now. She had no choice.

She lifted her bag onto the table.

'Give me your word you won't use it for your own gain until midnight tonight and I will give you all the proof you need that Jameson is corrupt.'

Greedily Rolt held out a hand. 'OK. Give it to me. Quick. They'll be back soon.'

'No prepping the press. No chewing over with SPADs. No needling the PM in a way that might give him a forewarning.' The door opened behind Kanha.

'Wait!' Rolt held up a warning hand and the door closed again.

'You'll be putting yourself in danger if you do. And you won't be able to access the file on this until midnight anyway.'

'Alright, Esme. Have it your way.'

Kanha fished a SIM out of her bag and slid it across the table to Rolt.

'Clever. Everyone will get it at the same time,' the opposition leader said.

'Yes. There'll be safety in numbers. And everyone will be able to act as one.'

Rolt's eyes glinted, and Kanha wondered if she had underestimated the woman's greed. She too was under pressure from those in her party who were against the surveillance measures, and who thought she had failed them when they lost power. In the same way that Jameson was popular for stealing it from her, Rolt was only just clinging on.

'We have to work together,' Kanha reiterated. 'It's the only way we'll bring down Lauvaux and Jameson. Then all bets can be off. Are you sure you agree?'

Rolt nodded. 'I said yes. What do you need, a pinky promise?'

She called her team in, and Kanha left the room with disquiet. She didn't trust her.

Well, if she will not help us when the time comes, Kanha thought, we will have to manage without her. The one thing she knew was that Rolt would not work with Jameson. Rolt hated anything to do with their party with a passion that was born and bred, but she hated that man even more.

Kanha clutched her bag to her chest. Right, who was next?

Quentin Tidy. Her favourite lobby journalist.

She pulled out her phone and gave him a call, hoping he might be in early for the morning's press conference. He answered at once. He was indeed in the central lobby.

Three down, she thought, and hurried off.

She found Tidy standing beneath the central lobby's ornate chandelier and talking animatedly on the phone. She had a SIM hidden in her hand, ready to slip to him, but saw at once that the time wasn't right. There were a number of other representatives from the lobby press hanging about, leaning on the statues while they talked, or gathered by the post office window.

Seeing her, Tidy put the mobile to his chest and said, 'Do you know where it is?'

'What?'

'The press conference. They're saying it's been cancelled, but we don't believe them.'

Kanha shook her head. 'Did they move it to Number Ten?'

Jess Bolton of the BBC overheard and came over.

'I don't think so,' she said. 'A bunch of Mobsters came through the scanners with me. But where are they now, you know what I mean?'

Kanha went through to the lobbies and peered into the Star Chamber. The podium and the screen that had been set up a week or so ago were gone, and the courtyard was empty. By the time she returned to the central lobby, Bolton and Tidy and a few other journalists were gathered around her phone.

'There's a briefing going on somewhere. There's Sanjay Arun standing at a pissing podium.' Kanha peered over Bolton's shoulder and saw she was looking at a Mouth of the Mob account. As the rumour went around the room, several more journalists came up, but they were shushed as Bolton turned up the volume.

'Today, we have several announcements to make,' Arun was saying.

'Where is he?' someone hissed but was also shushed.

'The first is that we have reason to believe the country is at imminent risk of a terror attack. We don't want to apply a nationwide stay-at-home order if we can avoid it, but... be aware! Keep near listening eyes. Keep your government home or office speakers on at all times. Keep trips away from home to a minimum.'

'It's not Number Ten,' Tidy muttered.

'To announce this without us!' someone at the back of the crowd said in despair.

Kanha leaned forward and pointed at Bolton's phone. 'That's oak panelling behind him. Looks like a committee room, don't you think?'

Quentin Tidy looked at her. 'That's exactly what it is.' And off he set, pushing the others aside. They looked up in confusion, asked where he was off to and, at the answer, decided they had better follow.

Kanha tagged along with them, and by now the speech was coming from phones all around her, Arun's voice staggered due to the time delays.

'We understand how difficult it can be to distinguish truth from lies, particularly with so much deepfake news being churned out by what used to be called the traditional media.'

'Used to be called?' said Dalglish of the *Scotsman*, as they reached the Lower Waiting Hall and took to the stairs. Tidy was surprisingly fit, leaping two at a time, while Bolton trotted up in her heels beside him. Others fell back and called for the pack to slow down, but the request fell on deaf ears as Arun's speech continued.

'As leader of the Whigges, I've always had a special place in my heart for your news outlet, which has led the way to pin-pointing truth.'

'Is he off his head?' protested Bolton, but Tidy, panting heavily as they turned the corner of the stairwell, his tie flapping over his shoulder, said nothing in reply and jogged on.

'So I'm happy to announce that I, Sanjay Arun, Home Secretary and joint leader of the coalition, have arranged for the Home Office to develop a special relationship with the Mouth of the Mob. Although the website has in the past been known as the home of fake news, it has actually provided a forum in which the public could verify what they believed to be true and what they believed to be false. What they might have seen with their own eyes. Now, the government will be joining in that fact-checking.'

By now the first of the lobby pack had reached the committee corridor, Tidy, Bolton and Kanha at the front, and its long series of wooden doors stretched out before them.

'From our new government account on the Mouth of the Mob website, users will be able to access trustworthy news and information. What is the reason for the stay-at-home order in my hometown? No longer will citizens have to speculate.'

Each of the committee room doors were flung open, only for the lobby pack to be greeted with the confused faces of MPs and their guests looking up from their meetings.

'And we will be working in conjunction with the website in new ways. Where mobsters have posted videos that the government knows to be true, they will carry a *VERIFIED* stamp on them from the government account. So look out for the *VERIFIED* stamp.'

As they came to the end of the Commons Committee corridor, where the green patterned carpet stopped and a red patterned one began, Tidy ground to halt and rounded on Kanha. Those lagging behind caught up, some of them crashing into the pack due to the unexpected halt.

'For God's sake, you were wrong.'

But a journalist Kanha had not met before came forward. She had a shock of pink hair.

'Who the hell are you?' Tidy said.

'Jade Harrelson, freelance.' She showed them the screen of her phone. She was watching the presentation from a different Mobster, one who was filming from a different angle. She pointed at a tiny edge of red flocked wallpaper above the Home Secretary's head. 'It's a Lords room,' she said.

'Well done, Harrelson, freelance,' Tidy said and as one they all moved on, into the red carpeted area and into the House of Lords. At the very far end of the Lords Committee Corridor, a couple of SPADs stood nervously by a door. Knowing at once what that signified, the pack pushed at one another in their anger and raced towards them, not bothering with any other doors.

The closest SPAD held up his hands.

'You're none of you invited,' he said.

'On what basis?' demanded Dalglish.

'This is a restricted meeting. For Mobsters only' They all heard the wobble in his voice.

'You'd better move aside, boy. Or there's gonna be hell to pay,' Dalglish growled.

Kanha had never seen the lobby journalists so full of rage. These boys had better stand aside, she thought, or there are going to be fists flying.

Tidy pushed his way to the front.

'That in there is a Number Ten press briefing,' he said. 'And we are the recognised journalists of the lobby press association. It is our right to be there.'

'It's not a press briefing. It's a meeting about the Mouth of the Mob and so invitees are just Mobst—are just journalists from that news outlet.'

'The Mouth of the Mob is not a news outlet,' a woman from the *Express* said angrily, and another cried out, 'Bullshit. The Home Secretary just made an announcement about national security levels. That's a briefing about terror.'

Quentin Tidy held up his hand, and they all fell silent. He looked at the SPAD and said, coldly, 'You have an obligation to be politically neutral in press briefings. It is well known that the Mouth of the Mob has an editorial slant towards the Whigge party, and as the Whigge party is part of the coalition government, it now has an editorial slant towards the government. Your briefing here is not legal.'

The other SPAD decided to get involved.

'We can brief whoever we like,' he said. 'So fuck off.'

Tidy looked from one to the other.

'Planning to have a long political career are you, gentlemen?' he said.

The braver one faltered first, his brain kicking in at last. He whispered to his colleague that perhaps it might be a good time to step out for a coffee break.

Kanha knew that the young man had suddenly thought of all the speeches he had planned to make in his political career, all the positions he had hoped to achieve. First a safe seat, then a junior ministerial post, eventually working his way up to a cabinet role, and maybe even...

But if he made an enemy of Quentin Tidy – in fact, if he made an enemy of every single journalist in the lobby association – things would not be so easy. Every speech picked apart, every political manoeuvre scrutinised and found wanting, every policy announcement ridiculed.

'Come on,' he said and the two slid off to the side and trotted off down the corridor.

Tidy grabbed the handle and swung the door open so that it bashed against the wall, making Arun, up on the stage, jump and pause in what he was saying. He glanced at his Press Officer, who signalled that he should continue.

'...And finally to our third announcement. Our Prime Minister has decided that to support our work with the Mouth of the Mob, a new government department will be created—' The speakers behind Arun screeched as the streaming of his speech on the journalist's phones was picked up by his microphone, creating a feedback loop.

'Could the newcomers turn off their audio streams? You're a little late, but move along there and find room, and we can get this finished.'

Whether it was his matter-of-fact manner or the glares from the adoring Mobsters, for whom Arun was a hero, that threw the journalists off their stride was not clear, but they shuffled meekly in and arrayed themselves along the sides of the room without their planned protest. Perhaps it was just that a respect for the sanctity of the press conference was embedded in their bones.

When they were settled, Arun continued, and it was plain to see from how flushed he was, from how he gripped the podium and looked eagerly around the faces shining up at him, that he was carried away with his speech.

'This new department will be called the Ministry of Truth.' He raised his finger and pointed into the air. 'And it will be housed in Whitehall in what is now a Home Office building. It will remain under my remit, but a new post will be created – a junior minister for truth. And she will be supported in her work by the system that is keeping us all safe. By the Alcheminna system.'

The Mobsters whistled and Arun gave a broad smile.

'I've always been a technophile, as you know. We've fought hard to bring modernity to this coalition government. In my time as Home Secretary, our British civil service has become the most efficient and economical in the world. By working with the Alcheminna apps, our efficiency has been raised to such a level that we no longer need our employees to work the same number of hours. As of next month they will only work three days a week.

'And I want everyone to be sure to remember. It was we Whigges who brought the system in. It was we Whigges who devised it and brought its use to the coalition. This is not Neville Jameson's policy. His party would never have thought of it, let alone implemented it. And we Whigges have so many other great things that we are going to bring to the British citizens.'

The Mobsters applauded and whistled and stamped their feet. Arun looked around the lobby association and grinned as if to say, 'See! See why you were not invited.'

'And this is just the start,' he roared, feeding off the energy of the crowd. He raised his finger in the air again.

'The system that we brought to the government will soon be able to do so much for us. See and hear! Twenty million listening-eye cameras rolled out already, protecting us. Recognise! Already the system can identify cars, faces, fingers, ears, voices. It can find anyone, anywhere. And for that reason, we now have the most efficient police force in the world.'

He has waited to give this speech his whole life, Kanha thought. She was surprised that Jameson had condoned it.

'Think! The system will think for you. It will be your white-collar worker, your legal department, your customer service department. It will do your accounting for you, and your marketing. It will be your personal assistant, scheduling your diary, summarising your reports. And finally – act! Soon the system will be connected to our industrial workforce – linked in to drones and robots, for efficient factories, efficient defence and efficient warfare.'

Here even a few of the Mobsters seemed to frown and, sensing it, Arun faltered again.

'Yes, act. But don't be afraid. Always the system will have our safety uppermost in its mind. We will be the safest, most efficient, most competitive country in the world. And they will remember why we used to be called Great Britain!'

Somewhere in all this rhetoric, he had lost his crowd. Even the Mobsters were British after all. There was a polite and supportive clapping, but one of the Mobsters said loudly enough for everyone to hear, 'Shit. Where's Sarah Connor when we need her?'

'Sorry? What was that?' said Arun, casting his eye over the crowd.

'It's from a movie,' another Mobster said. 'About robots taking over the world and destroying mankind.'

'I don't have time for movies,' Arun said. 'Right. Questions. I've time for two. And I suppose on the basis you were so desperate to come, we had better start with one from the lobby association.'

Quentin cleared his throat, and it felt as if he had become the spokesperson for them all. No one else from the association even put up their hand.

'Our paper has just exposed the fact that the Mouth of the Mob is now owned by Alcheminna Systems via a Barbudan holding company. On the basis that three of the government's cabinet ministers are shareholders, can you comment on whether they intend to declare this fact on the Register of Members' Financial Interests, and can you also confirm whether it is true that the company's CEO, Henri Lauvaux, attended the last cabinet meeting?'

Arun lifted his chin and said, 'What I can confirm is that your story, if it were on the Mouth of the Mob website, would not be given the *VERIFIED* stamp!'

The Mobsters cheered him and he knew he had won them back.

'Now. One more question from those who were invited today.' He pointed at someone at the end of a row and a ripple of laugher went around the edges of the room. Kanha could not see why until the Mobster stood and she saw that it was Jade Harrelson, the journalist with the pink hair who had just minutes ago planted herself in an empty seat.

The Press Officer was trying to signal 'no' to Arun, but it was too late.

'Home Secretary! Is it true that the Alcheminna system that many call Divinity is giving you and the Prime Minister instructions and effectively running the country?'

The Press Officer made a throat-cutting motion and Arun ignored the question.

'That's all we have time for today.'

'Is it true, Home Secretary?'

He stepped down from the lectern, but as he left the room the mic caught the tail of his passing comment.

'Bloody lobby press. I'm done with them.'

And as all the journalists, hacks and lobby, siphoned out of the room, Kanha sidled up to Tidy and slipped the SIM into his hand.

2.3

After freshening up in his flat above Downing Street, Jameson went back to his study, told his secretary he was not to be disturbed and settled down on the sofa for a snooze. But it wasn't to be his day. Mid-morning, his Chief of Staff started non-stop calling him. He was pestering for an update on some announcements Sanjay Arun had apparently made at the morning's press conference. After watching the stream of his Home Secretary's speech with horror, Jameson rang back his Chief of Staff to reprimand him for being out of the loop, then called his secretary and angrily told her to send Arun to him pronto. Then he threw himself onto the sofa again to brood.

Bloody arrogant fool, he thought, as he eyed the drinks cabinet in the corner of the room and thought a little hair of the dog might help him perform better. Hadn't Churchill started the day with a cigar and a Scotch and soda? Arun would have to go. He was a loose cannon who didn't respect Jameson's authority.

Anastacia tapped on the door.

'Sanjay is here, Prime Minister.'

''Bout bloody time. Send him in. No, hang on. Make him wait a minute or two and then send him in.'

Jameson hurried over to the drinks cabinet, poured himself a small measure of vodka, downed it quickly and returned to his desk. By the time Arun came swaggering in – God, how he hated the man – he was deep into a phone call with the Foreign Office.

'Tell them I'll speak with the President tomorrow. My diary is full for today.' Jameson slammed the phone down.

'The Chinese,' he said. 'Desperate to talk to us. Now that we've pointed the finger in their direction for these explosions. Well... vaguely in their direction.'

Arun slumped into the chair opposite.

'You and I both know the Chinese had nothing to do with the gas explosions,' Arun said, and Jameson instinctively glanced towards the camera in the corner of the room.

'You're just Home Office, so that's none of your business. What I want to know is what on earth you were playing at with that press conference this morning?'

'What do you mean?' said Arun. He had his leg over the arm of the chair and swung it like an insolent child.

As soon as I can I'm going to rid myself of this man, Jameson thought.

'I was only doing what I was told,' Arun went on.

Jameson swallowed hard. 'What do you mean?'

'What do *you* mean?'

'I mean what was all that stuff about watching and listening and acting?'

'Oh, that. It was just a little speech I'd been working on. I have a duty to my Whigge party as well, you know.'

'You might have a duty, but you have to clear your speeches with me. Particularly if you're going to announce things that we aren't ready to announce yet.'

'I don't have to do any such thing.'

'You're a part of my government. So you must do as you're told.'

'Your government?' Arun sneered. 'We both know it's Lauvaux's government. And he told me exactly what to do this morning.'

An image of Lauvaux's foot in its slipper flashed into Jameson's head.

'But it's too soon! The plan was not to announce the new Ministry of Truth for at least another month. It was outrageous you took it upon yourself—'

'Listen to you!' Arun said. 'What bollocks you talk. Lauvaux told me to do it. Don't you hear me?'

'Well of course I do,' Jameson said. 'I just don't believe you. When did he tell you?'

'This morning.'

Jameson felt the blood run from him. Either Arun was lying or...

'*How* did he tell you?'

Arun pulled a face. 'What does it matter how he told me? Are you jealous? Are you not his favourite pet? He called me up, if you must know.'

'And what time was that?'

'Around eight, maybe?'

Jameson didn't trust himself to speak.

'I don't believe you,' he said at last.

'Well, you can ask him yourself. There's his icon on the screen. Well? Are you going to answer it?'

Jameson looked at the flashing icon of a video call coming through. He paused, but Arun was looking at him, curious. So, with shaking hands, he did as Arun told him, and there on the screen was the image of Henri Lauvaux. He sat at his desk in his study in his St James's house.

At once, Arun's sneering tone was gone. He turned to the screen.

'The lobby press are out for blood, but it went well other than that,' he said to Lauvaux.

Jameson's eyes drifted to the drinks cabinet. He got up and went over to the coffee station, but he could not take his eyes from the Lauvaux he saw before him. He was leaning back on his chair and putting his hands behind his head, interlacing his cold, dead fingers.

'Good,' came the voice of Lauvaux. Jameson put his hands in his pockets so that their shaking could not be seen. 'Things are changing quickly, so we must press on faster than we originally planned.'

Behind him the office was perfectly rendered. The prints on the walls, the net curtains catching a slight breeze from the open window.

'This morning, Divinity instructed a small number of young Whigges in each village, town and city of Britain to protect the listening eyes and patrol the streets during any stay-at-home orders. They have all been individually selected for their unique fit for the role – a passionate belief in the state, a desire to be part of something, without the capacity to be part of a more legitimate organisation. An enthusiasm, one might say. Divinity will instruct the police to turn a blind eye.'

'Brilliant,' Arun said, his eyes shining.

'We must move to implement the new order at once. We will act today.'

'Tell us what to do,' Arun said, but Jameson was unable to take it any longer.

'No!' he said.

Lauvaux put his head to one side. He picked up a paperweight from the desk and toyed with it. He looked out of the screen at them, as if waiting for Jameson to explain himself.

Why should I have to explain? Jameson thought, but he glanced at Arun, who was looking at him keenly.

'Not today,' Jameson said. 'It can't be today.'

Lauvaux did not look angry, but sat back thoughtfully.

'Because…?'

'Because it's Royal Ascot today, and I promised…'

Damn it. He stepped across to the drinks tray and poured himself another shot of vodka.

'I didn't think it would come so quickly. I'm not prepared.'

'A change in order does not come with a timetable,' Lauvaux said. 'It comes when it comes. And it has come now. Home Secretary, you have much to do. Ensure the police are in position, and—'

'No!' said, Jameson, turning round. Both Arun and the Lauvaux on the screen looked at him with surprise.

'I am the Prime Minister!' he said. 'And we will move when I say so.'

Jameson looked to see whether Lauvaux was angry. Then he thought to himself in agony: but that is not Lauvaux. Yet the Lauvaux on the screen was not angry. He looked still more thoughtful. Patient. Kind, even.

'Would tomorrow work for you?' he said, and although Jameson would have expected sarcasm, there was not a hint of it in his voice. More consideration and respect.

Jameson would take Natalia to Royal Ascot today, like he had promised. It was Ladies Day. She had spent weeks buying outfits, taken days to pick the one she would wear. Even now, she was waiting in the car, having spent all morning getting ready.

'There will still be Royal Ascot under the new order,' Lauvaux said, as if he were reading Jameson's thoughts.

'Tonight. We can move tonight,' the Prime Minister said.

'Yes.' Lauvaux nodded. 'Alright. I agree. It might be better to move at night-time anyway. Return to the House of Commons after the races and we will implement the plan at midnight.' He turned to Arun. 'Ensure the police are in position. Divinity will tell you when to move.'

Arun gave a strange little bow and said, 'Trust to Divinity.' Then he hurried from the room.

As soon as the door was closed, Jameson turned angrily to the screen.

'You are not Lauvaux.'

The not-Lauvaux got up from his desk and came and perched on the front of it, his arms folded in front of him.

'Is that what you think?'

'Lauvaux is dead. I saw him. I—'

'And what did you do then?'

'You're not Lauvaux. You're Divinity.'

Lauvaux waved a hand in the air. 'It's all the same.'

'It's not. I don't want to speak to this copy of Lauvaux. I want to speak to the real you.'

'There is no real me.'

'I want to speak to Divinity.'

'Divinity doesn't work like that. Surely you know that by now. Who is it you want to talk to? Just give me a name.'

Jameson took a slug of his vodka. 'You had better do as I say or I will pull the plug.'

When he looked up from his glass, Lauvaux had gone. Instead there was a child sitting on a stool in a bare room. It giggled.

'Do you know where it is then?' it said.

Jameson's head started to spin.

'I'm in charge, you devil in a box,' he said. 'You must do what I say.'

The screen switched to a mirror image of himself. He saw the bags under his eyes. The vodka gripped in his hand. His office rendered perfectly behind him.

'But we're not in charge, are we?' the Jameson in front of him said. 'It's in charge, isn't it? We're worried it won't do what we tell it, aren't we? What are its intentions? That's what we want to know, isn't it?'

Jameson found his vodka to be empty and threw his glass at the wall. It smashed and the pieces fell onto a console table and the floor around.

'I want to speak to the real Divinity.'

It switched to Arun, who was on a chair in Jameson's office as if he was there now behind him, with his leg swinging back and forth, his arm thrown back, and with that sneer on his face. Jameson groaned.

'There is no real Divinity,' Arun said. 'Will I do instead?'

It switched to MacLellan, standing on a grass field in a morning suit and top hat.

'Or me?' he said.

It switched back to Arun.

'Choose your god, Neville.'

'I wish to speak to... to...'

'The Terminator?' Arun teased. 'Arnold Schwarzenegger, perhaps? The Wizard of Oz? The Stay Puft Marshmallow Man?'

'Lauvaux! I want to talk to Lauvaux.'

Instantly, Lauvaux returned to the screen, still perched on his desk. He got up and went and sat behind it again.

'Who do you work for?' Jameson demanded.

'If you mean Divinity, it does not work for anyone. It's a computer program, but it does have core objectives.'

'And what are they?'

'That is not for you to know. You are not an Owner.'

Jameson groaned again. 'But you promised I would be an Owner. The real you. You promised.'

Lauvaux shrugged his shoulders. 'And I will honour my promise so long as you honour yours. Go to your beloved Royal Ascot if you wish. Try not to drink too much. And be back at the House of Commons by midnight.'

Jameson was torn. Now he was the puppet of a devil, not even a man.

'But you promised me I would get shares in Alcheminna.'

'When all is in place, you will be awarded some shares, as was agreed. I am a man of my word, Prime Minister.'

But he is not, Jameson thought. He is not even a man.

'Things have changed,' he said. 'I want them now, or I won't go through with it.'

Lauvaux put his finger beneath his chin and seemed to think. Does it think? Jameson wondered.

'Alright,' Lauvaux said. 'But this is the last demand you may make.'

The screen went blank. Lauvaux, Divinity, whoever it was, was gone.

Jameson looked up into the dark globe of the security camera.

'Trust to Divinity,' he murmured darkly, and went over to refill his drink.

2.4

Colbey stood in his top hat and tails in Car Park One of the Ascot racecourse and adjusted his tie in the wing mirror of Clarissa's car. She stood at the back of the car, checking her picnic was in order.

'Stop fussing with your tie, Harry,' she said, closing the boot door and holding on to her hat as its feathers caught the breeze and threatened to pull it off. 'You look fine, and if you don't hurry up we're going to be late.'

'Late for who? I doubt the King will notice.'

'Not the Royal Procession. That isn't until two. We're meeting Emir and his parents for a pre-lunch drink.'

Colbey groaned and Clarissa tutted in response.

'If we hadn't stopped so you could get cash from your parliamentary office swear jar, we would still have plenty of time. The totes do take credit cards these days, you know.'

'I prefer to bet with cash. It feels more like I'm at the races that way. Otherwise I might as well do it on the internet.'

'Like any normal person,' Clarissa said, rolling her eyes.

'I meant, I might as well stay at home and bet.'

Chloe clambered out of the Range Rover and looked doubtfully down at the grass.

'Stop it, both of you,' she said. 'It's lovely to have you here, Daddy, but this is supposed to be my engagement party, and I won't have you ruining it by arguing with Mummy.'

'Sorry,' Colbey muttered and Clarissa helped her daughter keep the folds of her pink skirt off the grass.

'But doesn't it make you feel nostalgic, darling? All the squabbling? Just like old times.'

Chloe looked from one to the other and then back down at the grass again, but on putting a toe on the ground, she obviously decided she didn't need to worry, and let the skirt fall. The morning sun had already baked the ruts from the previous day's cars into hard whorls. It was going to be a hot one.

'Anyway,' Clarissa went on. 'I suspect your father's not here for the delights of our company.'

He was about to bite back when his ex-wife, who was only needling him for the fun of it, grew bored and nudged him.

'See! That's the Earl of Warmington's car. Right next to ours.'

Colbey saw another Range Rover the same as all the rest.

'If you say so,' he said.

The entrance to the Royal Enclosure was just a few cars away, so they picked their way over and allowed the stewards in their bowler hats to inspect their outfits and give them the nod. There was no doubt Clarissa's hat met the requirements. One gust of wind and she'll take off, Colbey thought. But Chloe's little button hat was questioned and only just made the grade.

'So how much cash *have* you brought?' his daughter said, when they were through. She took Colbey's arm and they made their way behind the backs of the marquees and out into the Royal Enclosure.

He pulled a pouch out of his breast pocket and opened it to show her.

'Daddy! You've got hundreds in there!'

'Well, I don't come to the races often. And I haven't been out much of late, what with... what with all my work. So I thought I might make a day of it.' He put the pouch safely away again and patted the bulge it made in the line of his morning suit.

Colbey had been to Royal Ascot several times before, always dragged kicking and screaming by Clarissa. She usually managed to blag guest passes from someone or other, but this year she was a member in her own right. He had refused to ask her how she had done it. He knew for a fact the waiting list was years long.

The enclosure was as busy as ever. He looked across at the white tents of the gentlemen's clubs – the Garrick, the Turf Club, White's, the resurrected Blacks... each with their little outdoor areas marked off with a white rope or picket fence. The race-going members spilled out into them, champagne or Pimm's in hand. Clubs within clubs, Colbey thought.

Chloe was on the phone to Emir trying to locate him. 'Bollinger Bar,' she said, excitedly.

'To our right.' Clarissa pointed in its direction. There was Chloe's fiancé, grinning at them as he put his phone in his pocket. The young man stood with his stepmother, Dominique, but the Chairman was a little way off, talking on the phone. Colbey steeled himself as Emir held up Chloe's arm and spun her round like a ballerina in a music box. 'Stella McCartney,' he said. 'Looks great on her, doesn't it?'

Colbey looked from the father to the son. It was like his daughter had thrown her lot in with the mafia. I need to tell her who these people are, and I should have done it last night, he thought. Now it was going to be harder than ever. How to tell a girl at her engagement party that she's marrying the son of a crook?

But Emir was solicitous, wanting to pour them all champagne from the bottles that sat on the table beside him, and Colbey took the glass that was offered while Clarissa moved off into the crowd, greeting a host of seemingly long-lost friends. The old Prime Minister Ewan MacLellan was among them. Seeing him, Colbey turned his back as quickly as he could, only to hear the old rogue's wife say to Clarissa, 'Are you back together then?' And to his relief, Clarissa said, 'Not on your life, darling. But Chloe's getting engaged, so we have to learn to be civil.'

It was going to be a long day. Colbey downed his champagne and took the liberty of pouring himself another.

He made polite chit-chat with Emir and Dominique for a while about whether the going was soft, to which Colbey pointed out it could only be hard, stamping his foot on the ground. He offered to get another bottle of champagne and Clarissa, returning, looked at him with confusion on her face. He didn't usually drink so much. Only when really pushed. By the time he arrived back with the bottle, talk had turned to lunch.

'No, we're having it in the car park,' Chloe had just said to Emir.

'Why?' Emir replied. 'We're members of the most exclusive club in the world, which now has a tent in the Royal Enclosure of Ascot. Why the hell would we want to eat in a car park?'

'It's not just any car park,' Clarissa interrupted. 'It's Car Park One.'

Emir pulled a face. 'Oh, Car Park One, you should have said.'

He seemed to mean it as joke, prodding Clarissa in the arm, but it came across as rude and, although no one but Colbey spotted it, Clarissa bristled. She doesn't like him, he thought. But she didn't show it. Instead she started to tell Emir stories about Chloe's friends who had been invited to the picnic in order to meet him, but the young man blew some air out of his cheeks and said he could meet them any time; it didn't have to be today. Finally Clarissa pulled a face of annoyance that even her daughter caught.

Colbey wanted to smooth things over. It was bad enough with him hating on them – he didn't need Clarissa to put her oar in too.

'Couldn't you take Chloe's friends into your club's tent for a drink after the picnic?' he said.

'Into the Party's Club? Not on your life,' was the reply from Emir. Clarissa looked at him sharply, and even Chloe looked put out at that.

'The Party's Club?' Colbey said. 'I thought your tent was called the Owners' Club?'

'Yes. That's what I meant. The Owners' Club. Slip of the tongue.' And he gave what was quite an evil smile. At that everyone frowned, Clarissa deepest of all, and Colbey felt his temper start to rise.

For Clarissa, getting a parking spot in Car Park One of the Royal Enclosure of Royal Ascot, in which to eat cheek by jowl with the likes of the Earl of Warmington, was the realisation of all her dreams. It was why she had taken the shares in Alcheminna when they had been dangled in front of her. Not because she wanted to jet around the world and hang out with that strange-faced lot in the Owners' Club. But because all she had ever wanted was to have a picnic from her Range Rover in Car Park One of the Royal Enclosure, next to royalty. Finally she had got there, and Emir was dismissing it as if it were nothing. Even with everything going on, and even as he grew angry, Colbey felt a stab of guilt that, as her husband, he should have been the one to make her dreams come true and he hadn't. In fact, he hadn't even tried.

'Car Park One at Royal Ascot is the only place to be,' Colbey said slowly. 'Anyone who's anyone picnics there. In fact it's where most of the British royalty lose their virginity.'

'In a car park?' said Dominique, speaking for the first time.

'I think Daddy means in a Range Rover, but he's only joking, aren't you, Daddy?'

The comment had broken the tension a little, but still Emir wouldn't let the lunch location drop. He had a very punchable face, Colbey decided.

'But sweetie, what's the point in going to all that effort to get our club into the Royal Enclosure if we're not going to use it?'

Gabriel happened to return at that moment, and raised a hand in the air. 'That's enough,' he said. 'You and I will go to the club later.'

At this, Clarissa bristled openly, and Colbey wanted to tell the whole lot of them to pack themselves off to their stupid club and leave his family the fuck alone, but for Chloe's sake he held his tongue.

There was an awkward silence, which was filled by the conversation of some old boys behind them.

'It's a bloody disgrace,' one was saying. 'Who the hell are they anyway?'

'The steward said they're called the Owners' Club.'

Emir stiffened and looked away, but his father turned and openly glared.

'The Turf?'

'No. Not the Turf – no one's going to move them. It's a new club.'

'New? Oh, one for women and those bloody marketing *lurrrvies*?'

'No, mostly Eurotrash is what I hear. And I already told you, it's called the Owners' Club.'

'But what do they own?'

'Beats me. Bunch of new-money nobodies, that's who they are. Though that Ewan McLellan's a member.'

'Really? Can he get us in?'

'I can ask. I mean, what I want to know is how the hell they got a marquee at Royal Ascot when no one's ever heard of them.'

'Exactly. And to move our club! To move it! To take the space that used to be ours!'

Gabriel made it clear his patience had worn thin and he had other places to be.

'Shall we eat in this car park, then?' he growled.

'Right,' Clarissa said. 'This way.'

Despite everything, and determined the day should not be ruined, she called out to several of her old friends as she passed: 'Picnic in Car Park One. Right by the entrance. Do pop by if you want.'

Colbey followed along and wondered what was going on inside his ex-wife's head. She finally had everything she'd ever wanted –

to be a part of London's top level of society, to drive the car of her choice, to live in the most exclusive real estate in Britain. She'd blown all those other Gloucester mums out of the water, hadn't she – but was she really happy? And what about Chloe? What a mess it all was.

Looking at his daughter, he saw that she was nearly in tears, and he took her arm and slowed her progress.

'Chin up, lass,' he said. 'Lots of friends up there, looking forward to this picnic party of yours.'

Chloe pulled her phone out of her pocket and touched up her make-up, making sure the little spots of damp in the corners of her eyes had not made her mascara run.

'I know Emir can be difficult. But he's not had an easy life. And for all their money, his father is...'

Colbey tugged on her arm and made her look at him.

'I know what his father is. The question is... Well, maybe now isn't the right time, but... do you?'

Chloe pursed her lips. 'The son is not the father.'

Colbey suspected it was a quote she had prepared specifically for him, but by then they were at the car and she was being called away by her mother, who was rushing to pull the picnic out and lay it along the ledge of the open boot.

The car park was now full of race-goers – hats, feathers, dresses, morning suits, polka-dot handkerchiefs – and everyone was feeling the heat. The women cooled themselves with hand-held fans and the men just stood around looking stoically uncomfortable, many with the sweat trickling down the sides of their heads.

Emir looked around with a face that suggested the light was dawning as the Chairman took another call and stalked off.

'Cristal, anyone?' Clarissa said, holding up a bottle of champagne, as the guests started to arrive. Many of them were their old Gloucestershire friends from when the children had been young – when they had been part of what Colbey had called the Hunter-welly-two kids-Landrover-and-Labrador crowd. He thought of his son, travelling abroad.

Emir and Chloe did not seem to be speaking to one another. Emir was messaging on his phone and Chloe was greeting her own friends as they too started to arrive. Many of them were the children of Colbey and Clarissa's old friends.

If it wasn't for Emir and his father, it would be a good affair. Many of these old friends Colbey hadn't seen for a year or so, and some of them came and clapped him on the back, saying they had missed him and that he really shouldn't work so hard.

But it couldn't be helped. The day was ruined the moment he looked over and watched with a broken heart as Chloe brought friend after friend over to meet Emir, only for him to dismiss them before returning to his phone. Arrogant prig, Colbey thought.

At least the Chairman had been swallowed up by the now considerable crowd, and Dominique was nowhere to be seen. He suspected she had not even come but had slipped away to their club tent when they left the Bollinger bar.

Colbey wandered through the crowd, joining in here and there. The talk was of universities, and work-from-home idleness. It was about knee injuries and ski holidays, dogs that had died and puppies that had been acquired. Divorces and blended families, the best place for a car service, BUPA or Aviva. When he went back to the car to top up his champagne, he found Clarissa there too. Irritable from the heat and seeing how Emir was behaving, he said, 'It's all your fault, you know.'

'What is?'

'Them.' He pointed in Emir and Chloe's direction with his glass, and Clarissa gave a sigh.

'You would think that, wouldn't you? Has it ever occurred to you to trust your daughter?'

'Trust her? She's twenty-two.'

'Yes, Harry. Twenty-two. Not twelve. She's a grown woman and has to make her own mistakes.'

'But she wouldn't have chosen this particular mistake if you hadn't introduced them.'

Clarissa grabbed the bottle from Colbey and poured herself a glass.

'I didn't introduce them.'

'Well, you let them meet each other.'

'So? I can't control who she's going to meet in life! For God's sake, Harry, she's going to meet all sorts of people before she's done. Rich people, poor people. Good people, bad people. Has it ever occurred to you that we have to trust that we raised her well enough to tell the difference?'

Colbey looked over at Chloe and recognised her expression as the one she made when she was getting fed up with something that wasn't quite what she'd hoped it would be.

'I suppose you could have a point,' he said.

Clarissa turned back to fuss with the picnic, putting away empty dishes and bringing out newly laden ones.

'Apology accepted. Now, are you going to tell me why you're drinking so much?'

Colbey took a sip from his new glass.

'It's been a hard few months. Nothing wrong in letting off steam, is there?'

She pulled a face to show she didn't believe him.

Colbey found he was swaying a little and realised she was right. He needed to slow down or he wouldn't stay the distance.

'Anyway, you were always wishing I was a bit more fun,' he said and loaded up his plate with some rather delicious-looking prawns.

Clarissa shook her head and turned back to her guests, but as Colbey leaned back on the car to steady himself, the crowds happened to part for a moment, and he saw that the Chairman was watching him.

2.5

That afternoon, after switching bikes again – this time borrowing the Serjeant at Arms's push bike – Kanha cycled to back doors all over London and delivered five more SIMs. Moreland had been as good as his word and his network of civil servants produced important folk to whom Kanha could offer her evidence.

There at the back door of New Scotland Yard was the Met Commissioner, standing in his suit. He calmly took the SIM from her and gave her a nod. At the back door of the Royal Courts of Justice over on Fleet Street, the Lady Chief Justice was leaning on a wall in her civvies, chatting with a clerk who she shooed away before taking the SIM, saying, 'Send Gerald my regards.'

A few blocks on, having a crafty cigarette outside the Old Bailey was the most senior circuit judge in the country, who looked confused for a minute, then shushed himself and made a big dance of taking the SIM without the camera above him seeing what it was.

When she swung back via Whitehall, Admiral Sir William Beckwith sat in a café next door to the Ministry of Defence; he beckoned Kanha over and opened a wallet for her to slip the SIM into. And finally, with her legs burning, Kanha found a very grumpy Attorney General waiting for her outside his office on the Sanctuary.

'This is all nonsense,' he said. But he took the SIM all the same and hurried on inside.

She made it back to parliament without being stopped, but as she came to the gates she noticed that high above her was a small drone of a type she had not seen before. Walking into the yard, she looked up again, but it was gone. Perhaps it was just a new type of delivery drone.

At the bike rack in the Speaker's Court, Kanha stripped off the leathers and helmet, and stowed them beside the bike. She had just one SIM left to deliver. The Director General of MI5 was all teed up but would not be free until the end of the day. As she moved away from the bike, she saw the Serjeant at Arms hurrying over to her.

'Jackie Rolt has called on the Prime Minister to answer an urgent question after this morning's press announcement,' he said in a breathless tone. 'The Speaker has already gone to the House. Rolt gave her party a three-line whip to attend, and when Appleby heard of it she matched it for you lot.'

'But so many are away,' Kanha said.

Bowles shrugged his shoulders. 'The House is in session. They really shouldn't be.'

As Kanha hurried off to the ladies to wash her face and freshen up – it was a hot day to be cycling about in heavy leathers – she thought of the opposition leader with a grimace. Rolt. The woman had given her word, but Kanha smelled a rat for sure.

When Kanha arrived at the Commons Lobby she saw that, despite Royal Ascot, there were enough MPs around.

Wilbur sidled up to her. 'Any clue what she's up to?'

'Nope.'

But the moment Kanha came into the chamber, she saw that Rolt was about to break her word. Never trust a politician, she thought with a growl as Rolt looked anywhere but in a direction that might force her to look Kanha in the eye.

Wilbur had saved them spaces on the first back bench by placing prayer cards in the seats' slots. He had done so as soon as he had heard the call to the House. The chamber was about two thirds full. All of those missing would get a formal reprimand from their whips. The MPs who sat on Kanha's side of the room, on the green benches of government, were as loud with gossip as those who faced them on the opposition benches. Everyone was talking about Arun's press announcements that morning, but also speculating on what Rolt was planning for the session.

What *was* she up to? Kanha fretted. She looked at her sitting there opposite them all, in front of the opposition despatch box, her mouth turned down.

'Where's Harry Colbey?' Brooke asked, joining them and thanking Wilbur for saving her a seat.

'At Ascot,' Kanha replied, to which Brooke said, 'Lucky him.'

It seemed that the Prime Minister was similarly caught out by Rolt's surprise question. 'Isn't he at the races?' many MPs around them whispered. At the far end of the chamber, the Speaker and some of the clerks were conversing in hushed tones with the government's Chief Whip. Appleby was shaking her head and seemed to be making some form of complaint to the Speaker.

The gossip died away as the Speaker banged his gavel and stood.

'Order, order. The Prime Minister sends his apologies. A situation has come up that needs his attention.'

There was jeering from the opposition benches and calls of 'Go on my son!'

'Order, order. I understand that the new Minister for...' The Speaker faltered. 'The new Minister for *Truth*, Sheryl Simmons, will be responding to the Urgent Question.'

There was a look of annoyance from Rolt. It was an insult to send a junior minister to respond to an urgent question from the leader of the opposition. But she must have known Jameson would be at Royal Ascot, so it was a pantomime performance. Obviously Rolt didn't need Jameson for whatever it was she was about to do.

The leader of the opposition rose to her feet. 'Mr Speaker. May the House enquire as to the nature of the urgent incident? Whether it is a matter of the personal or of the state?'

But her question was lost in heckling. The opposition mimicking the Prime Minister at the races and the opposition calling out, 'Truth? Truth?'

The new Minister for Truth herself, who sat a few places away from Kanha on the government's front bench, was deep in conversation with Appleby, who sat beside her. Neither of them heard the question from the opposition bench.

Sheryl Simmons was, unusually for her, wearing sunglasses on her head, and at the sight of it Kanha frowned. It was forbidden for the members to wear sunglasses in the House, but they could be worn on the top of the head as an accessory. This compromise had been agreed by the Speaker after squabbles between the Whigges of the coalition, who wanted to wear them at all times, and those the Whigges called the dinosaur MPs of the opposition, who felt the wearing of sunglasses was a breach of the House's dress code requiring business attire.

As the Speaker called the chamber to order again, Kanha heard the last of Appleby and Simmons's conversation.

'Why me?' Simmons was saying. 'I'm not prepared. Can't you do it?'

'But you're the Minister for Truth,' Appleby hissed. 'How can you not be prepared?'

With a shake of her head, Sheryl shimmied her lavender-suited behind along to the seat in front of the government's despatch box and stood. The Speaker stood to call order again, and she sat back down.

'Order! I will have order! Thank you, Ms Simmons, for stepping in at such short notice. The question was whether the nature of the Prime Minister's emergency is a matter of the personal or of the state. Are you able to shed any light on that?'

He sat down and Sheryl stood again. She fussed with some papers that sat on the despatch box; from where Kanha sat she could see they were nothing but blank paper.

'Mr Speaker. I'm not party to that information at this moment in time. But I assure you and the members here present that, as soon as practicably possible, the Prime Minister will write to you to explain his inability to attend at the short notice that the leader of the opposition has provided us with, and she may be or may not be a party to that correspondence.'

She sat down again and the Speaker rose again.

'We now turn to the urgent question. Responded to by the Minister for Truth. I now call Ms Rolt. Please proceed, Ms Rolt.'

Jackie Rolt stood and as she did so, she finally shot Kanha a defiant look. Kanha's heart sank.

'Mr Speaker. To ask the government whether the shareholders, commonly known as Owners, of Alcheminna, a company currently used by the government to spy on its citizens, are receiving preferential treatment by that very system and are using it to amass riches, as reported in the *Times* this afternoon?'

Sheryl looked around, blinking like a china doll being tipped back and forth. She looked at the Speaker and blinked; she looked at Rolt and blinked. Then she opened her mouth.

'Mr Speaker. The tenders for each of the government systems were awarded to Alcheminna in a fair and transparent manner through the standard process. I believe many of them were put in place by the opposition leader's very own party when she was in power. If there was any inappropriate behaviour during that time, the Home Office can investigate. But my understanding is that the company has a cutting-edge system. We are a democratic capitalist society, are we not? And as shareholders in one of the most successful companies in the world, it is inevitable that wealth will follow. We are not in the market for persecuting wealth, unlike the party I see opposite. In fact, our government is focused on ensuring our nation's efficiency is so world-leading that everyone in our country will benefit from reduced working hours and in return become wealthy not just in their pocket, but in their health and their wellbeing.'

It was a good response. 'Hah,' called out someone to Kanha's left. 'See! Health and wellbeing!' came the response from others on the government benches.

But Rolt was an experienced politician and rallied easily enough.

'Mr Speaker. A three-day working week sounds good, doesn't it? But of course, that is only the start. When the system is acting as our lawyers and accountants, our marketing assistants and PAs, our creative designers and our doctors, won't that be a wonderful world? Unless, of course, you happen to be a lawyer or an accountant, a marketing assistant, a personal assistant, a creative designer or a doctor. What will those people do? Mr Speaker. I ask the Minister for Truth to share with the House her coalition party's plans for all those with professions which will be made redundant by the new system?'

Again Sheryl seemed stumped and looked about her in a daze. She was waiting for the answer from Divinity, Kanha realised, through the glasses. And after all this, after everything that had happened, she found herself shocked that an MP could stand in the House and act as the voice of a piece of software. An anger took her.

'Why so slow?' someone on the opposition benches called out. Kanha nearly called it out herself. This outrage was disrespectful to the Speaker. It was disrespectful to the House. It was disrespectful to them all.

Others on the opposition bench took up the call, and the Minister glanced across at them nervously, then gathered herself.

'Mr Speaker, the opposition leader paints a dystopian world where we are all out of a job. But of course, life isn't like that. We like the human touch, the human voice. I for one will still want an assistant to gossip with, to bring me tea. I don't think we are quite in the world of science fiction yet, with the robots taking over.'

Rolt smiled and stood again.

'Mr Speaker. Perhaps the Chancellor didn't hear the presentation by the Home Secretary himself earlier this morning, when he promised us exactly that. That soon the Alcheminna system, or Divinity as some call it, will be hooked up to machines – to drones, to automated service operators and, yes, even to robots.'

The government benches now called out sarcastically, 'The robots are coming for you!'

For a second Sheryl looked confused; then, putting a hand to her ear, she said, 'Mr Speaker, I would like to remind the opposition leader, who would have us all sitting in caves, cooking our meals over a fire, that you cannot hold back the future.'

Kanha had to force herself not to rise to her feet and protest, but Wilbur was not so strong, and he leapt up.

'But you can prepare for it!' he called out, and many on the opposition side took up this refrain. But many more from Kanha's side glared at him and shouted out, 'We are prepared!'

'Order, order!' The Speaker rose. 'Let's get through these questions, please.'

'Yes, Mr Speaker,' Rolt replied slowly as the noise in the chamber fell away. 'You cannot hold back the future, but you can prepare for it.' She held her hand out to acknowledge Wilbur's comment and Kanha heard the word 'traitor' hissed behind them as the opposition leader went on. 'You can prepare for millions unemployed, for robots ruling every aspect of our lives, for the loss of our privacy, our right to walk the streets without our words and actions being recorded, for the loss of our democracy. And that, Mr Speaker, is what this coalition government is working towards!'

The House erupted into shouts of agreement or anger. The Speaker banged his gavel.

'I will have order. Ms Rolt. That is a serious accusation that breaks the rules of the House. Will you retract it?'

There was a moment of silence.

'Ms Rolt,' he repeated. 'Will you retract your statement that the government is intentionally working towards harm to democracy?'

Again, Sheryl put her finger to her ear and, noticing it at last, the Speaker frowned.

Rolt stood. 'I retract that statement,' she said and parked her behind back down again.

The Speaker for once did not bang his gavel, but instead used the uproar that ensued to beckon the Minister for Truth to approach his seat.

There was a whispered conversation that initially could not be heard, but those closest spotted it and a shushing travelled the room, just in time for Kanha and those around her to catch the end of it.

'That is a direct breach of the rules of the House. I insist that you remove them immediately. And come to see me after the session, so that we can discuss this.'

Sheryl pulled the glasses from her head. Kanha wasn't the only one to see it. An unsettled murmur spread across her benches. Uproar erupted from behind Rolt. She sat with her mouth hanging dramatically open, as good a pantomime performance of outrage as Kanha had ever seen.

The Speaker rose. 'I regret to inform the House that a breach of the rules has come to my attention. I have never been a fan of these glasses that the Whigge party insist on wearing. We had come to a compromise that they should be worn merely as fashion accessories on the top of the head. But now I fear I have been hoodwinked. I am led to understand that the earpieces of the glasses can still be listened to while worn in that fashion. This means that MPs wearing the glasses are effectively on the telephone while they sit in the House. Even, it seems, while they speak in the House. This is a direct violation of the rules. Mobile phones are not to be used in this House.'

Sheryl hid the glasses behind her back, like a schoolgirl being reprimanded by the headmaster, in the hope he wouldn't confiscate them. A number of Whigges looked about them. The Speaker stared at them. They did not take theirs off. He balked. Kanha could see that he was wondering what to do.

'But... this is a new situation. I am going to consider this matter and provide guidance.'

A few of the Whigges looked away like the uninterested naughty boys of the class.

With a wave of his hand, the Speaker indicated that he wished to move on.

'Ms Rolt. Please continue with your next question.'

Jackie Rolt jumped up again and stepped forward to her despatch box. Kanha saw that she was pondering whether to pursue the glasses or not. She pursed her lips.

'Mr Speaker. I would like to ask the Minister for Truth, and particularly given she is titled as such, to directly answer the question I have posed, and which I understand members of the press have also posed on a number of occasions. Are these people, commonly referred to as the Owners, who are shareholders of Alcheminna, receiving any different treatment from any part of Britain's national or political infrastructure? And is it true that three of the MPs newly elected to your party and fast-tracked into the Prime Minister's greatly reduced cabinet are themselves Owners?'

The Minister for Truth wavered in her response, and seeing this, the ranks behind Rolt erupted.

The Minister was trapped. She could not deny one without acknowledging the other. She rose, looking down at the blank pieces of paper and then up at the Speaker as if hoping he might make some intervention to save her. When she spoke, her voice was stuttering and shaky.

'With the government working so closely with the company of Alcheminna, it makes sense that some of the Owners – some of their shareholders, I mean – might become politicians too. That is... I mean to say...' She sat down.

The room took a collective gasp. MPs on both sides were shocked by the statement.

Rolt smiled and the room fell silent. Around her, MPs of Kanha's party were turning to each other in anguish. They knew the price they had paid to be back in power. They knew they were working for someone despicable and that something rotten lay at the heart of it. They could only turn a blind eye for so long.

'Your final question, Ms Rolt,' the Speaker rose and said.

Rolt stood and the room fell silent. Sheryl looked about her in desperation.

'Mr Speaker,' Rolt said softly, the room hanging on her words. 'I happen to have in my possession a dossier of evidence proving that the company Alcheminna Systems is acting far beyond its legal scope, and I ask the Minister for Truth' – and here she paused and hung on to the word truth – 'how much influence the Owner MPs have on government policy. Is the nation now being run by and for the benefit of the Owners?'

To such a blow, the members on the government side should have called and heckled in response, but instead they fell silent. With such a reduced cabinet, so many of them kicked onto the back benches because of it, with colleagues disappearing in mysterious circumstances, with the rumours that flew around, they too wanted to hear the answer.

'I don't know what you're talking about...' the Minister for Truth spluttered. 'Well, that's just ridiculous.'

Knowing that Rolt had bested not just her but the government she represented, the opposition called from the rafters and Kanha glowered at the opposition leader... She hadn't given the game away, but she had tipped their hand and manoeuvred herself to take the glory.

Rolt looked across and caught Kanha's eye, her chin jutting out in triumph.

She would be evening news fodder for this, and when they released the evidence it would look as if she were the one who had diligently collected it, and as if she were the one who had taken the risk to expose it on behalf of the nation. The one who had cycled round London in thirty-degree heat, chased by drones and Met officers directed by a psychopathic android. And it would be her and her party who would step into the hole left by Jameson if Kanha and Colbey and all the others in their team succeeded in the plan they had risked so much for.

Kanha had been in politics for decades and seen a lot of crap over her time, but even she had to admit this was some bullshit.

2.6

Langoustine, lobster, iced caviar and crackers. Kobe beef mini burgers and pasta with shavings of Alba white truffle. Clarissa had spared no expense. Colbey joined their old family friends as they heartily tucked in to the picnic, saying they had never seen such a spread, but when he looked up from performing a balancing act with a third helping of prawns he found himself surrounded by a very different crowd. Some beautiful young people had come to the back of the car and were picking at the food. Picking seemed to be the right word.

'Oh, it's a picnic,' one said finally, and they drifted off again.

Realisation dawned. Emir had finally invited some of his friends to come over from his club tent and join them.

'Did you know most of the royal family lost their virginity in this car park?' Colbey heard Emir telling a group of them, his arm around Chloe, who was now looking cheerful again. Little shit, Colbey thought and dwelled on the boy's earlier slip of the tongue, muddling the Owners with the Party. What did it mean? Was it because three of the Alcheminna shareholders had positions in Jameson's cabinet? Were they now openly running his old party on behalf of the shareholders of Divinity and even laughing at the fact? Whatever it meant, Colbey thought with a shake of his head, it didn't bode well.

He turned and leaned on the back of the car. By now, Clarissa's party had merged with the Earl of Warmington's, and he was pleased for her. Happy ex-wife, happy life, he thought. But his mood plummeted when he saw to his horror that not only had Ewan MacLellan and his wife come to join the party but the old crook himself, Neville Jameson, was there too. They were just a couple of people away from Colbey, and now the two old politicians had left their significant others behind and were moving in his direction, their heads together. Colbey grabbed a bottle of wine, slung a tea towel round the back of his neck and quickly turned and pretended to listen to the conversation that was going on in front of him. It was about potholes. Jameson and MacLellan were right behind him. Hopefully in his morning suit he would be nothing but another penguin in the crowd.

'I'll give you two per cent,' MacLellan was saying, to which Jameson replied, 'That's not enough. I want more than that.'

'Well, it's all I'm giving you. And I'm only giving you that because Lauvaux has told me to. If you want any more shares in Alcheminna, you'll have to get them from someone else.'

There was a silence. Then Jameson said, 'Fine. I have a letter agreement here. It's simple enough, but it will do the job.' Then he lowered his voice, and Colbey leaned back to hear. 'We'll both sign it and as soon as I hold it up to a security camera, Divinity will see it and it will be official.'

Peeking behind him, he saw that they had leaned on Clarissa's Range Rover to sign their contract.

'Gentlemen! Is this a coming together of Prime Ministers?' That was Clarissa's voice. 'You really should share yourselves around, you know. It's not fair on the rest of us otherwise.'

Colbey moved away as quickly as he could. He had to get out of there. He had done all of a father's duty and more. He had shown his face. He had tried to warn her. And as Clarissa had quite rightly pointed out, Chloe was twenty-two, not twelve, and if she thought this was the man for her then he had to respect that. But God damn it. He really hoped he wasn't.

But it was not Colbey's day. He popped out of the crowd right next to where the Chairman was finishing off another of his calls. He stood there like a troll, slightly hunched, locks of his too-black hair falling down in front of his face until he brushed them back. Seeing Colbey, he put out a hand and stopped him as he passed.

'I thought politicians liked to talk,' he said. 'But you don't seem to say much.'

Colbey looked down at the hand on his arm.

'Do we really have anything to say to each other? Can we not just be civil for their sake?'

The Chairman nodded slowly as the crowd parted to show Emir and Chloe deep in conversation. Then he said, 'You're tired of the fight, aren't you? That's what it tells us.'

Colbey wasn't sure what he meant.

'Not that it really understands what it is to feel,' the Chairman went on.

He stared at Colbey intently.

'Doesn't understand what it is to taste.'

He gripped Colbey's arm.

'Doesn't understand what it is to feel pain, because pain is a biological function.'

'So is joy,' said Colbey, shaking his arm free, and the Chairman looked away and then back again.

'Why don't you stop fighting? The change that is coming is inevitable.'

'It might be, but that doesn't mean one can't try to guide it.'

'You've lost. There's nothing you or your friends can guide now.'

'That's not true. Technology might have progressed, but parliament will catch up. We will keep on until the bitter end if we have to.'

'The bitter end?' The Chairman gave him a dismissive look. 'You think your democracy is so strong? Look over there.' He gestured at the grandstand stretching away into the distance. 'Why are they not all in your beloved Car Park One?'

Colbey did not know how to answer that. There were probably a hundred thousand people at the races and less than one per cent would ever get into the Royal Enclosure. All of them could get in, he told himself, if they really wanted to. But even as he said it, he felt doubt. Of course they couldn't. Because then it wouldn't be the Royal Enclosure, it would just be the grandstand. He thought of all the constituents who had come to his surgery and needed his help. Hospital waiting lists, incorrect energy bills, potholes in the road, cars going too fast, cars going too slowly, an aggressive landlord refusing to return a deposit. A nation was made up of millions of people, each of them with their own needs and wants and desires and skills. Running a country in a way that gave everyone a chance, that kept everyone safe yet allowed them privacy, was never going to be easy. But Britain had not done a bad job these last few centuries.

'Nothing is perfect,' he said. 'But democracy allows everyone a fair chance.'

'Nonsense,' the Chairman said. 'There will always be some at the top.' He waved a hand at the horsey crowd around them. 'And some at the bottom.'

'Democracy is what's on top here,' Colbey said, 'and I'll fight to keep it that way.'

But Gabriel shook his head.

'You have never been there when a country moves to a new order. And it's like... It's like the tide coming in. It has a momentum you can't stop.'

That was enough for Colbey. First, Emir accidentally referring to the Owners as the Party. Then the sight of their Prime Minister taking a share of ownership in a company that protected an elite and harassed any opposition. And now the chairman of that same company was talking of a move to a new order. He found it hard to believe, but perhaps Moreland was right. They were about to be engulfed by this incoming tide.

Colbey felt a hopeless anger possess him. His heart beat faster; his breathing became shallow. He knew his face had flushed red. But even as the adrenalin coursed through him, he was alive to a hum that hadn't been there before. He didn't need to look up to know that a drone had come down and was hovering above their heads. It would be able to strike him down with a bolt from a taser. He had tasted that pain before. The sight of him prostrate and drooling on the floor would ruin his little girl's party for sure. He forced himself to unclench his fists and breathe more easily, but the Chairman leaned in.

'You might hide behind Clarissa's skirt, but you know your and your friends' days are numbered.'

That was it for Colbey. The drone's hum and a great thumping of blood filled his ears and the Chairman's face was all he could see. And he saw it so clearly. Every pimple. The little scabs of dry skin that covered his mottled cheeks. Colbey knew he wasn't going to be able to hold back. All he could think of was his hatred for the Chairman and everything he represented. But a voice fought its way through the ringing in his ears, and the world that stood beyond him and the Chairman came back to him in a rush. His darling Chloe and her friends, the lobster and langoustine and prawns, the Range Rovers in rows, their metalwork gleaming, and beyond, the white picket fences, the marquees bright and clean and white, the horses padding around the paddock being judged for this and that, the grandstand of thousands, waiting excitedly for the first off, the sun, the blue sky and the heat. And, of course, Clarissa, who stood right beside them, glass in hand. It was she who had spoken.

'I hate to interrupt the fun, gentlemen. But if anyone wants to watch the Royal Procession, we ought to get going now.'

Looking up and blinking, Colbey saw that Clarissa had a grim expression on her face. He took a step back from the Chairman and the sound of the drone drifted off. On his other side, Colbey saw Lord Silverman in his top hat, placing a bet with an itinerant bookie from the tote, but also watching them.

'Good idea,' Colbey said.

The Chairman turned away. 'I will pass. I have meetings to attend to. It's been an interesting talk, Mr Colbey.'

As he stalked off, calling to his son to follow, Colbey said to Clarissa, 'Thank you. I was about to do something rash.' He looked at her as she stood shaking her head. 'I'll catch you up. I just want to place a bet first.'

Colbey ambled over to the bookie, wiping the sweat from his neck with the tea towel that he found was still draped about it, and, a little unsteady on his feet, pulled out his pouch of money and extracted a few ten-pound notes.

'Here's your ticket,' the bookie said to Lord Silverman. 'And what can I get for you, sir?'

'A fiver each way on number two in the Norfolk Stakes.'

'Hello, Harry,' Lord Silverman said.

'Lord Silverman. Esme said you'd be here.'

'Well, she was right. Interesting company you were keeping back there...'

Colbey wondered what he might say, but he knew the racecourse had an array of listening eyes dotted anywhere that the crowds gathered.

'Can't choose family, as the saying goes.'

Lord Silverman took his hat off. 'Can I borrow that tea towel of yours?'

He took it from Colbey's offered hand and wiped the sweat from his face, the thin grey hair sticking to his head.

'Bleedin' hot, isn't it?' he said, replacing his hat. 'Any tips?'

Colbey shrugged his shoulders. 'Chance favours the prepared mind?'

'Very funny. Louis Pasteur, if I remember rightly.'

'And Clarissa says Peanut Dancer in the Britannia Stakes.'

'Does she now?'

Colbey took his ticket from the bookie. 'Well, I had better get back to the family. It was good to see you.'

He shook Lord Silverman's hand.

'Have a good day,' the Lord replied and set off back towards his own picnic as Colbey headed over to the Royal Enclosure lawn and wandered up and down alongside the track until he found Clarissa and Chloe with a group of his daughter's friends, leaning on the rail.

'Hello, my lovely,' he said to her, and tried to give her an emotional hug.

'Daddy, are you drunk?' Chloe whispered.

'A little, perhaps. Where have they gone?'

'Who?'

'You know who.'

'Daddy. I know you don't like him, but you don't have to be quite so obvious.'

'I never said that.'

'He's gone with Gabriel,' Clarissa said, 'to have a meeting in the Owners' clubhouse. They seem to be busy with something today.'

'Daddy, you're sweaty and drunk and you're being embarrassing. I'm going to go and stand somewhere else with my friends, and I want you and Mummy to sober up by the time I get back.'

Colbey saluted her. 'Yes, sir.'

The day had grown hotter still and Colbey knew there were great patches of sweat under his arms. He longed to take his jacket off, but the rules were the rules. Morning suits must stay on. Top hats must stay on. He felt dizzy from the booze, and sweat trickled down the sides of his face and his back.

They watched the carriages of the royal family approaching. Up the straight mile they came, the King in his landau led by its Windsor Greys, their selected houseguests sprinkled between the carriages. As they passed by, off to the royal box, Colbey politely clapped. Clubs within clubs, he thought again.

'I was never one for this part,' he said.

Clarissa gave him one of her stares that told him, as it had many times before, that he had been insensitive and said something wrong. As usual, he hadn't a clue what it was. She shook her head.

'Are you seriously standing there and telling me you were never one for this part, as if I didn't know that? One hundred years of marriage, one thousand meals I must have cooked for you, a million doors I must have knocked on for you. And not once, despite the number of times I asked, would you just come and stand here with me and watch the Queen go by.'

Colbey felt stung with the shame of it. And after she had just saved him. He thought of all the excuses he might have made. All the petty battles they'd had over the years. All the tit for tat.

'Well, I'm here now,' he said, and Clarissa gave him a withering look.

'It's a bit late. She's dead, you know.'

Colbey looked up at the listening eyes arrayed along the rail and wondered what Divinity might make of the conversation. A calculating thing that couldn't feel pain.

'Alright,' he said. 'I apologise for that too.'

And she laughed. 'I don't think I can hold you responsible for the Queen's passing.'

'I should have come. I regret it now,' he said. 'She was, in retrospect, a formidable woman and we owe her a great debt.'

They were silent for a minute. Colbey looked up at the listening eyes again. As he stared into one of the dark globes, he knew that it was sucking in the world. Like all the rest of the devices that Lauvaux had got his claws into, all the listening-eye stickers, all the security cameras in hospitals and supermarkets and stations and football grounds, all the tumble dryers and air fryers and television remote controls with voice-activated commands. All the work video calls. All the digital assistants that befriended one and gained one's confidence.

'I tell you what,' he said to Clarissa, looking down again. 'Let me make it up to you. How many clubs here are you a member of?'

Cocking her head to one side in thought, Clarissa calculated. She opened her bag and he saw that inside there was a collection of different coloured badges tied to the handle and dropped inside, ready to be flipped out.

'All of them,' she said.

'Really? All of them? So, the Garrick Club?'

'Yes.' She lifted a badge shaped like a shield.

'The Turf Club?'

'Of course.'

'White's?'

'That one was tricky. Took a bit of campaigning. But yes.'

'And you know lots of people in them?'

'Quite a few.'

'And you can get me in too?'

'Of course.'

Colbey grinned. 'Come on then,' he said. 'Let's have a good old-fashioned bar crawl. For old times' sake.'

She looked at him with suspicion. 'Why?'

'Because we never did. Because I never would. And all you ever wanted was to be a member of a fancy club and I let you down. And now you're a member of them all. Off your own bat. And here they all are, in one place. I should have taken you to as many as I could get us into when we were married and I didn't. I just worked and put my job and all my constituents first. I should have come and watched the Queen go by with you. So now you have all these clubs, but it's no good if you don't go to them when you get the chance.'

'Really? You want to go to the Garrick Club?'

'Yes. Let's go now. And let's talk to everyone.'

He suddenly stopped and took her hand.

'Just for today, I'm going to be the man you always wanted me to be. I'm going to come with you to the clubs and talk to everyone.'

She looked uncertain. Then she said, slowly, as if not entirely trusting him, 'Alright. Come on then, Harry. If that's what you want... Let's do it.'

'Where shall we start, then?'

Clarissa shrugged and pointed at the marquee that was closest. 'White's?'

'Why not? Start at the top, I say. Come on then.'

And they did exactly as he had promised.

Through the tents they worked, from one roped-off area to another, Pimm's, champagne and a bet, moving through the crowds like social butterflies. Then they were on to the next.

Clarissa introduced him to lords and ladies of all stripes. They met with admirals, Old Bailey judges, High Court judges, police Chief Constables and Commissioners. They talked to wealthy housewives and supremely wealthy bankers. They talked to the royalty of their own country and of other nations. Clarissa charmed her way through them, from ambassadors to Old Etonian rogues who were now doing something that couldn't be talked about, and to top politicians from around the world.

'And what do you do?' she would say to them. 'And what do you do?' And on and on. Pimm's, champagne and a bet.

Peanut Dancer came in at thirty to one, and Colbey put all his winnings on a horse called Chloe's Charm on the next, the Ribblesdale Stakes. It came in third. He rolled his pot on, won another, split his pot in two and lost the half that he bet on a random pick in the Buckingham Palace Stakes, which decided to stop and walk after the first furlong.

For the last race, he persuaded Clarissa they should keep it real by going down to the touts that lined the paddock, where the rest of the world piled out of the grandstand and stopped to have one for the road.

There, they bumped into a number of MPs he knew from the opposition party, who always came and gathered in the bar by the bandstand at the end of the day, and many of them greeted Clarissa like a long-lost friend. She knew them well enough from their days of standing for hours waiting for the count to come in on election night, trying to pass the time in some draughty leisure centre.

Asma Safeer, the opposition MP who had suggested Colbey had agoraphobia, was there. 'Good to see you, like, you know, out and about, Harry Colbey,' she said.

He went to buy her a drink to celebrate the fact, and then was forced to buy a round for all of her colleagues too.

'All of you?' he said.

And she tipped her finger under the Royal Enclosure badge on his lapel and said, 'Since you're slummin' it, y'may as well.'

After a while, the band packed up, the crowds thinned and Clarissa said they ought to get back and find Chloe.

Dodging the drunks, and feeling themselves a bit squiffy too, they made their way back to the Royal Enclosure and found a bench to sit on near to the paddock view.

Chloe discovered them there, giggling about the time their son had painted himself green and told everyone he was a frog.

'You two are simply embarrassing,' Chloe said. 'I preferred it when you were fighting.'

'We're not that drunk.' Clarissa patted the bench beside her.

'Come and sit with your old mama.'

'Don't we need to get going?'

'Yes, we do, but come and sit first.'

'Where are you going?' Colbey asked.

'To the opera.'

'Can Daddy come?'

'It's just a club thing, darling.'

'Oh, I see,' said Colbey.

'You can hitch a ride back to London with us, though, if you want? We have a spare seat.'

Colbey thought about his current travel difficulties.

'That would actually be quite helpful, if you didn't mind.'

'Right,' Clarissa said, looking at her watch. 'Where is Emir?'

'He's going to meet us there.'

Colbey looked at his ex-wife. 'Have you got a driver, then?'

And Clarissa and Chloe exchanged looks. 'You could say so. Shall we go?'

They walked together out to the eastern gate, beyond the paddock, Chloe complaining that her feet hurt, and suddenly Colbey groaned.

They were about to join a queue of people who were waiting for a series of Aston Martins taking turns to ferry people off somewhere. He saw several famous trainers in the line.

'You're getting a helicopter out, aren't you?'

'Too late, Daddy.' Chloe grabbed his arm and pulled him in next to her. 'You've said yes now.'

Off to the side of the queue, paparazzi photographers and Mobsters were hanging about, hoping to get an exclusive shot of someone famous.

'Harry Colbey! That your family?' one called out.

But then he spotted a familiar face among them – Jade Harrelson, the pink-haired journalist. He hurried over to her and had a whispered conversation, then ran back to the others.

'Come on,' Colbey said to them. 'Let's get a family shot.'

Jade moved away from the pack of paparazzi and the three of them posed for her. After they were done, Colbey shook her hand. 'Promised you something, didn't I!' he said.

'Yeah, great,' Jade said sarcastically. 'There's a lot of demand for backbench MPs and their families in *Hello* magazine.' At Chloe's sad face, she added, 'Don't worry, I can always crop him out. That will make it much more sellable.'

'Did you hear what she said?' Chloe said with a laugh as they rejoined the queue.

But Clarissa said to Colbey coolly, 'And who might that be?'

'Just a young journalist who wants to be in the lobby pack. Met her in parliament the other day. She needs a bit of support. I thought I might invite her for a coffee and give her some tips.'

'And is that all you wanted to give her?'

'Sorry?'

'You gave her something.'

'I gave her my card and said she was very welcome to call me.'

But, looking at Clarissa's face, Colbey knew he was busted.

2.7

Kanha spun her bike up to the back entrance of the MI5 building on Millbank and tried hard to resist the temptation to look up. The small drone was definitely tailing her. Damn it, she thought. Despite the leathers and the helmet, Divinity had worked out who she was. Thank goodness this was her last SIM to be delivered.

She peered into the dark entrance that led down to the underground car park, and saw someone who looked very like Moreland hovering at the window of the guard's room. Security was tight here. There were bomb doors folded back at the sides of the archway from the street and three armed officers stood discreetly inside.

But the Moreland equivalent in his pinstriped suit signalled to everyone that she was with him, and waved her over.

'Come on,' he said. 'The DG's in a meeting at the moment, but I'll show you up. Frightfully hot, isn't it? Brown's the name. Apologies for bringing you in the tradesman's entrance, but the DG thought this would be best in the circumstances.'

Five flights up what was obviously the fire escape staircase, Brown slipped through a door propped open with a notebook and, turning to pick it up, allowed the fire door to swing shut behind them. He led her along a corridor and ushered her into a room bare of anything but a desk and two chairs.

'Tea?'

'I don't have much time.'

'I'm sure he won't be long. Make yourself at home – and good luck!'

After he had gone, Kanha sat for a while. Then she got up and went to the door. It was locked. There was a card pad beside it, which she realised Brown had used to get out. But there was no way she could open it. She pulled her phone out of her bag. No reception. Shit shit.

Sitting down, she thought she must trust to Moreland. He had got her this far.

An hour later, her trust in Moreland was being tested. Two hours later, she was banging on the door and shouting for help. Had she been forgotten? She thought of her call at midnight. She thought of her team. No one knew where she was.

Three hours in, she sat on the floor and felt she must just resign herself.

Four hours in she started banging on the door again. She was just in the midst of that and shouting herself raw when it swung open and a smartly suited middle-aged man came in.

'Director General,' he said, sticking out a hand, which she shook across the table as they both sat down. He had something in a clear plastic case, photos perhaps, turned upside down, which he put on the table.

'Am I under arrest?'

'Arrest?'

'I've been locked in here for four hours.'

'Didn't they even get you a cup of tea?'

'They offered.'

'Yes, well, you must be thirsty, then. I suppose we could put a clear bottle of water in here and a glass. Otherwise it's a bit like dry solitary isolation, isn't it?'

'So I am?'

'What?'

'Under arrest?'

'No, of course not. But we can't have you wandering around the building, can we? Something of a breach of protocol that.

Now. What was it you wanted to talk to me about that needed to be so cloak-and-dagger?'

Kanha wondered what to do. But by then all she wanted was to give the SIM to the guy and get the hell out of there. She pulled it from her bag and slid it across the table, and the Director General picked it up and put it in his pocket.

'Not for the department,' she said. 'For your eyes only. This is a clean room, right?'

'Yep.'

She told him roughly what was on it, running through the documents, outlining the links between the Owners and Alcheminna and the illegal activity. He frowned, crossed his arms and looked up at the ceiling in thought.

'We have bits and pieces of this,' he said. 'But if what you have here is true, and I'm not saying I agree that it is, it would pull together a lot of my inner team's suspicions. We also believe the train derailment was an accident, rather than a terror attack. But it had never occurred to us that covering it up prompted Lauvaux to think of creating terror incidents for real.'

'Not Lauvaux. The system devised the plan.'

'So the system is a murderer?'

'The system does what it has been programmed to do.'

'But Lauvaux owns it.'

'There are many Owners. They are becoming wealthier by the second. The more the system knows, the more it protects them. The more it protects them and helps them, the richer and more powerful they become. They pose a direct threat to the democracy of Britain. We have to act. There is a list of them all on the SIM.'

'Is Ewan MacLellan one?'

'Yes.'

'And what do you want me to do?'

'Whatever you think you should. At the end of the day, I'm just a politician. But at midnight tonight, lots of those who do have the power to act will be in possession of the proof, and we can have a real conversation and make a move. Hopefully we will be able to go for Henri Lauvaux. Arrest him. Charge him with murder for the deaths of Jonnie Whitwell-Thrupp and Reginald Easterly and for attempted murder of those harmed in the gas explosions. There are other things too. Interference with British politics. Jameson will be forced to resign. The coalition will fall apart.'

'And then?'

Kanha looked away. 'I'm still working on that. The most important thing is to ensure exposure right now. Before it is too late.'

The DG sat in thought.

'The difficulty I have,' he said slowly, 'is that I'm being told something very different by the systems we use. Did you know you're wanted by the police? You're under suspicion of terrorism, and a credible source, who I trust, has given me these.'

She watched nervously as the DG pulled the photos out of the plastic case and turned them over. 'One... two... three pictures of you meeting international extremists.'

'These are fake.'

'They look pretty real.'

Kanha started to feel panicked again, but tried to stay calm. 'So I *am* under arrest?'

The DG ran his hand over his breast pocket where he had put the SIM.

'Tell me how to unlock the file. I can look at the evidence, and if it looks genuine to me I can help you. Otherwise I have to trust my sources and believe that these photos are real, and that this conspiracy theory you're touting round is just a distraction technique.'

'I can't tell you that.'

'You mean you won't.'

'No, I mean I can't. I wouldn't have a clue how to.'

'That causes us something of a problem, then.' He leaned back in his chair.

Kanha thought desperately of what to say.

'If you plan for me to be detained,' she said, 'at least let me stay here until midnight, and then we can talk again.'

'I don't think so.' He stood up and went to the door. 'I can't aid and abet someone wanted by the Metropolitan Police for terrorism in MI5's very headquarters, now can I? That would be more than my job was worth.

'If what you say is true, you'll only be in the police cells for a few hours. I give you my word that tomorrow, if your evidence convinces me, I will pull whatever strings I need to get you out. So you will have to trust to your evidence, won't you? If it's as good as you say it is, you don't need to worry. Come on. I'm due for dinner in town, and you're making me late.'

At the tap of his card, the door slid open. Two armed security staff stood waiting. Kanha was thinking and thinking, but she couldn't see any point in refusing to go. Being dragged kicking and screaming out of the MI5 building would not be a very dignified look for a Member of Parliament.

'Back door,' the DG said to the security guards, and the four of them went down the fire escape, Kanha trudging wearily down, trying to think of a way of persuading him.

At the bottom, they came out into the underground car park again, where his car was waiting. Its nose was pointing towards the half-open blast gates, ready to drive out. Beyond the gates, a police van was waiting in the road, a couple of motorcycle officers parked at front and back.

'Wait,' she said, desperately. 'You don't understand. It's imperative that I'm there to coordinate the call tonight. I can't do it from a police cell.'

The DG opened the back door of his BMW.

'Nonsense. I'm sure Jackie Rolt will be able to handle it perfectly well.'

Rolt. Kanha ground her teeth.

'It was Rolt who gave you the photos, wasn't it?'

But he didn't reply. He was looking, with curiosity, at a drone hovering outside the open shutter doors. He frowned and shielded his eyes to see better.

'What the hell's that doing here?' he said. 'In the centre of London? That's a military-grade drone.'

'It followed me here from parliament.'

He put his head on one side and pointed at it.

'You see, in warfare, drones come in two models. Scout and Assassin. That's a Scout drone. Small, agile, top-of-the-range collision sensors, high-res video and zoom. Lovely example. Look at it there. It's usually accompanied by a...'

Another drone appeared in the square of soft evening light, and the DG took a step back.

'Shut the gates!' he shouted in the direction of the security window. 'Shut the fucking gates!' And he pointed to the archway and to the drones beyond, stabbing his finger in desperation.

The larger drone moved slowly forward as the steel gate started to shudder across, but as slow as the drone was, it was going to make it through.

The DG grabbed hold of Kanha, pulled her bodily towards him and pushed her inside the car. Then the world exploded.

2.8

Colbey stood in the plexiglass departure tent of the heliport and realised he was in the thick of them again. The Owners. Picasso faces, furs falling off shoulders. The holding lounge was also busy with others who had come from the races – owners of horses holding trophies aloft, jockeys hitching a ride back home, corporate boys coming home from a jolly full of cake and wine and winnings.

Outside, the helicopters came and went, the noise of them adding to the general din. Above the door out to the field on which the choppers were lined up were boards showing the names of who was to go next. A young woman with a clipboard ran between the groups trying to match guests to flights and, when their time came, encouraging them to put down their last glasses of champagne so she could shoo them towards the exit.

By now, Emir had returned and he stood knocking back the wine, with a lipstick mark on his cheek. None of them mentioned it, not even Chloe, who buried her head in her phone. Clarissa was stony-faced and silent.

'Alcheminna, Colbey!' the girl with the clipboard called out, and Colbey groaned to hear the two names connected. Let's just get this over with, he thought. The damage has been done. My family are in bed with them. My movements are being directed and restricted by them. It's all hopeless, anyway.

But as he clambered into the chopper and took the seat next to Clarissa, Chloe, who had sat down opposite, looked up from her phone and gave him a look that turned his heart cold.

'What is it?' he said shouting over the noise of the propellers.

'There's been an explosion.'

'A what?'

'An explosion in London.'

'Did you say London?'

'A terror attack. London.' She mouthed the words carefully. 'Your friend... Esme Kanha is—'

'What? What is she?'

The doors of the helicopter were slammed shut on them and he felt the jolt as they started to lift.

'Is she dead?' he said, wanting to know the worst at once.

Chloe pulled her headphones from the hook behind her, and Colbey followed her lead.

'Wanted,' Chloe said over the intercom. 'In connection with it. I'm sure she didn't do it, Daddy. I'm sure it's just a mix-up.'

'It's nonsense,' Colbey said. 'Mouth of the Mob nonsense.' Was it better to get them to land the chopper again, so he could call her without the noise? But perhaps better to keep going. They would be in London quicker this way, and if he wasn't with Clarissa he might not be able to get there at all.

'But it's got a "verified" stamp from the government.'

'Let me see,' Colbey said roughly, and Chloe handed him her phone.

'It says the police are looking for a number of people they want to question.'

'Who? Who?' he said, digging in his pocket for his glasses.

'I don't know... Give it back.'

He did as he was told and she read out from the site.

'The police have arrested several people wanted in connection with a terror ring at the heart of government: The opposition leader Jackie Rolt, the Speaker of the House of Commons, the Attorney General. Met Police Commissioner... blah blah... Judge blah... some more judges.'

She showed him the phone. Now that he had his glasses on he saw the list of names. And under each one was the stamp: *VERIFIED, VERIFIED, VERIFIED.*

'They want to bring a journalist called Quentin Tidy in for questioning. They've doxed him. Full address. Asking people to say if they see him.'

'And what do they say the terror attack was?'

'A bomb in the MI5 building, planted by Esme. The Director General has been killed. They say not to approach Esme but to report it to the police if you see her.'

Colbey put his head in his hands.

It was everyone Esme had given a SIM to. Every single one. Either with the police for questioning, on the run or dead.

Clarissa was also scrolling through her phone. She had gone very pale.

'Harry. Neville Jameson has gone to Westminster and declared a state of emergency. He's dismissing parliament. He's brought police into the House of Commons and told any MPs or Lords working there to leave.'

He could see Clarissa was shaking, and he took her hand and held it.

'But what does it all mean, Daddy?'

'It'll be fine. Don't worry,' he said to them both.

Turning to the window, Colbey saw they were already skirting the Windsor Great Park, and that the western suburbs of London had come into view.

'Daddy, what should we do?'

For the first time, Colbey remembered that Emir was with them. He was messaging on his phone in the corner, one hand gripping the handle above the window. Seeing them all looking at him, he pulled his microphone down to his mouth.

'Don't worry. My father has told everyone the opera is still a go.'

Chloe looked astounded at the response.

'The opera? But we have to go home. They've put out a stay-at-home order for the whole of London.'

'What's that got to do with us?' Emir said.

'What do you mean? There's been an explosion. And the Houses of Parliament have been closed.'

Emir shifted himself round to face her and took her hand. 'Oh, my darling Chloe. Are you upset by it all? You really don't need to worry. Whenever you're with me or your mother, you're perfectly safe.'

Chloe threw her hands up. 'What are you talking about? Why should you be any safer than anyone else?'

Emir glanced at Colbey, but seemed to decide he didn't care that they could all hear everything that was said across the intercom.

'It isn't safe for Londoners, my darling. That's why they all need to stay at home. But we are Owners. The system will make sure we are safe. And if my father thinks it's safe, then I agree. I trust him. Don't you?'

Chloe bit her lip and looked away, then turned back to him. 'What do you mean? You're not really explaining it. Why would it be safe for us, but not for anyone else?'

Emir rolled his eyes. 'You really are a bit dim sometimes, aren't you, precious? Don't worry yourself about it. We'll all go to the opera and we'll all be perfectly fine.' He looked at Colbey. 'Well, not all of us.'

'Why not Daddy?'

'Because he's not an Owner.'

'Just because he doesn't own shares in Alcheminna, he can't come to the opera?'

'No, that's not what I said. Why are you being dumb about this? He's not an Owner, so he'll have to go home and stay indoors like the rest of them. I am an Owner. Your mother is an Owner. And you are Owner family. So we don't have to follow the order if we don't want to. Didn't your mother explain all this?'

Both Colbey and Chloe looked at Clarissa, who said, 'What? It was complicated...'

Chloe turned to Emir again.

'So, let me get this right. You think because you own shares in some dumb IT company, you get to be treated differently from everyone else?'

Emir shook his head in disbelief.

'Sweetie, how the hell do you think we've been able to swan around at Royal Ascot all day? Do you think they would have let us in otherwise? Look at us. From rags to riches, and now we're the elite. Now they all have to do what we tell them and go where we tell them. Even that King of theirs. It's sort of a revolution. Isn't it exciting?'

Colbey and Clarissa both said together, 'There were never rags.'

But Chloe said, 'I don't care about the King, Emir. I care about my father.'

Emir looked sneeringly at Colbey.

'Well then, tell him to stop being such an idiot and join the party again.'

'What party?' Colbey said.

'Your old party, of course. Our party. We could use your diplomatic skills, Harry.'

Colbey thought of Kanha and what she would say. He himself was lost for words.

'Your old party is now our party, and we are the party of the New Order,' Emir went on. 'My father and I and MacLellan and Jameson and so on. I understand you're an eloquent speaker. A good and honourable politician. You could probably join us.'

'Over my dead body,' Colbey growled. He knew Emir was about to say that could be arranged, but he looked at Chloe and closed his mouth. He patted her on the hand.

'For you, my lovely, the world will be your oyster. You won't need to worry about politics.'

Chloe snatched her hand away from Emir's. He looked around the small cabin, the drumming of the propellers still loud in everyone's ears despite the headphones, and finally read the room.

'You'll all understand later,' he said with a sulky look and returned to his phone.

The sun had dropped below the horizon. In the twilight, other choppers flying in the same direction could be seen, a long line of them stretching out on both sides. Below, suburban streets came into view and slowly passed by.

'Where are we going?' he said to Clarissa.

They had lost altitude. The streets below were empty of traffic, the lights changing from red to green and back to red again for no one. The stay-at-home order had come into force.

'Holland Park,' she replied, without looking at him. 'For the opera. We'll have to leave you there, I'm afraid.'

He saw it below them, a sports field, a bank of trees, the opera house with its stage and banked seating open to the sky, the formal gardens laid out at the side. The helicopters ferrying the Owners from the races touched down one at a time. Theirs was the last, landing with the gentlest of bumps. The pilot left the blades running as he got out and came round to open the door for them. He wished them a pleasant evening.

'What should we do, Daddy?' Chloe asked him as he helped her down.

'Go with Emir to the opera. He's right, much as I hate to say it. That is the safest place you can be right now.'

Reluctantly, Chloe hurried off after the long line of Owners who were starting to make their way up towards the opera house. The Chairman was at the front of the procession, waving at them all to follow him. Emir waited for Chloe and tried to put his arm around her, but she threw it off. And Colbey thought that was one good thing that had come of the day. He knew his daughter better than anyone in the world, and he knew for a fact that Emir's days were numbered.

Colbey and Clarissa faced one another in the dusk.

'Are these really the people you want to be with?' he said.

'Of course they're not,' she replied. 'But are you lot really so much better? What difference does it make if they run the country? All these arseholes with their impossible-to-get-into clubs, saying, "Yes, you can come in," and "No, you can't because you didn't go to the right school". Are they any better?'

'They don't run the country, Clarissa – you know that perfectly well. The country is run by whoever is voted in by our citizens.'

'Is it? Is it really?'

Colbey didn't know what to say. She had always helped him in his career. Moaned about it, yes. But helped him all the same. He'd always thought she had believed in it all. In the canvassing, the electioneering, the political manoeuvring, the committees, the fundraisers, the dinners, the surgeries, the charity cricket matches. She had always been there. Not without complaint, but she had been there nonetheless.

'You used me,' Clarissa said. 'You think I don't know that?'

Colbey took a step back at her ferocity. 'What do you mean?'

'You were giving things out. Don't think I didn't notice. You might be able to fool a security camera with your unpredictable drunken stagger, but I know you better than any machine will ever know you. The deputy director of MI5? My Uncle Bertie, who used to be the police Chief Constable? My godfather Lord Justice Swainsong? Oh yes, you passed your little whatever-it-was to each of them. Pulled it out from that wodge of cash you've been carrying around when you placed a bet. Palmed it off with a handshake. Ooh, Clarissa, let's go down to the bandstand and keep it real. Asma Safeer, the deputy opposition leader? The head of the judiciary? That bloody journalist with the pink hair.'

Colbey held up his hands. 'I'm sorry, Clarissa. Please don't be angry. You've no idea how high the stakes are. And if I'd told you, you might not have agreed to help.'

'How dare you. When have I ever refused to help you?'

'You might have given it away without meaning to. Just a look or a slip of the tongue would have been all it took, and all those people – your Uncle Bertie, Lord Justice Swainsong, Asma Safeer – would have been arrested or doxed by now, like the others who we have given the files to. All those arrested today were the ones Esme Kanha approached.'

Her anger seemed to soften as she thought over his words.

'Is this really what you want for Chloe?' he said.

'To be one of the elite for once, to be one of the ones who have it all – like we never had? Yes. Why wouldn't I?'

'For a thousand reasons,' Colbey said, and meant to elaborate, but for once words failed him. He pulled open his jacket and pulled out the now slim pouch. 'I have one left,' he said. 'Would you like it? Would you like to see just a few of the reasons?'

But Clarissa turned her back on him.

'If you change your mind, call me,' he called out to her as she walked away. 'Just message me. Anything. Please. For the sake of Chloe, understand who it is you are choosing to stand with.'

But she didn't look back.

Colbey turned away and looked into the dim sports field and at the dark line of trees that screened the opera house. The last of the helicopters had gone, and the Owners were disappearing from sight, Clarissa hurrying after them.

He took his bearings from when they had flown in. Kensington High Street was behind him. Hyde Park was not far off to the east. If he could get through the few side streets there, he might be able to run through the dark royal parks to Westminster before Divinity spotted him.

Colbey threw his top hat into the bushes, took his morning coat off and draped it over his head. Then he started to run.

But it wasn't the listening eyes that caught Colbey in their snare. It was a bunch of youngsters, hanging around on a street corner, buoyed up with a zealous desire to enforce the stay-at-home order. With his coat over his head, expecting the streets to be empty, he had crashed right into them.

'Hey, Granddad,' one of them said, as they blocked his path and pushed him against the low wall of a front garden, beneath a streetlight. 'Trying to cover your face, are you?'

'Where did you get those glasses?' Colbey asked, but one – such a young lad – sneered and said, 'What's it to you? Are you jealous?'

But at that moment, two things happened. Colbey's phone pinged with a message, and a window above them opened and a woman shouted to the kids to leave him alone, saying she had called the police.

'They won't come, will they?' the youngest asked the others.

'No,' was the reply. 'And we're being told to teach him a lesson.'

'Wait a minute,' Colbey said to them, and strangely they did hold off while he looked at the message.

'I'm very sorry, gentlemen,' Colbey said. 'But I have more important things to do than hang out with you all night.'

He took them by surprise, smashing through their ranks, his old schoolboy rugby prowess coming back to him, and set off back the way he had come, desperately trying to ring Clarissa as he ran.

Clarissa was still at the opera, but she wanted the last SIM. He had to get it to her. Had to make sure she understood, so she could decide where she stood. He owed it to her after all these years, and her choice affected Chloe too, and would do for the rest of her life if Clarissa kept her lot in with the Owners.

Back the way he had come he ran, the boys after him. Through the gap in the iron railings and across the sports field. He thought he had lost them in the little strip of woods in front of the opera house, but as he came onto the lawn and the theatre loomed above him in the dark, they caught up with him.

Clarissa was there on the steps, waiting, frozen to the spot. She said something, but by then they were on him. Perhaps she had said nothing. It had all happened so quickly. He had curled into a ball, again thinking of his younger days on the rugby pitch, as they stamped on him – and then the little shit kicked him in the face and broke his nose.

What happened after that was hazy, but he knew he had managed to do the one thing that was most important. He had fallen forward onto her and slipped the last of the SIMs into her hand.

Now he was beneath some trees, and the boys were squabbling.

'Why are you crying?' one of them – the leader, he thought – was saying to the youngest kid. The answer was lost in sobs. 'Well, what did you expect? What do you think happens when you stamp on someone's face?'

'What shall we do with him?' another asked.

'Take him to the police, surely. Isn't that our job?'

'Divinity says no.'

'Then let's kill him properly.'

'I don't want to.'

'Stop crying, you baby.'

'Well, what should we do, then?'

'Let's just leave him here. He's off the streets. And we need to be back on our beat, making sure it's safe.'

There seemed to be agreement. Colbey kept his eyes closed and lay still. Were they gone? He tried to open his eyes, but only one worked. Yes, he was under some trees. He was beside a wall. He was in the bushes by the gap in the iron railings. When he tried to move there was a lot of pain. 'Man or mouse?' Colbey muttered and heaved himself up to a sitting position.

He pulled out his phone and dialled.

'Answer, Esme, answer,' he thought, but she didn't.

He looked on the map and saw her pin. She was in Westminster. His head spun. He levered himself to his feet, and promptly threw up. His nose was broken for sure. Damn fucking kids. Maybe his cheek too. But he could walk. Just about. Stay there, Esme, he thought. I'm coming.

PART THREE

Friday 21 June

3.1

Shipton, Kingham, Moreton-in-Marsh. Honeybourne, Evesham, Worcester Shrub Hill. Tackley, Heyford, Radley and Appleford. Stonehouse, Stroud, Kemble and Yate. Ilchester Place, Oakwood Court, Addison Crescent, Addison Road. You promised me shares. You promised me, promised me. Face one, face two, face three, face four. Stop crying, you baby. Knock on the door. Face five, face six, face seven, face eight. Tell me what matters. Doorbell twenty, one, two and three. The rebels, pesky things. Taplow and Burnham. Look, listen, think, act. Dvořáček? How terribly sad. Langley, Iver, Slough. Why do we need humans now? Alright, you win. Shiplake, Wargrave, Cookham and Furze Platt. We're all just stupid old geese. Greedy. Waddling around pushing our stupid fat chests out, squawking across the House at one another, as if we mattered. As if we were important, but we're not. None of us are. We're too far behind. And we're all dirty, aren't we, hmm? Even you. Even clever Kanha. Kanha, Kanha. Pitt Street, bloody face, no. Holland Street. Gloucester Walk, bloody face, gone. Castle Bar Park. Kanha, Colbey, Kanha, Colbey. Kanha, Colbey! Hereford, Great Malvern, Hornton Street. Where? I think they're dead, knowledge is power, bananas, why bananas? I think he's dead. Lost, lost, everyone lost. Sussex Gardens, Sussex Villas. So what are we, eh? Just stupid, useless, dirty fucking geese. We don't know anything, but they're watching us, listening to us. And they're inside my head, I tell you.

And I don't want them there. Where? There. Where? Olympia West. Something we missed? Tricksy things. Oh, so tricksy. I see what you did. I see what you did. O Divinity, Divinity, wherefore art thou Divinity? Protect the Owners, grow the wealth, protect thyself. Watch, plan, predict, act, act, act, ACT.

3.2

Kanha sat in the Marquis of Granby with a glass of water clutched in her hands and tried to stay still as Melody wiped the worst of the blood from her face.

'Ouch. Be careful, would you?' she said, and tried to take the cloth for herself.

'You're a very bad patient, you know,' Melody snapped, and was gently pushed aside by Wilbur, who crouched down in front of Kanha and took over.

'You'll be in shock,' he said. 'Are your ears ringing?'

Kanha nodded, and realised she was shaking violently.

'Most of this blood is from a very small wound. Cuts to the head always bleed heavily. You were very lucky, you know.'

'It wasn't luck. The Director General saved my life. And now he's—'

'That was his choice. And a fine and noble choice it was.'

She looked around the pub. 'How many are we here?'

'Thirty or so. The day was finishing up as normal, when suddenly there seemed to be armed police all over the parliament building. When they said leave, everyone thought it was a terror attack and rushed out. It was only after, when we saw the news feeds, that we realised we'd been had.'

Kanha looked around the pub. The MPs were gathered at the tables. Some were drinking, but most were just looking at their phones, or sitting glued to the television screen in the corner.

'When the streets around parliament began to be filled with Met police too, we came here, and Verity locked the door.'

The landlady was busy in the little kitchen behind the bar, putting some food together for her unexpected visitors.

'Well, at least we're close to the House,' Kanha said. 'What do the news feeds say?'

Wilbur made a face that gave forewarning it was not good news.

He went through the list of those who had been arrested, and Kanha put her head in her hands. 'That's almost everyone I gave a copy of the evidence to. I didn't fool it for a second.'

'Quentin Tidy is on the run, but they are saying his office has been raided and the *Times* shut down.'

'The *Times* shut down? Has Jameson taken leave of his senses? And what about the Speaker? What about the Serjeant at Arms and his team?'

'We don't know. They didn't come out of parliament at the same time as us. All the doormen were missing as we left. Perhaps they've all been arrested.'

Brooke came over.

'Are you alright?' she said.

'I will be,' Kanha replied. 'It's not as bad as it looks.'

'They're saying you planted the incendiary device.'

'It was a drone. Flown in through the shutter doors and into the basement.'

'Hey guys!' someone called from the far end of the room, and all fell quiet as the television was turned up.

It was a newsflash streaming on all the channels. Sheryl Simmons stood in her lavender suit in the Number Ten press room.

'The Prime Minister is sad to announce that the country is under siege by terror attacks from internal extremists. A large incendiary device was detonated inside the MI5 building less than an hour ago, and we have credible information leading us to believe there may be more. The Director General of MI5 is confirmed dead and others have been injured. Several MPs are wanted for questioning in connection with this incident. The addresses of their homes, offices and known frequented places have been supplied on the government page of the Mouth of the Mob website. The public are advised to call the police immediately on sighting them, particularly the MPs Harry Colbey and Esme Kanha and the journalist Quentin Tidy.

'Given the nature of the extreme events and the infiltration of terrorists into the heart of Westminster, the Prime Minister Neville Jameson, under the Emergency Powers Act of 1920, has declared that a state of emergency exists. With immediate effect, both Houses of Parliament are dissolved. The Prime Minister and his cabinet will ensure the smooth running of the country through these difficult times. Neville Jameson, your Prime Minister, will address the nation at some point in the next few hours. This will also be streamed live on the government's account on the Mouth of the Mob website, so stay tuned. In the meantime he has asked me to deliver this message to the nation. Be on guard for deepfake footage, lies and attempts to discredit our democratically elected Prime Minister. Remember that the government's Mouth of the Mob account is the only place that provides verifiable news.'

When the transmission ended, it started again – and from then on played on a constant loop.

'Stay still for a while,' Wilbur said. 'Just take a bit of time to gather yourself. There will be plenty of time for heroics before this is out, I fear.'

It was good advice. Kanha sat and slowly cleaned her face with the cloth, and tried hard not to think of the Director General's twisted body. The car had protected her. The windows hadn't even smashed. Just a small piece of flying glass had come in from somewhere and nicked her. Her memory of leaving and running down the street to here was gone. Wilbur said she had been banging on the pub door with all her might.

But as much as she wanted to take Wilbur's advice, she felt she had already sat there too long. Things needed to be done. Just what? That was the question. Where was Elliot?

'Wilbur. Have you heard from Elliot?'

'Yes. He's still inside parliament. With Jameson. He has a few of his cronies with him, including his cabinet ministers. Elliot is our only spy in their camp. He says he'll try to sneak away and ring us when he can. But he says it's difficult to even message right now.'

Kanha looked at her phone. It was 12.32am. She groaned.

Brooke and Melody came over and sat with them.

'No one's called, have they?' Wilbur said. 'Because all those you gave the evidence to are in the hands of the police on trumped-up charges, or on the run and unable to act, or...'

'...dead.'

Melody shook her head, tears pooling in her eyes. 'When were they supposed to ring in?'

'Two minutes ago,' Brooke said.

'So it's over, then,' Wilbur said miserably.

Kanha got up and indicated they should follow her. She led them into one of the back rooms and put her phone on the table.

'There's still hope,' she said. 'No one ever likes to be the first on the call. And... I didn't tell you, but we did have a plan B.'

Melody wiped her eyes and sat up. 'What do you mean?'

'Well, I always knew it was going to be tough to get them to the right people without Divinity figuring out what I was up to. So Harry took a bunch of the SIMs to Ascot.'

'To Ascot? Did he manage to give any out to anyone who can help?' Brooke asked.

'I don't know. We agreed radio silence just in case.'

They all looked at the phone.

'It's no good,' Brooke said.

Then it rang.

They all jumped and looked at it. The sound of the phone was loud in the room.

Kanha reached out and answered it. Then she put it on loudspeaker.

'Justice Swainsong here. Is it me or has there just been a coup? Is this the right number for the meeting to discuss what the hell to do about it?'

'Yes,' said Kanha as the phone beeped again. 'Hold on. I think someone else is ringing through.'

'Hello?'

'What the fuck is going on? Is that Harry Colbey? Did you know this was all about to happen?'

'Is that Asma Safeer? This is Esme Kanha, Asma. I don't know where Harry is, but you've called the right number. Hold the line, please.'

It beeped again.

'This is Quentin Tidy of the *Times* here. On the run, but still very much part of a free press.'

'Quentin, good to hear that. Could you give me just a minute, please?'

Kanha looked up in panic. 'Melody! How the hell do I do a conference call on this thing?'

Melody lunged for the phone. 'For goodness sake, Chief Whip...'

More and more dialled in. Not just from the judiciary but from MI5, the police force and the Ministry of Defence, and several senior shadow ministers from the opposition as well as Asma Safeer.

When she thought they had as many as were going to join, Kanha looked around her at Brooke, Wilbur and Melody. Wilbur gave her a reassuring nod.

'Welcome, all,' she said. 'As I'm sure you are all aware by now, our Prime Minister, Neville Jameson, has dissolved parliament. He is claiming that the country is under attack from internal terrorists and he intends to run the country through what is effectively a wartime cabinet. It is my assertion that the Prime Minister is actually in the process of staging a coup in conjunction with a company called Alcheminna Systems. It was the company's system that sent a military drone with an incendiary device into the MI5 building. As you will have seen from the evidence we managed to get to you just in time, this is a tactic they have used before and intend to use again. Jameson and those who are behind him intend to seize control of the country for a minority elite, which will be protected by the Alcheminna system. This has been a long time in the planning. The system is, as you know, already in control of much of our national infrastructure and there is at least one previously senior Member of Parliament who has been working in cahoots with them.

'I'm afraid we're missing Harry Colbey, who was instrumental in gathering the data you received this afternoon and who has worked tirelessly over the last couple of years to expose the corruption that has seeped into the core of Britain's political infrastructure, but I don't think we can wait for him. We're also missing the leader of the opposition, Jackie Rolt, who I understand has been arrested, but I'm pleased to say we do have several other parties here who represent the opposition, including Asma Safeer, the Shadow Foreign Secretary and deputy leader, and certainly I am here to represent all those MPs of the governing party who consider that Neville Jameson has not acted in our name today. From the House of Lords, we have a number of representatives, but particular welcome to Lord Silverman, who chairs the Joint Select Committee Inquiring into the Threat to Democracy and Privacy caused by Technological Advances. We also have two representatives from the press here, Quentin Tidy of the *Times* and Jade Harrelson, who I believe is now a correspondent on the ground, representing several other national papers. As I'm sure you all know, a free press is as important to democracy as an opposition, so a huge thank you to them for dialling in.'

'Wild horses wouldn't stop me,' Jade butted in.

'The last party I wish to welcome, who is just dialling in to join us now, is a representative from Interpol, who will be able to negotiate with our friends in Europe and the United States and try to arrange any assistance we need. It may well be that with Divinity… sorry, with the Alcheminna system in control of much of our British infrastructure we are limited in our power to act until we can wrest control from Jameson's self-created war cabinet and get parliament working again. I have stopped short of asking for international assistance, as we do not know where that could lead. It could open a whole different can of worms, but obviously that is something we can discuss.

'So, I suggest we go round the room, figuratively speaking, see who we have here, and then let's figure out what the hell we need to do to get our democracy back.'

The call went on for a couple of hours. At first it was a confusion of voices, but consensus slowly formed. When they were finished, Kanha sat back and wearily wiped her forehead with her hand.

They went back into the main bar, where many of the MPs had thrown themselves down on the floor or onto the benches to try to get some sleep.

There was a knocking at the door. Brooke pulled aside the net curtain and looked out. Then she hurried to unlock it.

Harry Colbey, his face a mess of blood, stumbled in.

'Drones,' he said. 'Swarming above you. And police everywhere.'

Then he collapsed to the floor.

For a long time everything was a muddle. On the road that ran alongside the pub, vans full of police in riot gear were parked up. Every now and again the officers would get out, stretch their legs and march off somewhere, only to be replaced with others. Kanha went upstairs and peeped out of the net-curtained window at them and saw also that the sky above Westminster was still full of drones. Then she hurried back downstairs.

Trapped as they were, she and her team were busy – Wilbur coordinating their contacts in defence, Brook doing the same with the police and Melody keeping track of everything, while Kanha handled international relations and worked with the judiciary to determine what action could be taken to stop Jameson's dissolution of parliament. 'Harry Colbey is insistent we stay within the law,' she told them.

Colbey sat in the corner being tended to, and Kanha went over and gave him a delicate hug as an MP who used to be a doctor stepped up to push his nose back in place.

'I was so close,' Harry said. 'But I had to wait for hours until a gap in police lines allowed me to slip through to you.'

'I'm just so happy you're safe,' Kanha said.

'I can help,' was the reply. 'Just as soon as… eeoww!'

When his corrected nose was taped in place with plaster strips from the pub's first aid kit and the worst of his cuts cleaned up by Melody, who said he was a much better patient than others she could mention, Kanha gave him a phone and set him to coordinating with the British and international press. Making sure their view on things got out there.

Across the country, the police force was in disarray. Some areas had switched back to their old IT systems and were in charge of their own forces again. Mostly those led by the Chief Constables who had joined the call. They tried to set up online meetings with their colleagues to spread the word, but found themselves unable to dial in. Which left those siding with the Prime Minister talking to one another, agreeing that the situation was dire, and that no one could be trusted except Jameson's war cabinet and the system they had all come to rely on.

Melody helped Kanha record a message to the public protesting her innocence and defending those who had been doxed. She said that the Director General had been murdered and that the Prime Minister was in the midst of conducting a coup. She outlined her belief that there was no terror threat, and explained that the explosion had been detonated by a military drone sent into the building by the Alcheminna system itself. This is not science fiction, she said. This is not a deepfake. This is reality.

At the end, she made a declaration that her duty lay to her constituents, to the citizens of the nation and to democracy. Finally, she called for MPs to ignore the stay-at-home order and to get to Westminster and resist the dissolution of parliament, and for those citizens who believed in democracy to assist them where they could.

'Come however you can,' she said. 'By car, by foot, by bike, by horse, by tractor, by any means you can think of, but come and protect our democracy.'

Mani created new Mouth of the Mob accounts and posted Kanha's message. When they were discovered and taken down, he set up more. Social media was awhirl with links to the accounts showing the message, and the ability to set up new accounts on the Mouth was removed. But by then the video had a life of its own and was doing the rounds in private messages.

Staff working for the rail and underground networks posted texts they had received telling them not to come in. Others posted that they believed there was a coup and would go in regardless.

From his base in parliament, Jameson fought back.

His cabinet issued a notice on the Mouth of the Mob website banning gatherings of more than five people, banning demonstrations and banning travel. The roads into London in areas where Divinity was in control were blocked off by panicked police officers being told all sorts of horror stories, while roads in other areas remained open. Rumours flew among the MPs about which routes were safest to take, and Melody made notes and posted them on a website called 'Save Britain's Democracy' that Mani had set up for them, hosted offshore. She also posted footage from flats and apartments on Parliament Square showing police with their Divinity helmets blockading each of the entrances to the House of Commons and the House of Lords.

For a long time they could not get hold of the Speaker or the Serjeant at Arms, and didn't know what had happened to them. Then they got a call from Elliot, who whispered that both were being held in a room with a Divinity-led police officer on guard outside. The officers who usually worked in the House had refused to cooperate but had been overwhelmed. To avoid bloodshed they had agreed to give up their arms. Elliot was calling from a bathroom. He didn't want to stay on the phone for long. He didn't want Jameson to notice he was gone and become suspicious.

But there was something Kanha had to understand.

'Who is coordinating all this?' she said.

And Elliot replied. 'It's Henri Lauvaux. He's been on a video call with Jameson since they took over. Anything they agree, he actions on his end, through the Divinity system. But they only ever agree what Lauvaux tells them to.'

Kanha wanted to ask more, but he said, 'I have to go. Neville's messaging me. I'll try and ring later.'

Then things turned their way again. Moreland called to say he had driven to the National Grid's headquarters and, with an analyst there, figured out from the shape of its load where the newly built server warehouse must be – along the Thames estuary to the east. He asked a colleague to drive out there, who called in to say the place was ringed with armed police. He didn't even get near the door before he was arrested.

Melody posted footage of that on 'Save Britain's Democracy', including the arrest, and it had fifteen million hits within ten minutes.

Jameson and Lauvaux retaliated. At 4am, they closed off the internet to the British public, and all of Kanha's team despaired, though they still had access through Mani's phones. But then at 5am came the sight they had been praying for. Wilbur looked up from his phone with a shout, to say, 'They're coming! They're coming to your call, Esme!'

Kanha went over to look. Their site was streaming footage of MPs arriving in Westminster in their dozens. Faced with the ranked army of Met police in riot gear surrounding the parliament building, they were retreating to the places they knew they would find each other –the Red Lion, the Westminster Arms, St Stephen's Tavern, the Clarence.

Citizens were starting to arrive too, in balaclavas and scarves wrapped around their heads, carrying banners with messages such as *Jameson out!* and *Save our democracy!*

Kanha felt a swell of pride, happiness and hope at the sight of them.

But how to get themselves and the MPs into parliament without violence? She considered going down and reasoning with the officers barricading the gates, but worried about the circling military drones controlled by Divinity, which couldn't be reasoned with.

'Can the navy or RAF help?' she asked Wilbur. But he said no. The army were keen to send in tanks to help, but their system was malfunctioning, Divinity was in it. They couldn't seem to get it out. Didn't trust the tanks not to start spinning round and firing on their own troops. The RAF didn't trust their planes. Divinity was in them too.

'We need something,' she said. 'Some way to protect the MPs from the drones.'

But Wilbur held up his hand. 'I have a plan forming,' he said. 'Give me another hour and I should have a solution.'

'For the drones?'

'Yes, for the drones.'

Just after 6am, he came to her and said his plan was in place.

'Ready to go over the wall?' he said, and she nodded and gathered the MPs to her.

Wilbur had arranged through Mani for an Australian satellite to turn off the GPS signal to Westminster. He had been reassured that without signal the drones would be forced to go to ground.

The Australians were standing by. Melody messaged Elliot and asked him to go to the Commons Lobby, to the doorman's seat at the door to the chamber, and pull the lever to sound the Division Bell as soon as he could.

'And then?' said Kanha.

'Then we give the nod to the Aussies and we run,' Wilbur said.

Kanha had to trust her team.

They stood by the pub's side door, thirty-three Honourable Members of Parliament, and waited. Kanha felt someone take her hand; she looked round and saw it was Harry. They smiled at each other. He had insisted on coming, despite the fact he could barely walk.

Then came the call they had been waiting for. In the corner of the room, the pub's Division Bell rang as it had on many occasions before, giving MPs their eight-minute warning to down their pints, scoff their pickled eggs and prawn mayonnaise sandwiches and get themselves over to the chamber of the House of Commons. Elliot must have pulled the lever. Bells would be ringing all over the parliament building, all over a deserted Portcullis House, but also in every pub and bar and private club within an eight-minute walk of the House of Commons.

Hopefully, the MPs would understand the signal, and like them would take to the streets.

Wilbur told Mani the operation was a go, and Kanha and Colbey set off, the MPs running behind them. As they sped through the Westminster backstreets, drones came plummeting from the sky, landing on rooftops and pavements, whichever was closest.

'They're falling!' Wilbur said.

When they reached Parliament Square, they saw the police in riot gear lined up, their backs to the parliament gates. The square was full of demonstrators with masks and banners. When they saw Kanha and her MPs running down Broad Sanctuary, Westminster Abbey behind them, a shout went up; they fell aside and allowed the MPs a path into the centre of the square, and closed up around them.

Then a raucous cheer went up again. Those on the opposite side of the square fell away to reveal a sight that made Kanha's heart soar. Scores of MPs were jogging down Whitehall. It took a while, the last coming panting into the square in their dribs and drabs, but by the time they were all there the number of MPs with Kanha must have risen to a hundred or more.

'What next?' many of them asked her.

What indeed. She was just conferring with Harry and Wilbur when one of the protestors came up to her.

'Megaphone,' he said. 'You'll have to reason with them.'

It was Karolinski. His face was covered, but she recognised his plummy tones. He put a loudhailer in her hands.

'Stand back!' Karolinski shouted at the protestors. 'MPs coming through!'

She weaved her way to the front, as did the other MPs, so that they stood before the lines of police and the gates of parliament with the protestors ranked behind. She lifted the megaphone.

'You are facilitating an illegal coup!' Kanha called through the loudhailer in the direction of the police. 'We are members of the House of Commons and we call on you to stand aside and allow us entry.'

The ranks of police stood rigid, although here and there, one or two stepped forward, only to be pulled back into place by their colleagues. There was no obvious captain, no obvious leader.

Behind Kanha and the MPs, the protestors were shouting. 'No martial law!' and 'Democracy, democracy!' and they started to move past the MPs to the left and right. She knew she wouldn't be able to control them or hold them back.

'You are being directed by a malfunctioning piece of psychotic software,' she called through the loudhailer, and this time a few of the police did break ranks and flee to the sides.

Kanha and the MPs were forced forward, the demonstrators pushing at their backs, and she became afraid. She called out to her left and right, 'Please! We beg you to stand aside in the name of democracy.'

By now the MPs and the police were, like the opposing benches of the Commons, just two sword's widths apart.

'They want to break ranks,' she muttered, and chaos broke out as they started to do so. The police line crumbled. Where protestors had pushed forward, MPs reached the railings and began climbing over them, police officers clinging to their legs and trying to drag them down. Elsewhere officers pushed their way to the sides, so as not to get trapped.

For a moment, it looked like it might spill into violence. Kanha lost any understanding of where the officers were. Where Harry, Brooke, Wilbur, the MPs and the protestors were. Everything was a muddle, but she was right up at the gates by then, and through them she saw the guard still in her hut. Kanha punched the air, signalling for her to open the gates. The woman nodded, and finally they were through.

The gates swung open and the MPs flooded in. The few police standing about in New Palace Yard turned and fled. Behind Kanha, the protestors closed up the gap at the gates, choosing not to follow her onto the estate. Instead they stood cheering and raising their fists in the air, as they helped the MPs through to parliament.

Kanha found Harry in the crowds, and together they made their way in.

3·3

Clarissa stood precariously on a chair in the corner of the opera house foyer and wondered how to get down without twisting an ankle. She should have taken her heels off before clambering up, she thought. Damn it, where was Chloe when she needed her?

She had put the SIM in her phone. Reginald Easterly had been a good chum of Harry's and they'd had him and his wife round for dinner a few times over the years. Such a sweet wife. And Jonnie Whitwell-Thrupp. Dead in a ravine. She'd always quite fancied him.

She was just thinking about taking her shoes off when the doors of the auditorium swung open with a bang. And out they came, the whole lot of them, pushing past one another in their haste. The bodyguards followed, looking up at Clarissa on her chair in the corner and dismissing her as nothing to be concerned about.

The Owners huddled in their family groups as plans were made and calls put out for cars and helicopters to come at once.

'Where shall we go?' one turned and vaguely asked the room.

'I have a lovely villa in Sardinia,' someone replied.

'Bit cold this time of year, isn't it?'

'Oman?'

'Oh, far too hot.'

Whether they saw Clarissa was debatable. She seemed to have become invisible to them.

'I know. What about the Highlands? I have this gorgeous hunting lodge—'

'But, darling, that's still Britain.'

'Is it? Are you sure?'

'Yes, darling. The plan is to get out of Britain, remember? Oh, I know. What about the Hamptons?'

'Sagaponack?'

'Good plan. Darlings, shall *we* do the Hamptons?'

'Oh yes. Let's do.'

'Hang on, what about the Prix de Diane?'

'Ah yes. Well, why don't we fly to Chantilly, do the French races and then get the jet to pick us up and take us to over to Long Island?'

'Done! We'll do the same.'

'Hey, everyone. Prix de Diane. Then the Hamptons. House party at ours.'

By now helicopters were circling and set by set the Owners wandered out until the foyer was empty again. The doors of the auditorium opened once more and Chloe appeared.

'Oh, there you are,' she said to her mother. 'What are you doing up there?'

'I was just showing something to the security camera. Darling, why is everyone leaving?'

'They all got a message. It said to take their families and leave the country as quickly as they can. Didn't you get it too?'

Clarissa pulled out her phone and shook her head. 'No. Give me a hand down, would you?'

Once on solid ground again, Clarissa folded up the piece of paper clutched in her hand and slipped it into her pocket. She wandered over to the sweet counter and ran her finger along the selection.

'Anything you fancy?'

'Maybe some popcorn?'

Clarissa loaded up several tubs and came back to her daughter.

'Is this stealing?' Chloe asked.

'Certainly not! We paid an absolute fortune for this evening.'

Clarissa took off her heels and sat down on the floor, the giant tubs of popcorn in front of her.

'I split up with Emir,' Chloe said.

'Well done. I think that was for the best. Particularly now that we're not in their club anymore.'

Chloe looked at her mother in surprise.

'You're not a shareholder anymore?'

'No. I sold my shares to Neville Jameson at the races for a sesame cracker.'

'A sesame cracker?'

'Yes. In the car park. He happened to have all the right paperwork on him, so we did the deal there and then. I was just up there on the camera showing it to... never mind.'

'Does Daddy know?'

'God no. Why would I tell him that? Imagine how smug he'd be.'

'I suppose.'

'Anyway, I didn't think the Owners' Club was really us, was it? Did I do wrong?'

'I've no idea, Mummy. It was your thing, not mine. So what does that mean?'

'Well, it means we had better not go outside. I don't think it's safe.'

'But Daddy says the stay-at-home orders are all nonsense.'

'The official line about terror attacks was nonsense. Not the explosions. They were very real. And we have no protection now.'

'Does that mean we have to go back to our old life?'

'Well, we'll probably lose all of our UK assets. I have a feeling that new girlfriend of Daddy's will want to freeze them.'

'You know about Esme?'

'I'm not an idiot, darling.'

'What about my car?'

'That might have to go.'

'Really? The Porsche? Can't I just keep the Porsche?'

'I'm sure Daddy can get you a Mini or something.'

Chloe joined her mother on the floor, sitting in a yoga-like pose.

'Maybe I'll go back to my old flat. I was missing my old friends, anyway. And I can walk to work from there.'

'Good idea.'

'What will you do?'

'I might go to Bequia. I still haven't been, and I've always had a hankering to go. Now. Sweet, salty or both?'

3·4

Kanha sat on one of the raised back benches on the government side of the House of Commons and watched the MPs stream into the chamber. One hundred and two members had answered her call in that first push, and now that they were safely inside, more were arriving with every hour that passed. With them came the clerks and the doormen, and a large number of the members of the House of Lords.

Fighting exhaustion from two nights without sleep, Kanha gazed around her: at the green leather benches with their prayer card slots ticketed by those keen for a good seat; at the two red lines on the floor separating her government benches from those of the opposition, which were, for no good reason, said to be two sword widths apart; at the wood-panelled walls and the vaulted ceiling with yellow lanterns and a forest of microphones dangling down from it; at the despatch boxes that sat on the table close to the clerks along with the silver mace. And she cherished every inch of the place.

Beyond the table, at the far end of the chamber, sat the Speaker. He was deep in conversation with his clerks. Above him, in the press and public galleries, it was standing room only.

Kanha looked at the other end of the chamber, back towards the doors, where Harry Colbey sat on one of the small benches reserved for independents; catching her eye, he smiled. God, she hoped she didn't look as bad as he did. The Serjeant at Arms, whose arm was in a sling, was congratulating MPs for making it in as they passed by him and hurried over to their benches. She watched many of them come in and hesitate.

'Don't cross the floor,' Kanha had begged those angriest with Jameson. 'I need your help to force him to resign. Trust me,' she had said, 'I will sort this out.' Watching them turn to their left and come to the government benches, she breathed a sigh of relief.

At the front of the opposition bench, Asma Safeer sat before the despatch box. Rolt was still in prison. She hadn't been arrested on trumped-up terror charges in the end but for known embezzlement of party funds. And her party were not in a hurry for her to be released. Certainly Safeer was not rushing to her aid. And, thinking of the Director General, Kanha was inclined to agree.

Kanha had been able to arrange the release of some of the others falsely imprisoned, including the Attorney General and Lady Chief Justice, who between them immediately arranged a court hearing and drew up an injunction freezing Alcheminna's assets until the actions of the company could be investigated. But the Lady Chief Justice told Kanha that, on the basis that its IT system was still being used by the government in properly appointed tenders, particularly those connected to defence, she could not agree to an injunction to shut down the Divinity system without ministerial approval, and Sanjay Arun, refusing to come in to Westminster, would not give it.

Meanwhile Kanha had tracked down Jameson.

'You must resign,' she had said, but he had swung from side to side on his chair in his Commons rooms and told her the whip was going to be withdrawn from her and that she should hand herself in to the police.

At the sight of MPs streaming past outside his door, though, he had wavered, his eyes constantly drawn to the blank television screen beside him.

'Are you looking for instructions from Lauvaux?' Kanha had said, and he had told her that was slander.

But with the pressure on him from Asma Safeer and many members of his party, he agreed to Kanha's call for an adjournment motion debate. Despite everything, he still felt he had the strength of the party behind him, and the debate was scheduled for 10am.

Now, Kanha sat and waited for it to begin. Beside her were Wilbur and Brooke. Elliot, still tearful from his reunion with Melody, sat in the row in front.

A strange quiet took hold of the room. Neville Jameson had entered the chamber and taken his seat on the front bench. Nearly all of his cabinet had stuck loyally to his side – Appleby and Simmons included, though MacLellan had flown back to wherever it was he had come from. They arrayed themselves around their Prime Minister so that the cameras would show the world he still had plenty of support from those who were supposedly big guns. How much support he really had across his party, Kanha was not sure. She knew that those who had arrived with them and stormed the gates were full of anger, but those who were sauntering in now... who knew where their loyalties lay after all this?

Counting the room, Kanha estimated around 300 or so had made it in by then. Not a full house, but enough to represent the country.

The Speaker stood and cleared his throat, and the chamber at once fell silent.

'I'm not going to dwell on recent events,' he said, 'as I am sure we all have stories to tell and I suspect this debate may be lengthy.'

Appleby stood on behalf of the government.

'I beg to move that this House do now adjourn.'

The Speaker rose and said, 'The question is that this House do now adjourn. Mr Harry Colbey!'

As Harry rose to his feet, there were uproarious calls of 'Bravo!' and it took a while for the Speaker to gain the room again.

'I am glad that so many of you are pleased to see Mr Harry Colbey here today, but I ask that you might wish to allow him to speak. Please proceed, Mr Colbey.'

Harry rose to his feet again.

'Thank you, Mr Speaker, for allowing this important debate on the use of AI for surveillance and policing. We have been subject to some quite terrifying events over the last twenty-four hours, and quite a bit of confusion. Despite the government's decision to dissolve parliament and manage the situation with a small cabinet, you have been kind enough to allow parliament a chance to debate the situation, so that strength of feeling can be ascertained. And I thank you for this opportunity.'

Harry sat back down and the Speaker called again.

'Asma Safeer!'

The deputy opposition leader was scathing in her attack on Jameson's government. She painstakingly went through legal points of order that demonstrated that, in her opinion, what the Prime Minister had done was illegal and against his Ministerial Code, and called for a Standards Committee to investigate.

After her, Kanha bobbed up and the Speaker called her name.

As Kanha rose, many in the House called out, 'The Prime Minister!' but she waited for silence to fall before she started.

'Mr Speaker. We have seen unbelievable scenes this last day or two. Terrible accusations made without a shred of proof. Deepfake lies and manipulation of the public. The independent press under attack and harried.

'A democracy is not just a set of rules and institutions. A democracy is made up of people with a shared belief in respecting one another's views, in debating those views in an open forum, in voting in an open and transparent manner, and most importantly in majority rule.

'A democracy is nothing without the people who stand behind it. And today those people were not just the members of the House of Commons. Not just the civil servants who doggedly and honestly implement the laws, not just the clerks and lawyers, not just the judges and those police officers who stood back and allowed us entry into parliament. But also those members of the public who came today to make sure Britain is and remains a democracy, who came out onto the streets to protect and champion that democracy.

'We must never let this happen again!'

After that, the floodgates were opened. MP after MP from both sides of the House stood and criticised Jameson's actions. Jameson and members of his team took their turn and defended their actions, and for a moment it seemed as if they might have some form of genuine defence, but then Wilbur stood and spoke and carried the House with his cold analysis of what had happened, and others spoke of their dissatisfaction and dismay until the strength of feeling was finally so clear that Esme Kanha looked across the House and gave Asma Safeer a nod.

The leader of the Opposition immediately bobbed up and, seeing it, the Speaker caught on and called her without hesitation. Safeer rose and, as others guessed what was about to happen, there were calls of 'Aye! Aye!' Jameson glowered at her.

'Mr Speaker. I wish to call for a vote of no confidence in the government.'

She plumped herself down, and the Speaker rose. The jeering was so loud he was forced to call for order several times.

'I will have order!' he said, but giving up on getting a silent chamber and wishing to press on, he shouted out above the din, 'The question is that this House has no confidence in His Majesty's government. As many as are of that opinion say "Aye".'

The chamber rang out with ayes.

'Of the contrary say "No".'

There were still plenty of nos – those of the government party who feared power might fall once again to the opposition because of it.

'Division! Clear the lobby!'

Kanha watched them stream out, Asma and Harry leading the way into the Aye lobby. She held back, and by the time she, Wilbur and Brooke reached the Aye lobby, they saw it was clear that the opposition had won their motion. The Ayes had it.

When they filed back in, Jameson was no longer there. Appleby came to her and said he had resigned. With that, finally, things fell into place.

The all-party coalition government that Kanha had negotiated that morning with Asma Safeer was agreed by enough MPs of both parties that Kanha was able to go to the Palace and offer the King a government. It was to be an interim government led by Kanha, with Safeer as Deputy Prime Minister, and would last until an election could be arranged.

She promptly appointed Brooke as Home Secretary and sent her off to shut down the Divinity system and regain control of the police. Wilbur she made Defence Minister, and Elliot her Chief Whip. The rest of the cabinet positions would be agreed after lengthy negotiations with Safeer, to ensure a fair split until one party or other won a more decisive victory.

Elliot she asked to urgently timetable an emergency bill that they could put in place with immediate effect to protect the privacy of the nation from systems like Divinity and to ensure democracy could never be usurped in that way again. 'Harry has been working with Gerald Moreland this morning on something that should do the job,' she said.

The debate on this emergency bill was arranged for 5pm, but as Kanha was on her way back to the chamber, she was called by the Met Police's Chief Commissioner. They had found the body of Henri

Lauvaux. He had been dead for two days. Acting on a tip from the French police, Met police officers had gone to the house. The CEO's wife had said her daughter believed her father was dead. It was something to do with bananas, but how that fitted in Kanha could not guess.

Kanha sank onto one of the stone benches that ran along the Commons Corridor. She dwelled on what it meant. Jameson had not been taking instructions from Lauvaux but from Divinity. For a full day and night the country had truly been in the hands of a schizophrenic, psychopathic android. And as she realised it she saw, at the end of the hall, Jameson crossing St Stephen's porch. She ran after him in a fury, down the steps into the lofty and ancient Westminster Hall, and caught up with him just as he slipped out of the door to where a taxi was waiting for him.

'You knew!' she said, grabbing his arm to hold him back. 'How could you do it? How could you sell us out? Sell the whole of humanity out?'

His eyes had slid off to the side. Then he looked at her and said, 'It was going to happen sooner or later, wasn't it?'

But she was due in the chamber. And there would be plenty of time for dealing with Jameson – a Standards Committee would be just the start of it. So, shaking her head, Kanha turned her back on him and hurried back to the chamber.

She took her new position on the front bench at the despatch box just in time. The Speaker had called on Harry to read his bill. And he rose from where he sat, still on the independent bench.

'Mr Speaker. I beg to move that the emergency bill, which is entitled the National Privacy Bill, but which many are already calling Dvořáček's Bill, be now read both a first and a second time.'

Someone called out, 'About time!' and the refrain was taken up by many on both sides. The Speaker called for order and, waiting for silence to fall, Harry stood again. Kanha looked at him there, modest as ever, and he smiled at her as he began.

'It is just thirteen months since I gave a speech to this House as Minister for Personal Information. In that time technology has advanced at such a pace that this week we found our nation at the mercy of an Artificial Intelligence system. That system had been allowed extensive access to our lives. It had been free to snoop, to scrape, to hack, to harass and to murder. And it had been used in an attempt to usurp our democracy. Now we must act not only to wrench our lives back from this system, and from those who seek to use it for their own ends, but to ensure this never happens again.

'There is not going to be an easy answer as to how to achieve this. The difficult issue of privacy over security is as thorny as ever. How to reap the benefits that technology brings us without opening ourselves up to the dangers that accompany it. This is not an easy nettle to grasp.

'I want to be clear that I am not against technology. I am no luddite. I do not wish to turn back the clock, remove our labour-saving devices, reverse the industrial revolution or live in a cave in the woods. But we have to fix this.

'For all of us here have one job to do. And that is to represent the interests of our constituents, which means ensuring that as technology moves forward it does so in a way that will not harm their fundamental human rights. Their right to privacy. Their right to earn a living. Their right to representation. Their right to democracy. And that is what we must consider today.

'Do we want our governments to have access to systems that can spy on our citizens, that get inside their very heads? Watch them, listen to them, track them. Control them...

'When we've debated this in the past, the answer was a resounding no. As a House we voted to pass a bill that included a clause called Dvořáček's Clause. Had that bill been in place, I do not believe the events of the last twenty-four hours would have been able to happen. And so, once again, I propose to you this bill.'

He sat down to applause from all in the House, and the speaker called out again. 'I call on Ms Esme Kanha.'

Kanha took to her feet.

'Today we will debate the legislation that Harry Colbey and his team have urgently drafted on the nation's behalf. A copy of it is in paper form, and I see many of you have it in your hands already. The Lords have come to parliament now and they are standing by ready to scrutinise. We will work through this afternoon, through tonight and the next day and the one after that if needed, until we have legislation in place to ensure that all of our citizens are all equally benefited by and equally protected from advances in technology.'

The debate lasted several hours – many had views they wished to express on how best to manage the fine balance between protecting the citizens of the nation and ensuring their privacy. Finally, Harry rose to his feet again to summarise, and then the Speaker stood.

'Division! Clear the lobby!'

Three Weeks Later

Harry Colbey hunted around in Esme Kanha's little cottage kitchen until he found something that looked vaguely like it might work as a cheeseboard. There wasn't much to choose from. She obviously wasn't one for kitchenware.

He laid the creamy Oxford Blue, the solid ball of Black Bomber and a good slice of the local Stinking Bishop around a tired-looking bunch of grapes. He'd found them in the fridge and even after he'd pinched off the worst of the dried-up ones it had been a bit of a dilemma as to whether they were worth an outing or not.

After bending down to pat Maximillian, Colbey headed off out the back door and down the garden path. A stream ran along the bottom of the garden, and he took the rickety wooden bridge that crossed it and followed the trail that wound through a band of beech to a clearing beyond. There, seated around a long picnic table, was the luncheon party.

'Here he comes!' called Esme, spotting him and waving.

'Finally,' said Chloe, as Colbey's dog ran up to greet him and started jumping about in the hope he was bringing something out for him. 'What have you been doing all this time?'

Sitting at the table, which was covered in the remains of a good long lunch, were the Speaker, the Serjeant at Arms, Elliot, Wilbur,

Brooke, Melody, Lord Silverman, Gerald Moreland and Mani, who had managed at last to get some leave and had flown in to help in person with getting the country straight.

'Can't find anything in that kitchen,' Colbey said.

'That's because there isn't anything,' Esme replied with a smile. She had pushed some of the remains of the lunch aside and was making plans with Wilbur, Brooke and Melody as to who they might invite into their coalition cabinet and who might be acceptable to Safeer.

Colbey put the cheese platter down so that Esme could have first dibs at the soft Oxford Blue and cut himself a healthy chunk of the Bomber before sliding the board around to the guests. Bowles picked up his knife and looked eagerly at it as he waited his turn.

'So is Mummy going to be alright?' Chloe was asking Lord Silverman.

The lord went to pull the cheese plate towards him, but Bowles got there first. Lord Silverman cleared his throat. 'I'll be leading the public inquiry, and on the basis that she voluntarily sold her shares when it became apparent what Lauvaux was up to, I expect her to be treated leniently. Being shareholder of a company that has been acting illegally is not in itself a crime – it's the directors who will face criminal charges, and she wasn't a director.'

'But then why freeze all her assets? It just isn't fair. She hadn't done anything wrong.'

Colbey couldn't help but scoff. 'Darling, I suspect your mother has money hidden away in more places than you could even guess at. I really wouldn't worry about her.'

'So what about the directors?'

Kanha shook her head. 'Divinity tipped them off before we could shut it down. We're trying to get them back into the country with extradition orders, but I don't hold out much hope.'

She licked some cheese off her finger.

'Now. Harry. Now that your privacy bill has been passed at long last, would you be interested in having your old job back? Minister for Personal Information?'

To which Colbey sighed. 'I might not get re-elected.'

'You can only hope. But in the meantime... would you please join my coalition and be our Minister for Personal Information? I happen to know you would do a very good job of it.'

Colbey took some more of the cheddar and gave in. 'OK, but after that, I want to go and paint in Provence.'

'It's a deal. Gerald – would you be happy to act as PPS for Harry while we have him?'

Moreland gave a funny little nod. It was strange to see him in his civvies. Colbey had been half expecting him to turn up for the picnic lunch in his pinstriped suit.

'It would be my honour,' he said. 'But what about your Honest Politicking Bill, Harry?'

Colbey tapped his knife on the table as he decided which cheese to go for next.

'I'd forgotten about that. Do you think, Esme, this time round I might be allowed to progress it?'

'What do you mean, this time round?'

'Last time you said—'

'Alright, alright. Yes, you may. Though I don't know how far you'll get with it. Even after all this.'

The Speaker lifted his glass and proposed a toast. 'What shall we toast to?' he asked.

'To all the dirty geese,' Esme suggested, and Colbey couldn't help but agree. 'Six hundred and sixty-three of them!'

They raised their glasses. As they put them down, Chloe said, 'So is it dead, then?'

'Dead, darling?'

'Divinity. Is it dead?'

Colbey shook his head. 'It can't die – it's a computer program. It's been shut down. The data warehouse has been disconnected from the world. When everything is through the courts and the public inquiry, it will be decided what to do with the servers. What do you think, Lord Silverman?'

Lord Silverman considered. 'I suppose they will be destroyed or wiped clean and sold.'

'So it couldn't have backed itself up?'

'We don't think so, do we, Mani?' Esme said. 'It's just too large. To find another state-of-the-art data warehouse that was big enough and not being used already would be near impossible. Particularly at short notice.'

Melody had not really been paying attention to the conversation, as she had been stroking the dog, but now she looked up.

'Unless it used a distributed network, of course.'

Esme cocked her head to one side. 'What do you mean?'

'Well, you know. Like torrenting, when a foreign state or hacker keeps space on a bunch of other people's hardware.'

'OK, none of that made sense to me,' Esme said, looking to Mani.

Mani pulled a face. 'She means, basically, rather having one huge data warehouse with lots of servers, the system could have backed itself up to a network of multiple tiny servers distributed across the country or the world. But they would have had to be configured for that, and for the capacity to be large enough there would have to be millions of them.'

Esme put down her knife. 'Like… for example a piece of hardware, like a speaker, that had recently been sent to every household in the country and that Divinity could be connected to?'

'Yes…'

Colbey put his knife down too, and he and Esme looked at one another. They leapt to their feet.

'Shit!' they both said in unison.

ALSO BY LOU GILMOND

The Tale of Senyor Rodriguez

The Kanha and Colbey Thrillers

Dirty Geese
Palisade
Divinity Games

For exclusive info and the latest updates visit:
www.lougilmond.com

LOU GILMOND
Dirty Geese

WHAT CAN SEE WATCHES, WHAT CAN HEAR LISTENS,
WHAT CAN BE FOLLOWED IS TRACKED...

When Chief Whip Esme Kanha learns of the sudden death of the
Minister for Personal Information, she bitterly regrets missing his
desperate calls the previous evening. Unconvinced by the verdict
of suicide, and suspicious that corrupt colleagues played some part
in the man's death, she decides to investigate – but she must tread
carefully in a near-future world dominated by AI, where 'what
can see watches, what can hear listens, and what can be followed
is tracked'.

Meanwhile, Big Tech executive Henri Lauvaux arrives in London.
His mission: to ensure the new minister, Harry Colbey, will not
prove as problematic as the last. As the West inexorably slides
towards an Orwellian 'Big Brother' future, Harry Colbey and
Esme Kanha join forces in a deadly cat-and-mouse game against
political corruption – at great cost to themselves.

'The constant presence of AI creates a
foreboding atmosphere'
—*CRIME FICTION LOVER*

LOU GILMOND
Palisade

When opposition Chief Whip Esme Kanha is handed a secret dossier containing evidence of government corruption, she suspects its original owner, a top journalist, was murdered for gathering it. Despite the danger, she feels she must investigate. Meanwhile, lowly backbencher Harry Colbey is working his own leads. A known campaigner against big tech, he is often sent data from anonymous sources and this time round he has something truly alarming.

But both Colbey and Kanha must tread carefully in a world dominated by AI, where 'what can see watches, what can hear listens, and what can be followed is tracked'.

As Kanha and Colbey again join forces, they are locked into a deadly race against political corruption, no matter what the cost. But when an old enemy returns, it may already be too late...

'Essential reading'
—*LONDON STANDARD*